The Body in the Shadows

Nick Louth is a best-selling thriller writer, award-winning financial journalist and an investment commentator. He self-published his first novel, *Bite*, which was a No. 1 Kindle best-seller. It has sold a third of a million copies, and been translated into six languages.

Freelance since 1998, he has been a regular contributor to the *Financial Times*, *Investors Chronicle* and *Money Observer*. Nick is married and lives in Lincolnshire.

Also by Nick Louth

Bite
Heartbreaker
Mirror Mirror
Trapped

DCI Craig Gillard Crime Thrillers

The Body in the Marsh
The Body on the Shore
The Body in the Mist
The Body in the Snow
The Body Under the Bridge
The Body on the Island
The Bodies at Westgrave Hall
The Body on the Moor
The Body Beneath the Willows
The Body in the Stairwell
The Body in the Shadows

NICK LOUTH

THE BODY IN THE SHADOWS

First published in the United Kingdom in 2023 by

Canelo
Unit 9, 5th Floor
Cargo Works, 1–2 Hatfields
London SE1 9PG
United Kingdom

A CIP catalogue record for this book is available from the British Library.

Print ISBN 978 1 80436 301 0
Ebook ISBN 978 1 80436 300 3

This book is a work of fiction. Names, characters, businesses, organizations, places and events are either the product of the author's imagination or are used fictitiously. Any resemblance to actual persons, living or dead, events or locales is entirely coincidental.

Cover design by Jem Butcher

Look for more great books at www.canelo.co

Printed and bound in Great Britain by Clays Ltd, Elcograf S.p.A.

1

For Louise, as always

Chapter One

The perennial sound of Slade accompanied Sam Gillard as she perused a rail of slacks in Marks & Spencer. She'd taken a day off to do some Christmas shopping at the newly opened Greenway Centre in Woking. Three floors of sparkling retail therapy were alluring when the weather outside was gloomy and overcast. She was in womenswear on the first floor, laden with purchases, wondering if she could justify a new pair of work trousers to accommodate her pregnancy bump. She'd already bought a new zip-up fleece for Craig, a toy car transporter for her nephew, and a coffeemaker for her mother. For herself she'd made an impulse buy of a pair of scarlet Mary Jane ballet flats. They looked great and eased her pregnancy-swollen feet, so she'd worn them straight from the shop.

In the distance, a tall young man wearing a grey hoodie and pristine white trainers stood out amongst the predominantly white female shoppers in the women's lingerie area. He was clearly bored, looking at his phone, and seemed out of place. Still, something about him snagged at her brain. He radiated a restless energy. Her years as a police community support officer had given her something of a sixth sense, and this intensified when the man began to look about him. She followed his gaze and saw a uniformed security officer at the far end of the shop. Sam moved to get a better look at the youth, perhaps fifteen yards away, and saw him brush past a middle-aged female shopper. She had her back to him as he slid past in the congested pinch point by the costume jewellery display. He obviously said something to her, perhaps an 'excuse me', because she smiled. His left hand rested briefly on her shoulder, the numerous gold rings on his long dark fingers catching the light.

So fast and so smooth that she almost missed it, his other hand slid into the woman's leather handbag, slipped out her purse and pocketed it.

Sam turned to see where the store detective was. Not visible anymore. The pickpocket was moving towards her now, his long legs eating up the distance between them. The first-floor exit was right behind her. Her first thought was to tackle the thief directly, but common sense dismissed it. She was six months pregnant with a carrier bag in each hand, and he was perhaps twenty, six foot three and clearly very fit. If he wasn't carrying a knife she would be astounded. She could ring 999 but, having worked in the control room at Mount Browne, she knew it would be a lucky day for a patrol car to arrive in ten minutes. Easily enough time for a fit young thief to be a mile away.

She turned to look at the clothing rail as he passed behind her. Her own hand was clasping the top of her handbag, but he made no attempt at it. The moment he was past she turned and took a quick picture of him on her phone. The generic hoodie, the high-top trainers, the dark tracksuit trousers with a double stripe of white. An urban uniform worn by millions. Only the Route 66 logo on the back marked him out.

She watched as the thief exited the store and turned left, striding nonchalantly towards the atrium bridge to the other side of the three-storey shopping centre. She then turned back to the victim, who was now browsing nearby.

'Excuse me, this young man's just stolen your purse.'

The woman, grey-haired and bespectacled, the classic middle-aged M&S shopper, froze in horror, and rushed to check her bag as Sam showed her the photo.

'It's gone,' she cried.

'Find the store detective and report it, and then call the police. I'm going to try and find where he went. Don't leave the store, I'll come back for you.'

Not waiting for a response, Sam turned and hurried to the exit, wanting to know where the thief was heading next. The store exit gave onto a broad balcony served on the far side by two escalators from the crowded ground floor, and two more to the higher floor. She quickly scanned the atrium and looked over the balcony to the floor below. No sign of him. To her left were WH Smith and Claire's Accessories, to her right Wilkinson's hardware store. There were plenty of shoppers up here, but the thief's height and hood should mark him out. She waited for a minute, choosing the vantage point of the bridge between the two sides of the first-floor balcony. She was about to give up and go back into M&S when she spotted him coming out of Accessorize. She followed at a distance of about twenty yards, and managed to get a good side view photo, widening her fingers on the screen for a close-up. She looked around for uniformed police or security guards but could see nobody. He made his way past her across the bridge towards a cafe where people were sitting outside. A skinny late-teenage girl walked

3

towards him, and as they passed each other, he slipped something into her shopping bag. She had a hard face, tattoos on her neck, short unkempt dyed blonde hair and a worn denim jacket. Sam risked a head-on photograph, and as she did so, the girl glanced in her direction. Sam wasn't sure if she'd been seen. The girl headed off left on the far balcony while the thief moved right. Sam knew she was in danger of getting out of her depth here, with two people to keep an eye on, so she rang 999. Put through to the control room, she told her colleague Helen all the details, all the while following the thief.

'You're walking, Sam, I can hear your breath. Stay away from him,' Helen warned.

'I won't take any risks. But this poor woman has had her purse stolen, and there are probably others. Ah, he's taking the escalator up to the second floor.'

Sam cut the call and headed towards the moving stairway. The tall man towered over the half-dozen female shoppers behind him on the escalator. Sam watched as the thief answered his phone, then turned to look behind him. She was just at the base of the escalator, and stepped on, but he appeared not to have seen her. She averted her glance, but kept him in her peripheral vision. She focused on her destination, gradually coming into view. The second floor had not been fully let, and she could see most of the units were still being fitted out. There were only a few people up here. The thief had reached the top, still on the phone, and stepped off and to the left. Leaning over the balcony, he looked right at Sam and nodded, still on the phone. He was glaring at her, and pointed a finger, ripe with unspoken threats.

She was being gradually transported towards him.

There was no way she could escape. She would be there in ten seconds.

Sam glanced behind, and saw with horror that thirty feet behind her, the skinny girl was just getting on her escalator, phone clamped to her ear.

Unconsciously, Sam lowered a protective hand to her pregnancy bump. *This is not what I would have wished for you.*

She assessed her options. She'd rather fight her than him, so she began to rapidly descend the moving stairs. She squeezed past two middle-aged female shoppers, who tutted and complained. But Sam only had eyes for the blonde below, all cold, dark eyes and sallow skin. They were five seconds apart. Sam was just a few feet away when the girl pulled a knife, its short narrow blade hidden from the view of others by the flap of her denim jacket.

Two seconds.

Sam took the biggest inhalation she could, and screamed, the sound filling the entire atrium, and echoing back from all angles. She threw the bag containing the coffeemaker into the face of her female assailant. The girl was knocked down three steps, but kept her feet, her shielding arm deflecting the bag over the side of the escalator rail.

A second later it detonated like a bomb on the ground floor.

'Help!' Sam yelled, again as loud as she could, pointing at the girl half a dozen steps below her. 'She's got a knife!'

But the stares were all at her, the pregnant shopper, losing it. *Poor dear*, they would be saying, seeing there was nobody near the shopper who had hurled her purchases over the side. *Drink, probably. Or maybe drugs. Or just too much lockdown. It can hit your mental health, can't it?*

The girl had hidden her knife, and was not advancing up the stairs, but she was laser-focused on Sam's face. Now both of them were being drawn inexorably upwards toward the thief leaning over the balcony. She turned back to him, aware that hundreds of people on the ground floor were staring up at her, an unwitting high-wire act. The escalator would transport her to the top in five seconds. At four, the last intervening traveller, a small teenage boy glued to his phone, stepped off and squeezed past the thief. She saw his brown eyes and yellowy bloodshot whites and thought: drugs. He's high!

At three, he leaned over and hissed: 'Give me your phone or I'll fucking kill you.'

It sounded like the best Black Friday deal she had ever heard.

With shaking hands, she passed the device up to him. He snatched it from her with one hand and with the other pulled her off her feet at the end of the escalator, so that she skidded and tumbled onto the polished tile floor. She crashed sideways, banging her head, hand bracing her midriff. She could hear the sound of running feet, shouts of help, someone coming towards her just as the woman with the knife reached the top of the escalator.

From the right-hand side of her view a stocky uniformed security guard was running towards her. Thank God. The thief turned, swore, and sprinted away. It was an Olympian turn of speed, which made everyone else look like they were frozen in time. The guard didn't even attempt to follow. Instead, he headed towards Sam, his radio to his mouth. Other shoppers, seeing the thief's rapid departure, felt emboldened to come up and ask her how she was.

'Where's the girl?' Sam asked breathlessly.

'Who's that, dear?' asked a kindly-looking woman in her seventies.

'The one with the knife.' Sam looked around and couldn't see her. 'She was just coming up the escalator.' Her breath came in sobs.

'You want to be careful in your state. Can I phone someone for you?'

'That's very kind. I'll just phone my husband.' Only then did she realise she did not have her phone. Everything was on it: her calendar, contacts, banking, you name it. It was this sickening realisation that brought her closer to tears than had the prospect of being stabbed. She asked if she could borrow one from the woman. The security guard had been joined by a colleague, and they were still scanning the various floors for the thief while their radios squawked. 'IC3 male,' said the first guard into his walkie-talkie. 'No, police are on their way.' Sam blinked away her tears as the woman passed across her phone.

Then, in her peripheral vision to her right, Sam saw her. Now wearing a beanie hat, no jacket, but the tattoo and the cold dark eyes were a giveaway. And the glint of the knife, held low. 'It's her!' yelled Sam as the girl, her face distorted with rage, pushed past the kindly lady, the knife aimed for her precious midriff.

'Nosy fucking bitch,' was all Sam heard. 'Take my photo, would you?'

Years ago, she had been fighting fit thanks to aerobics and even a few self-defence classes. Not now. But she had two lives to fight for, not just one. One hand braced on the balustrade, she kicked sideways at the girl's knife arm. She made contact and the arm jerked, the blade spinning to the ground, then skating along the tiles towards the feet of the security guards.

But her assailant wasn't finished and moved with fury and speed. She had grabbed hold of Sam's leg after the kick and lifted it so that she was off balance, using it as a ram against its owner. Sam's other foot was no longer in contact with the floor, and she was in danger of being twisted and flipped over the balcony. Sam screamed, and gripped an ornate wrought iron balcony support with her free hand, even as her hips were now almost level with the guardrail.

'Help me, help me!' she yelled, but the faces of the shoppers hung passively open, phones pointing at her, astounded but not willing to intervene. Just drama on film, nothing to do with them. Even the security guards seemed to be set in treacle, turning and moving in slow motion towards her. Only the older woman remonstrated. Sam kicked with her free foot, trying to smash the girl in the face, but to no avail, as she clung to the metalwork with all her strength, winding one arm into the metal curlicues. Then another hard shove, her hips slid and she was over, falling.

Falling.

She screamed, long and hard, as if to shatter with her dying anguish every sheet of shop glass in the place.

No! My child, my child!

Her drop was arrested in a second by an agonising pain. Her arm, knotted into the ornate balustrade and stretched painfully over the rail at the elbow, felt it was being torn from its socket. With her other arm she lunged for the handrail and got three sweaty fingers on the warm, greasy wood, while her legs kicked frantically for purchase on the blank panelling underneath the balustrade.

She lost a shoe.

The scarlet Mary Jane, its price label still on the sole, looped the loop before diving into the spinning kaleidoscope of shoppers a hundred feet below, staring up at her.

Feeling sick, she looked up and into the dead eyes of her assailant, who was leaning over, unpeeling Sam's fingers from the handrail. The stout security guard arrived just in time, pulling the girl away, an arm around her neck. Through the bars of the balcony, Sam watched her twist rapidly from his grip and launch a fierce knee into his groin. The man crumpled with a groan, and the girl punched him twice with sickening speed in the face. She then leaned over to Sam, spat copiously into her face, and sprinted away. Sam felt the vile liquid on her eyelashes, on her lip, on her hair, and hadn't a free hand to wipe them.

The assailant gone, strong male arms reached down and hauled her gently over to safety. Her arm was agony where it had been twisted and jammed in the balustrade ironwork, but her first plea was for someone to get a tissue to mop the vile mess on her face. As she sat on the floor, buzzing with shock and surrounded by well-wishers, she had one thought.

What on earth had she done to deserve *that*?

Chapter Two

'So what did he look like?' the PC asked as Sam sat on a chair in the stockroom of a nearby store, catching her breath.

'Very tall, mixed-race. I got a photo on my phone.'

'Ah, but he took your phone, didn't he?' The police-woman looked at her kindly, as if the assault had robbed her of her wits.

'Yes, I know. But the picture will be on the server of the service provider, and if I give you the number, the police should be able to retrieve it,' Sam said as a staff member brought her a cup of coffee.

'He'll probably have deleted it, love,' the PC said. 'He's probably on CCTV, so there's no need for you to worry. What we need to do is check you over, and make sure your baby is all right—'

Sam closed her eyes in frustration. 'Even if he tries to delete it, it will still be there on the server. My husband is a detective. I do know what I'm talking about.'

Sam felt a kick inside her, the first she had experienced. It was as if her unborn child was in agreement. She gasped, and the PC took it as a sign that all was not well.

'Just relax, the paramedics will be here in a minute,' she said.

'Can I give you this?' Sam said, handing across a soggy tissue that she had kept. 'She spat in my face. I want to be sure that she hasn't got anything horrible. It went in my eye. And it'll have her DNA.'

The PC looked at the soggy tissue with disdain.

'Just poke it into a rubber glove if you don't have an evidence bag,' Sam said.

The officer felt in her tunic pockets, clearly irked at being told how to do her job. She passed across a blue disposable glove, and Sam poked the tissue inside and then gave it back.

The shop manager, having earlier been given Craig Gillard's direct line, came over with a phone in her hand.

'It's your husband for you,' she said.

Sam's spirits soared as she grabbed hold of the receiver, and she could hear herself begin to sob once again as he began to speak.

'Are you okay, Sam?'

'She tried to throw me over the railings from the second floor.'

'I heard the initial report. I'm about twenty minutes away.'

'Craig, I was trapped on an escalator and I threw my Christmas shopping at her.' She began to laugh within her sobs. 'It was a coffeemaker on special offer!'

'We'll get a new one, even if it's full price. Just hang on in there, it's going to be okay.'

'And a man came to me from downstairs with my shoe.'

'Your shoe?'

'The one that fell off. It just missed him. He asked to see Cinderella, to see if it fitted.'

'That's a fairytale ending, I suppose. I love you, Sam, and everything's going to be fine. I'll be there soon. Nothing's more important to me than you and our precious child.'

And with those kind and loving words, she really began to cry.

—

Gillard had interrupted his shift to give Sam a lift home. In the car on the way back from Woking, she told him the full story.

He listened carefully and then said: 'The case has been passed to DI John Perry, who I've been assured is giving it the highest priority. This isn't simply aggravated theft, but attempted murder. Thank God you were able to hold on. It just doesn't bear thinking about.'

'Is there CCTV of them?'

'Bound to be,' Gillard said. 'It's a newish shopping centre, so it should be high quality too.'

'He was wearing a hoodie, but it's her I really want.'

Gillard looked at his wife. Less than two years ago, she'd been kidnapped and locked in a steel box, and nearly drowned. She had undergone therapy for the PTSD, and in recent months her nightmares had receded. He just hoped this wouldn't bring them back.

'The baby's been kicking,' she said. 'First time I've felt it. It's a good sign. In fact, I was planning to get some advice seeing as I was after twenty weeks without a kick.'

Gillard glanced at her bump, and rested his hand there, feeling the warmth. 'Quite an exciting start to his life, isn't it?'

'You could certainly say that. If he's not a she.'

Gillard paused and then asked: 'Was there anything on the phone that would reveal your home address?'

She blew a sigh. 'You don't think that they could come after me, do you?'

'On balance no, but it's always a good idea to think the unthinkable.' Gillard looked at his wife, with their unborn child still nestling in her body. He felt even more protective of her now. He'd double-check the locks on the windows and doors at home, but that would never be enough. When it came to looking after her, he always felt there was more he should do.

Chapter Three

Next day in the first floor CID office at Mount Browne, Gillard sat with DI Perry looking through CCTV footage from the Greenway shopping centre. There were numerous images that caught the thief with his distinctive Route 66 hoodie. However, the hood was drawn sufficiently low that none they had seen so far showed his face.

'Have you got any from the start of the first floor ascending escalator where Sam got on?' Gillard asked.

'I'm not sure,' Perry said.

'Centre floor plan shows that there is an Edinburgh Woollen Mill facing the escalator.'

'No, their cameras are all in-store,' Perry said. With his hangdog expression and prematurely greying hair, the forty-four-year-old detective inspector looked like the worn-out schoolteacher he once was. He liked to joke that now he was dealing with crime rather than education, he only ran into the bottom five per cent of the pupils that he used to teach.

'What about the girl? Have you identified her?' Gillard asked.

'No, but we do have some better images.' Perry selected a series of stills, which showed the washed-out looking bottle blonde. There was even some footage which showed the moment when she brushed past the thief and received what looked like the stolen purse.

'She's definitely a better prospect,' Gillard said.

'We've got fewer but better images of her. I've talked to half a dozen store security from the usual high target retailers, and the only one who recognised her was a guy at Primark who used to manage an off-licence in Knaphill. She was caught shoplifting there about eighteen months ago, after which she was banned from the store.'

'No prosecution?'

'No. It's the usual problem. They claim they have to wait so long for the police to arrive it's not worth the staff time of holding them, so they normally just get the money or the goods back. It's a familiar pattern, I'm afraid.'

Gillard wasn't surprised. He was rarely involved in shoplifting or street robbery cases now, but was aware that a slowing police response due to limited resources made it much harder for retailers. To get a prosecution meant staff waiting with the suspect, sometimes for an hour or more. The problem had very much been thrown back into the laps of retailers themselves.

'So do we have a name?'

'He was going to check and get back to me. I'm going to offer the best images to the media, see if the public can do the job for us.'

Gillard stood up and rested his hand on Perry's shoulder. 'All right, John, let me know as soon as you have it. I want this dangerous young lady tracked down as soon as possible.'

–

Gillard got back to his glass box office to find an internal mail envelope on the top of his in-tray. Inside it was a sheet of headed Metropolitan Police phone message note-paper and a two-liner. 'Caller rang Croydon Police Station asking for you, wouldn't give his name. Refused to speak to anybody else.' The number below was a mobile, and the date of the message was three days ago, late evening.

Gillard hadn't worked at Croydon for almost three decades. His curiosity piqued, he rang the number, which after ringing out for a minute went to a robot message. Gillard left his name and, not wanting to hand out his direct line, the Mount Browne switchboard number. He then rang the Met police at Croydon and asked to speak to whoever had taken the message. The receptionist knew nothing about it, and while he was on hold, asked around. Nobody knew anything. Gillard thanked her and hung up.

Research Intelligence Officer Rob Townsend knocked on his door.

'Sir, we've traced your wife's phone, and retrieved some of the images.'

'Well done. Where was it?'

'It was turned off five minutes after the attack, just a few hundred yards north of the shopping centre. The suspect deleted the images, then presumably tossed the phone away somewhere. The last signal shows it was close to the canal.' Townsend, studious and fresh-faced, looked younger than his thirty-two years, and had recently grown a beard which turned out more gingery than the hair on his head. He now ran a team of three civilian technical experts who were always busy looking at the contents of mobile phones.

'Let's look at these pictures then.' Gillard followed Townsend across to his desk, where a picture of the female assailant had been magnified so that it showed her face. It was a good picture, and captured the cold dead dark eyes, some of her neck tattoo, and a knife with a curlicue handle.

'That's excellent, pass it on to Perry and see if we can get it in the papers for tomorrow.'

By the time Gillard had got back to his own desk terminal, there was an email from DI Perry. The saliva in the tissue provided by Sam had yielded no evidence of HIV or Covid infection in the assailant, but had produced a DNA sample which matched someone on the database.

Lydia Marasova, aged nineteen.

Gillard pulled into the gravel car park. He hadn't been to the Fox and Goose for a couple of years, not since before the makeover. It had for years been known as the Rince of Wales. The large plastic P on the sign had fallen off decades before. Now it was a trendy rural gastropub.

Sam was wearing a sling, and he helped her get out of the car. By some miracle, her arm wasn't dislocated, nor the tendons torn, but it was very bruised. This was to be his treat. As they entered the bar to the sound of soft jazz and saw the well-heeled clientele, the candlelit tables and potted palms, it was clear that the place had changed enormously.

As the waiter led them to their table, a secluded booth in the large glass-ceilinged extension, Gillard spotted a familiar face.

'Hello Kirsty, what are you doing hiding away in the darkness?' Gillard asked.

Kirsty Mockett was a young and fast-rising crime scene investigator, normally to be found swaddled in bulky Tyvek coveralls at some blood-spattered incident. Tonight, she was wearing a dark green velvet dress that hugged her figure. She coloured at Gillard's remark and introduced the dark-haired man sitting opposite her.

'This is Matt Culshaw, and this is—'

'Craig Gillard, well, well,' said Culshaw, standing up to greet him. 'And you must be the charming Sam. Delighted to meet you,' he said, cracking a wide smile. 'A bit of a high-wire artist, I hear?'

'An unwilling one,' she said, smiling back. A bit too readily, in Gillard's opinion.

'So pleased to hear that you and the little one are fine,' Culshaw said smoothly, resting a hand on her good arm. 'And if you ever want to join a real circus, we've always got room at the Met.' He winked.

'So how do you know each other?' Sam asked.

'We worked on a couple of cases together years ago,' Gillard said, then turned back to Culshaw. 'So where are you based now?'

'Flying Squad,' Culshaw said. 'I've just been promoted to DCI.'

'Is it still called that?' Kirsty asked. 'I thought it was called S07.'

'Or the Sweeney,' Sam said, with a chuckle.

'It's M07 now, and anyway, where is the romance in that?' Culshaw said. He had an easy laugh, a very sharp suit and a skin-fade haircut that would surely need to be touched up once a week. Gillard wasn't surprised that Culshaw had ended up in the most iconic of the Met's detective groups, one with a hundred-year pedigree in the fight against robbery and organised crime in the capital.

Anxious not to intrude on what was clearly a date, Gillard eased Sam away from the table to their own, which was a good fifteen feet away. As they sat down, Sam looked at her husband's face and said: 'From that smirk there is clearly a story there.'

'Several, in fact. Kirsty was going out with Rob Townsend until a few months ago – you know, the research intelligence officer. There's obviously been some speculation in the office about who…'

'You mean because she's so pretty?'

'Is she? I really hadn't noticed,' he said with as much insouciance as he could manage.

Sam pinched his cheek playfully. 'Oh, come on.'

He counterattacked. 'So what do you think of Matt Culshaw? You were giggling at everything he said.'

'Was I?' She raised an eyebrow and pursed her lips. 'Well, he clearly fancies himself, not without reason. He's got a dazzling smile and there's a great physique under that jacket.'

Gillard laughed. 'Are you trying to make me jealous?'

'I wouldn't know how.' She reached across the table and took his hand in hers.

'From what I've heard, he's a rising star. Last year he managed to put away a whole crowd of young moped-riding bag snatchers and phone grabbers, as well as one or two of the major kingpins who fence the proceeds.'

'So what's he doing in Surrey?'

Gillard looked over his shoulder. Culshaw was caressing Kirsty's arm, and there was clearly an intimacy between them. 'Need I say more?'

'He's clearly putting a message out, knowing you will probably blurt it out in the office. He's staking ownership.'

'That's a rather brutal analysis, though I'm not sure I disagree with it.'

'You like Kirsty, don't you?'

'I have an extremely high regard for her work, if that's what you're asking.' He looked at his wife meaningfully, hoping that she wasn't asking anything deeper.

'Then do her a favour. Don't mention this. In a man's world, a woman loses half of all the respect she has ever earned when everybody knows who she is sleeping with.'

'Okay, I'll say nothing then.' He got out his phone. 'I'll just send her a text. To tell her to put him down as she doesn't know where he's been.'

'Don't you dare.'

'I was only joking.'

The waiter arrived and tried for the second time to interest them in the wine list. Gillard explained that he was driving, while Sam just moved her hand gently over her belly. The young man got the idea and took their order. Once he had gone, Sam said: 'Did you want to come with me tomorrow?'

Gillard was momentarily baffled.

'I've got my long-delayed ultrasound tomorrow,' Sam said. 'Do you remember?'

'Ah, yes. That's why you're on the late shift.'

'I did explain it.'

Reaching into his memory, Gillard recalled it. 'They're looking for eleven rare conditions the baby might have, yes?'

'And the condition of the spine, brain, heart and other organs. And obviously they want to see if there's any ill effects from my little encounter the other day.'

Gillard squeezed her hand. 'Yes, I'll come. And keep my fingers crossed.'

'I saw the photo of the woman on the regional news at 6.30. It was the photo from my phone, wasn't it?'

'Yes, it was way better than any of the CCTV images. We've got a name now, you know. Lydia Marasova, aged nineteen. Last address was in Farnborough. The DNA matches. Previous convictions for shoplifting, possession, anti-social behaviour. It's all pretty low-key up until now.'

'What about the pickpocket?'

'Nothing so far.'

'And still no sign of my phone?'

'No.'

'I need it back, Craig. There is so much on there, and a lot of it might not have been backed up on the cloud.'

'Like I say, it's probably in the canal. That's roughly where it was last triangulated.' He wondered whether the thief had looked at Sam's personal information, her Facebook account, emails to him, and to her friends. He could quite understand why the loss made her feel so raw and violated. Though it wasn't too common, there were cases when such personal information had been abused in pursuit of further crime. After her kidnap, and the subsequent PTSD, that was the last thing she needed.

–

While Gillard and Sam were in the restaurant, DI Perry and two uniformed officers were standing in the lounge of a dingy two-bedroom flat in Farnborough, Hampshire, the last known address of Lydia Marasova. The landlord who let them in, a sari-wearing Asian woman, looked with disgust at the mess. Clothes strewn all over the room, half-eaten takeaway food, piles of dirty crockery.

'Always late with the rent, that one. And then a week ago, poof, she disappears, leaving me with this.'

'Did you ever see any of her friends?' Perry asked.

'No. I live two streets away, but the downstairs neighbour complained to me about noise.'

'I'd like to see all the documentation she lodged with you,' Perry said. 'Previous addresses, references, that kind of thing.'

'But who is going to help me with this?' she asked.

'We will be finished here in an hour,' said the female PC.

'Occupational hazard for you, isn't it?' said the other, peering into the kitchen. 'Non-payment and mess.'

'Normally, it is not this bad. Most of my tenants are very good, actually. But yes, occasionally, we have a bad one.'

'Do you have any other contact details apart from her mobile phone?' Perry asked.

'I have her father's address. He stood as guarantor.'

'We'll start with that.' Perry rubbed his hands together.

–

Two hours later Perry and the two constables were standing outside a semi-detached 1930s house in Slough. The front garden had been paved over to provide hardstanding and now hosted a newish white Mercedes saloon. They squeezed past on the way to the front door. It took three rings before the door was answered by a smallish man with a neat grey beard. He was wearing a bathrobe.

'Mr Marasova?' Perry asked.

'Yes, what is it?' He looked extremely nervous. 'I was just about to have a shower.'

He introduced himself and the other officers. 'We're looking for Lydia. Is she here?'

The man blew a long sigh. 'No, she's not. Is she in trouble?'

'Yes, it relates to an incident in a shopping centre near Woking. Did she tell you about it?' Perry asked.

'No, I'm sorry. I haven't spoken to her for two weeks. She is such a disappointment to me.'

'May we come in?'

'She's not here. I told you.'

'I hope you don't mind if we check for ourselves,' Perry said. 'It won't take a couple of minutes and saves us having to get a warrant.'

'I suppose so,' Marasova said, opening the door wide. The officers trooped in, wiping their feet carefully, noticing the pale and pristine carpets, and taking in a framed certificate of merit on the wall.

'What's that for, Mr Marasova?' asked the male PC.

'I build and repair sound mixing desks, for music. This is from an institute in my country.'

'And that country is?'

'Romania. I was born in Romania, in Bucharest. But I have UK right to remain.'

'It's all right, we're not the Home Office gestapo, we only want to find your daughter.'

'She's not here.'

'So you say,' Perry said. 'Mind if we look around?'

'I will take you on a tour,' Marasova said with a shrug. They began in the kitchen, where Marasova pointed out the cupboards, cooker and washing machine.

'It's all right, Mr Marasova, we don't want to buy the place,' Perry said. There were a couple of mugs in the sink, and a series of fridge magnets holding some family photographs.

'How many children do you have, Mr Marasova?' the female officer said, scrutinising a picture of two adults and two teenage children.

'Two. My son, Tador, is in Bucharest to study. Lydia, she is God knows where.'

'And your wife?'

'I am separated. She lives with my son.' Marasova led them into the lounge, into the dining room, and upstairs into each of the three bedrooms. Everything looked tidy and normal. The beds were neatly made, and having seen the mess that Lydia Marasova left in her flat, she didn't look to have been staying here.

'Would you be good enough to ring her from your phone?' Perry asked.

'Of course.' Marasova brought out his own mobile from the pocket of his overalls and tapped out a number. 'There is no reply. Even to me, her father.' He gave a large shrug, his downturned mouth indicating: what is a father to do?

'What about your garage?' Perry said.

'You want to see in my garage? Sure, come and have a look.' The internal door into the garage revealed an enormous model railway which ran right around the perimeter. The whole thing was painstakingly constructed with scale model houses, bridges, stations and rolling hills, with woodland and farms, all with their own livestock. It was clearly the work of many years. 'Do you want to see it in action?' he said, pivoting up a section so he could reach the centre where the consoles were. 'I made all the electronics myself.' The faint smell of solder seemed to underline that.

'No, you're all right,' said the female PC.

Perry, something of a railway enthusiast in his youth, would have been tempted to say yes. Instead, he peered under the waist-high layout to see if anything was concealed. All he could see was a metal cabinet full of neat wiring and electronic bits and bobs, and a few boxes of tools and spare parts. He felt a frisson of boyish excitement.

'As you can see, she is not hiding here,' Marasova said, ducking under to speak to Perry.

The detective inspector stood up. 'Please let us know if you see her again,' he said. From his jacket pocket he took out a photograph of the male pickpocket taken from the CCTV in the shopping centre. 'Do you know this man?'

'No. Who is he?'

'He seems to be working with your daughter, stealing purses and handbags,' Perry said.

The man grimaced and passed his hand across his face as if to wipe away an unwelcome image. 'It is the drugs, you know. She did well at school, and then she fell in with a bad crowd. You know?'

'We know very well,' the female PC said. 'It's all too common, unfortunately.'

'Will you let me know if you find her?' Marasova asked. 'She is a pain in my heart.'

'We will,' Perry said. As they made their way back to the car, he reflected on how many of his own former pupils had set off on a similar journey of self-destruction; starting with a rift with family, bad choices of friends, and misguided attempts at self-discovery through drink or drugs. And then there was his own wild daughter, Vanessa, estranged from the family since the divorce. If all this could be stopped in childhood, you would hardly need a police force.

Chapter Four

Gillard slid his unmarked car into a parking spot near the base of the council tower block. Thamesway Tower. He peered up at the twenty-storey construction, one of the first concrete monstrosities built in south London in the 1960s, and now shrouded in gaily coloured insulation which did nothing to hide the misery of living there. Somewhere up there, on the sixteenth floor, was Keith Sutton, former armed robber, convicted way back in the seventies of GBH and much else. It was his message that had been passed on via Croydon police station. Gillard hadn't seen Sutton for at least a decade, but he must be in his seventies. He had been an important informant when he finally emerged from Wandsworth Prison in 1995. Though he been long retired from criminality, Sutton still knew everybody in the ageing cadre of bank robbers, safe crackers, burglars and hard men. Gelignite and crowbar boys. All those who for decades had been the hard core of British criminality.

Nobody had ever suspected that he'd become a grass.

It was the death of his youngest son in a drugs overdose in 1993 that changed everything. In the early years when Gillard was a DC in the Met, he had interviewed Sutton about a car theft. A BMW had been taken from a nearby street and used in a robbery before being abandoned. Sutton knew nothing about it but said he would ask around. A week later a cryptic message was left on Gillard's phone indicating the address that he should be looking at. The local tearaway he implicated wasn't part of any major crime gang, so Sutton was only doing what any community-minded neighbour would do. Except that being a snitch crosses the line. Once a grass, always a grass.

Gillard checked his watch. Sutton was late. He peered towards the graffiti-stained doors of the tower block. Beside it a bunch of youths, white, Black, and Asian and mostly hooded, sat on bikes, smoking and chatting. Nearby, an abandoned car, side window smashed, sat in a sea of broken bottles. He was glad he didn't have to police this area anymore. Surrey wasn't exactly a cushy number, but it didn't have the problems of poverty, deprivation and inequality which existed here.

Finally, the door opened, and an old bent man wearing a stained car coat and a woolly hat shuffled out behind a walking frame. It took a moment or two for Gillard to realise that this was Keith Sutton. The youths stared at Sutton as he made his way slowly towards the car. Gillard agonised over whether to get out and help him. His face was widely known after some of the cases he been involved in recently, and the arrangement had been that he would stay in the vehicle. So that's what he did. When Sutton got up to the passenger-side door, Gillard buzzed down the window.

'Hello Keith, how are you doing?'

'Can't complain,' he wheezed, as he pulled open the door and folded his walking frame. 'Lungs are buggered, and I've got arthritis of everything. Are we going for a jar?'

'Not here,' Gillard leaned across and put the now-folded frame onto the back seat. He knew that in any pub around here, he would be sniffed out as a copper. 'You like Italian food?' Gillard asked. 'There's a nice place up the road.'

'Nah. Don't like it,' Sutton said, looking up towards the glass and steel towers which were encroaching on his manor. 'It's all trendy metrosexuals and foreigners. What about fish, chips and mushy peas?' He eased himself into the car and closed the door.

'All right, if you know somewhere open at two o'clock on a Tuesday afternoon.'

Half an hour later, Gillard and Sutton were sitting side-by-side in the car eating fish and chips out of crackly white paper, the car filled with the tang of vinegar.

'Not a bad place that,' Gillard said. The chips were nice and crispy, and the fish seemed fresh.

'Used to be owned by Cypriot Joe, you remember him?'

'Wasn't he involved in the Midland Bank job in the nineties?'

Sutton nodded as he laboriously chewed and swallowed a large mouthful. 'He was a good fence. You don't get ones like him these days. All these modern tearaways, they just stick stuff on eBay and get caught. Amateurs, the lot of 'em.'

Gillard let the reminiscences continue for a few minutes before returning to the main subject.

'So what's this about a big job in the offing?'

'I heard a whisper, that's all.'

'From who?'

'Can't say. If I finger my source, you'll just pull him in, wontcha? And he'll put two and two together about who squealed.'

'Okay.' Gillard could tell that Sutton was enjoying stringing out the tale as long as possible. Given that he probably spent most of his time stuck looking out of the window at an ever-changing London, while his old mates died one by one, the chance to tell a story was probably the highlight of his week.

'All I know for certain is it's big. No, not big. Huge.'

'How much?'

'Half a billion nicker.'

Gillard was taken aback. 'Are you having me on?' He couldn't quite imagine anything that big outside of a central London diamond or safe deposit box heist. Frauds could be bigger, but Sutton didn't move in those circles. His mates were all old-fashioned criminals. Gelly and jemmy blokes.

'Can you give me any other names?'

'Do me a favour,' Sutton said, posting a chip into his mouth.

'Fair point. Anything about when?'

'Christmas, in the run-up.'

'Where?'

Sutton stared long and hard at Gillard. 'For fuck's sake, you want it all on the plate, dontcha?'

'I could do with this on a plate,' Gillard said, indicating the greasy bundle in his hands.

'Guv'nor, I have no idea where. Believe me.'

Gillard couldn't remember the last time anyone had called him guv. Still, this was useful information. He was happy to let the conversation fall back into small talk as he drove his source back home to Thamesway Tower.

'Do you want a hand?' Gillard asked as Sutton was laboriously clambering out of the car.

'You couldn't lend us a fifty, could you?' Sutton asked. 'For old time's sake.'

He had expected this. He pulled out his wallet and extracted two twenties and a ten. 'There will be more, a lot more, if you can get me some details.'

'I should cocoa,' Sutton said.

As Sutton shuffled away, Gillard wondered what to do with this nugget of information. In theory, seeing as the informant was in the Met's patch, it was up to them. But Sutton had made it very clear he didn't trust anyone that he'd come across in the Met police, particularly after the way his son was hounded, as he saw it. That's why he'd come to him, someone he trusted from years ago.

Once he'd seen Sutton safely away inside the building, Gillard drove off. He felt sorry for the old geezer, adrift in a world where everything had changed, even the once-familiar nature of crime.

–

Gillard didn't need to ask a favour of Kirsty Mockett to find Matt Culshaw's direct number. The DCI's number was on half a dozen different press releases, the most recent of which related to the moped gangs that he had been involved in cracking down on. He dialled the number and it was picked up by a female officer who said that Culshaw was in an important meeting. Gillard explained who he was and said that he was in receipt of a tip-off and would appreciate a return call.

'I can put you through to his deputy if you like,' she said. 'DI Florence Latimer.'

Gillard agreed and was soon talking to a husky-voiced woman with a Caribbean lilt.

'It's about a big robbery around about Christmas time,' Gillard said.

'Any idea how big?'

'Half a billion.'

'Wow. Are you sure?'

'I'm sure that's what I was told. Whether my source is correct or not, I have no idea.'

'Who is the source?'

Gillard chuckled. 'I'm sure you won't be surprised that I'm not going to tell you. My source would only speak to me.'

'I appreciate that, detective chief inspector. It's an interesting corroboration to something we have heard ourselves.'

'Are you going to share with me?' Gillard asked.

She laughed, a delightful sound. 'You scratch my back and I'll scratch yours.'

'Maybe later,' Gillard said, thanked her and hung up.

The call back from Matt Culshaw took only fifteen minutes.

'Craig, fascinating titbit. Sounds like a case for us.'

'Maybe, depends on the location.'

'It would be too big for Surrey, even if that's where it happens.'

'Then maybe it would be the NCA,' Gillard said. The National Crime Agency tended to get anything that smacked of organised crime outside of Greater London.

Culshaw laughed. 'Half the time the NCA needs our help. We've got all the contacts, you see. We've got more informants in the Met area than the rest of the country put together.'

'But this one's mine.' Gillard wasn't just being stubborn. Anyone who grassed up a major criminal was putting their life on the line. For the police, informants needed handling with the greatest subtlety and care. It was often a fine balancing act of turning a blind eye to minor criminal transgressions in order to get information about major ones. Public money paid on the quiet to those in the know was another procedural minefield. And in the end, you had to keep your successes quiet. Not only for the safety of the informant but to leave the door open to future flows of information.

'Look, Craig, I'm going to be down in Surrey tomorrow evening.'

Gillard smiled to himself. *Yes, and we all know why.*

'Why don't we meet up somewhere in your neck of the woods for a quiet pint, say seven o'clock?'

Gillard would be off duty at six, and suggested the George in the Tree, a very quiet rural hostelry in a wooded fold of the Surrey Hills, which was pretty much on his way home.

Wednesday 2nd December

Culshaw was already sitting on a stool at the bar when Gillard arrived. In his sharp suit and highly polished black shoes, he looked a little out of place amongst the mock Tudor beams, horse brasses and hand pull pumps.

'What'll you have?' Culshaw asked. He appeared to have a pint of lager.

'Just a half of bitter shandy for me,' he said.

Culshaw addressed the barmaid by name as he ordered Gillard's drink. It was served immediately, the young woman making prolonged eye contact with Culshaw as he tapped his card on the proffered payment terminal.

As she moved away to serve another customer, Gillard muttered: 'You're a fast worker.'

'Nah, I just like to be sociable,' Culshaw said. 'Let's shift to a more secluded table.' He eyed a round wooden table at the back of the lounge by the dartboard. Gillard followed him over.

Culshaw took a deep draft of his drink and smacked his lips, his eyes flicking briefly again towards the barmaid. 'So what is it that you've heard, Craig?'

'No more than I told your deputy. A big job, around about Christmas.'

'Half a billion,' Culshaw said, looking Gillard in the eye.

'That's what I heard.'

'We're hearing it too. Only the faintest whispers.' Culshaw looked about as if they risked being overheard. The only nearby occupied table had two elderly men of whom one wore a hearing aid, a grey metal sliver visible behind his ear.

'The only possible element I can add at this stage is that it's likely to be old school,' Gillard said. 'More Brinks Mat than Bernie Madoff.'

Culshaw chuckled at the reference to Britain's biggest bullion robbery. 'Yeah, if it was a fraud, we'd never get to hear about it in advance. In fact, you might not even hear about it afterwards. I'd say that what we are hearing conforms to that too.'

'So do you have any leads?' Gillard asked.

'A few, and they all point to a London connection. Given who our grass is.' Culshaw smiled at Gillard, clearly enjoying fencing with him. 'What interests me is how you came to know about it down in leafy Surrey. I know you worked out of Croydon in the 1990s. I think that's the connection. It's as rough a patch now as it was then. I've had a look through some of the cases you worked on.'

Gillard smiled. *You'll not find out my source that way*.

'Kept out of the paperwork, was he?' Culshaw asked.

'It's pretty much a health and safety requirement, given how many bent coppers there were in London in the 1990s,' Gillard said. 'Look, I'm happy to work with you on this, but you have to keep me in the loop. Not who your informant is, but all the details. Then at least I can go back to my grass and put it to him for confirmation.'

Culshaw took a deep swig from his pint, and scrutinised Gillard through semi-closed eyes. 'Every snout worth their salt knows they can't go back asking more questions. It's a bit suspicious, isn't it? If it doesn't end up getting them killed, it might still scare the robbers off. Intel goes both ways.'

'It's always a judgement call, Matt. Always was, always will be.'

'All right, Craig. Here's a name for you. Mal Scattergood. See what you can find out.'

'I never heard of him.'

'Son of Les Scattergood, fence and jewel thief of the seventies. Scattergood senior died a few years ago, having done a twenty stretch. Les' missus, Vera Scattergood, still runs the Railway Tavern in Bermondsey. Always dreamt of retiring to Spain but never did. Son Malcolm's record is much more small-time. Truant at school, shoplifting, some minor drugs, youth custody, got involved in some dodgy one arm bandit deals. Six months inside in 2002. Now he's a shopfitter working for one of the big firms.'

'He'd be out of his depth, wouldn't he? Half a billion?'

'Yeah, we can't see where he fits in.'

'Did his dad teach him about fencing jewellery?' Gillard asked.

'Well, old Les Scattergood used to melt down and recast stolen gold and silver in his workshop under the railway arches at the back of the pub. I'll email you his record, see what you think. More to the point, see what your grass can come up with.'

Culshaw drained his pint, checked his watch and said: 'Best be off now.'

'Don't want to keep Kirsty waiting, do you?'

Culshaw smiled and twitched his eyebrows.

'Treat her nicely, Matt. I don't want her getting upset. She's a real asset to our CSI team.' He looked meaningfully towards the barmaid Culshaw had been eyeing earlier.

Culshaw laughed. 'One other thing I forgot to mention about young Scattergood. His mum is the sister of Jackie Norris.'

Gillard's jaw hung open. Now that *was* an interesting connection.

–

After Culshaw had gone and Gillard was driving home, he considered what he knew about the legendary criminal Jackie Norris. Brought up in Bermondsey, Norris had a prison record starting in 1965 when he was fifteen. Shoplifting, GBH, then in the 1970s a couple of bank jobs. He briefly became involved in the south London-based Richardson gang before setting up on his own. His highest profile job, and the one that brought him notoriety, was the theft from a Piccadilly jeweller in 1983 of a £4.5 million diamond jewellery collection that had once belonged to Czarina Alexandra Fyodorovna, on loan from St Petersburg prior to an exhibition. He did seventeen years for that but none of the items were ever recovered.

All of this might have been just of academic interest had Norris not turned up in Gillard's patch in 2006. He purchased and renovated the old Lord Russell Hotel outside Guildford, turning it into an upmarket spa resort now called the Swallowtail Hotel. Norris, having been divorced by his wife in prison, had remarried a glamorous *Sunday Times* investigative reporter who had come to profile him. Sally Winchester, who kept her maiden name, then produced the bestselling biography *Redemption: The Jackie Norris Story*. It was serialised in an ITV three-parter in 2010, with Norris himself being played by Ray Winstone. As an exercise in public rehabilitation, it could not be bettered.

But everybody still wondered where all the money for the hotel came from.

Over dinner with Sam that evening, Gillard asked if Sam had ever been to the Swallowtail Hotel. She poured him a glass of Pinot Grigio and replied: 'No, more's the pity. Have you suddenly come into some money?'

Gillard laughed. 'No I haven't, but I think we could stretch to the weekday lunch.' He had looked at the hotel website and seen that the taster menu was £90, excluding wine. The mini spa break was £400. However, the website slideshow was very slick, and only on the 'about us' section was there any mention of 'Mr Jack Norris, our celebrity owner with a colourful past'.

'Sounds great to me,' Sam said. 'We could get an early bird sauna and massage first.'

'I suppose I asked for this, didn't I?'

'Don't be tight on me. I'll pay for it. Besides, after the physio had a go at my arm, it's even more bruised. A nice massage should help.'

'I'm not sure I need the massage,' Gillard said.

'I don't know *anyone* who needs a massage more than you do,' she scoffed. 'You've got more stress than a football manager in the relegation zone. You don't swim so much anymore, and the cycling days are few and far between. You're *always* at work.'

'Well, if only people would stop killing each other...'

'Then you wouldn't have to be killing yourself, right?'

'All right, all right, I'll go for the massage.'

Sam got out her new phone and swiped through the Swallowtail Hotel website. 'I'm booking us in before you change your mind.' She tapped in the details on the booking form. 'Right, that's it. A week on Saturday, 9.30 a.m. I'm going for a deep cleansing facial and an Indian head massage. I've got you down for the full body. Do you want the hot stones?'

'No thanks. Sounds like a medieval punishment.'

'Don't be so cynical. You'll love it. And I'm paying for lunch afterwards.'

Chapter Five

It was technically his day off, but Gillard had no other time to visit Keith Sutton. He'd left several messages on the informant's landline, for the sake of safety just identifying himself as Craig, and had eventually got a return call from Sutton's daughter Dawn explaining that he had just come out of hospital, and was on oxygen. Apparently, he could barely speak.

Traffic was just as clogged as ever, and despite heavy cloud cover and intermittent showers, there was the usual gaggle of youths by the windswept base of Thamesway Tower. Gillard emerged from the unmarked car, which he parked within view of a CCTV camera. He'd dressed down for the trip in bomber jacket, tatty jeans and trainers. The lads grudgingly parted to let him past and go through the aluminium doors and into the lobby. He feared that the lifts would be broken, but at least one of them seemed to work, arriving with a clatter and then wheezing open. He stepped inside the cramped and smelly metal box, in which almost every possible surface had been burned with cigarette ends and tagged with graffiti. He turned to hit the close button, but a large Puffa-jacketed arm prevented the door from closing. A large and intimidating Black guy in his early twenties with an intricate razor cut and diamante stud earrings stepped in with him.

'Which floor?' Gillard asked.

The man ignored the question, and his finger snaked forward and jabbed the button for eleven, just an inch in front of Gillard's chest. Once the lift shuddered into its upward crawl, he got out a marker pen, and unhurriedly scrawled out 'death to cops' on the metal doors, finishing with his own tag. He then capped the pen and stared into Gillard's face for the entire agonisingly slow journey. Gillard let his gaze drift away, not wishing for a pointless confrontation or to confirm the man's suspicion. The unerring radar of the neighbourhood hoodlums had discerned something about the way he dressed or his demeanour. Perhaps if he'd been wearing a suit and if it wasn't a Sunday, he might well have passed for some local authority official.

At eleven, the door opened, letting in a rhythmic blast of rap. The man made an unhurried departure, swaggering down the corridor towards the sound. It took several jabs of Gillard's finger to persuade the door close button to work, as if the lift somehow thought he should be confronting the miscreant.

Sutton's flat was on the sixteenth floor, past a series of graffiti-stained windows, on a corridor bathed in the aroma of bad cooking. There had been an attempt to make the entrance look homely with an external doormat and a small cactus in a pot, seemingly dead. To one side there was a metal grille secured by padlocks, which could be folded across the door for extra security.

Gillard rang the bell, which was answered by a big-built woman of around thirty-five, heavily made up, with marker pen eyebrows.

'You Craig?' she asked.

'I am. You must be Dawn.'

She looked behind him nervously before letting him in. ''E's in 'ere,' she said, leading Gillard into a cramped lounge, oppressively heated. Sutton was sitting in a battered chair, staring at the football on the TV. He had an oxygen mask over his face, but his eyes smiled. He beckoned Gillard to sit on the chair opposite and lowered the sound on the game. Sutton's voice was a barely audible gasp, but Gillard heard it as a greeting.

'Fancy a cuppa?' Dawn called to him.

'Please. No sugar, just a dash of milk.'

She was looking at him curiously. 'You're not from the social, then?'

'No.'

'He don't get many visitors, except official ones. So which are you?'

'I've known Keith for years. Craig Roberts. I used to be his probation officer.' It was a tenable lie. The surname was his mother's maiden name.

She scrutinised Gillard's face, looking for some evidence of this past connection. 'Okay then.'

'Dawn, you can leave us alone for a few minutes,' Sutton rasped. The slow hum of the oxygen machine behind the settee and the rising roar of the electric kettle in the kitchen almost drowned him out.

She closed the lounge door and left them to it.

'This place has changed a bit, hasn't it?' Gillard said.

'I've been here since they built it. Moved out of the terraces, down there. All demolished now. All gone. Still, I'll be here 'til they take me out in a wooden box.'

'How do you get on with the neighbours?' Gillard asked.

'Oright.'

Gillard told the old man about his encounter in the lift.

'A lot of drugs in this building,' Sutton said. 'There's a Rasta gang on the eleventh floor, and there's loads of noisy parties. There's some advantages to going a bit deaf. But on the other hand, there are fewer break-ins because the young kids are scared of 'em. Jerrold, one of the dealers, knows about me. I get some respect off of him. He even went to get me shopping in a couple of times when Dawn couldn't come during lockdown.'

Dawn briefly came in to leave them each their tea, Gillard's served in a cup and saucer, Sutton's in a chipped mug.

Gillard scrutinised the old man, physically decrepit but mentally flexible. Most people of his age couldn't deal with changing times. This area had always been rife with crime, but most of the families then had been known to each other, looked after each other's kids, a cohesive if fractious community. Now, all over the country, there were estates dotted with the elderly whose kids had moved away and left them marooned and isolated, surrounded by new, more racially diverse and occasionally intimidating people. But those like Sutton were able to see that new cultures brought at least as much respect for the elderly as those that they replaced. Even, it seemed, the drug dealers.

'No, it's not them I'm worried about.'

'Who, then?'

'You come back for more, aintcha? You want me to spill the beans.'

Gillard had planned to work his way round gradually to the subject of his visit, but it would be obvious to Sutton with the insistent phone messages. What other reason could there be?

'If you have any more,' Gillard said. 'What about the name Mal Scattergood?'

Sutton coughed violently, and waved a dismissive hand towards Gillard while reaching for the oxygen mask. A few deep shuddering breaths and he was able to remove it.

'You shouldn't have come here,' Sutton whispered. 'It's bad for my health and safety.'

'I'm not going to ask you to go back and ask any more questions, I know that wouldn't be sensible.'

'Dead right. You should make your own enquiries without mentioning me.'

'So this job is still on?'

'I've heard no different.'

'And you've no idea where?'

'He didn't say.'

'And Scattergood?'

Sutton started to laugh, which turned into a cough, which in turn caused him to spill his tea. It took a few more breaths on the oxygen before he was able to speak again. Dawn came in and chastised Gillard as he was attempting to wipe up the spill with a tissue from a box by Sutton's side.

'You're upsetting him. He's not well.'

'I'm all right, stop yer fussing, gal,' Sutton gasped.

'I'm doing this for you,' Dawn said, then turned to Gillard. 'He's an ungrateful old sod. I come round here twice a week to clean the place up and look after 'im, and what thanks do I get?'

'Have you got Carer's Allowance for him?' Gillard asked.

'Nah, the forms are a nightmare. He gets a bit off the rent, and he's got an extra bit on his pension.'

'Council Tax Reduction and Pension Credit,' Gillard said.

'Yeah, that's it.'

'With his mobility problems, you should be able to get Carer's Allowance.'

'I've got the form, but I didn't get very far,' she said. 'Someone told me he couldn't get it because of all that time he spent in prison.'

'That's not true,' Gillard said.

A few minutes later he was sitting at Keith Sutton's dining table going through the Carer's Allowance form with Dawn. It was a hefty document with lots of notes in bold and he soon realised that Sutton would need to be in receipt of something called Personal Independence Payment, or an equivalent benefit, to prove that he needed the help. No wonder Dawn had struggled.

'I'm a bit rusty on these,' he admitted. 'Half of the benefits have new names since I helped a neighbour apply. Ask at your local Citizens Advice, they can help you with the forms.'

'Oh, right, thank you.' She seemed mollified. Gillard got up and returned to the lounge, where Keith was watching the football again.

'So where were we? Scattergood, wasn't it,' Gillard whispered.

'I told you, I can't ask questions 'cos it looks iffy. All I can do is listen.'

After another coughing bout, Gillard asked what they said at the hospital about his lungs.

'Totally buggered, basically. Too many fags for too long, and of course I lived through all the years of the smog an' all. The consultant said my lungs look just like a kipper.' He looked up at Gillard and said, 'Got taken to

43

the seaside once, Herne Bay in Kent, when I was a nipper. You know, I fainted with all the oxygen and fresh air. Me mum and dad had to wave a full ashtray under me nose to bring me round.' The anecdote, clearly much-repeated, set off another bout of mixed laughter and coughing.

Gillard chuckled along with him.

'Seven years, they reckon. That's how long I've got.'

'Not too bad, I suppose.'

'Wouldn't be so bad if hadn't spent most of it inside.' Sutton pulled out a packet of cigarettes, its cover depicting a horrific wound of indeterminate location. 'I better start hurrying up and finishing off my stash,' he said, propping one in the corner of his mouth and feeling in his pockets for a lighter. 'I wouldn't want to pop my clogs with an unfinished packet, would I? That would be a waste of dosh.'

As the room filled with the acrid smell of tobacco, Gillard decided it might be time to go.

Sutton waved his hand in the smoke, as if that had any chance of dispersing the smell. 'Dawn goes on at me to give up, but I can't. Sod all left to live for anyway.'

'Have you tried nicotine patches?'

Sutton laughed and slid up a sleeve of his shirt. The pale almost grey skin had a large patch on it. 'Been there, done that,' he said.

Gillard stood up and thanked Sutton for talking to him. 'I've got to get back now. You know, if you can prevent this crime, we might be able to stop somebody spending the rest of their life locked up like you did. All I need is just a little bit more information.'

'All right. I overheard the whisper that it was Norris that was recruiting.'

'Jackie Norris?'

'Yep, big Jackie. And his son Damian.'

Interesting. That at least corroborated what Culshaw had heard.

–

Monday morning was a day out for Gillard, away from his normal duties in Surrey. He had been called to a confidential meeting of M07, the serious and organised crime group, at New Scotland Yard in central London, to discuss the rumoured robbery. After getting off the train at Waterloo, he made his way along the South Bank, enjoying the watery sunshine and the unseasonable mildness, and across Westminster Bridge, then turned right onto Victoria embankment and the imposing edifice of the Metropolitan Police headquarters. At reception he was given two additional security lanyards and escorted up to the third floor, where he was ushered into a room that was smaller than he expected. He recognised Matt Culshaw, and next to him a tall Black female officer who he took to be DI Latimer. The meeting was led by Assistant Commissioner Kay Thompson, and the head of the unit, Commander Digby Snow.

After thanking them all for coming, Thompson said: 'This meeting is absolutely confidential. We are at the early stages of uncovering what could be a major robbery, which relies on covert intelligence and under-cover officers. But intelligence travels in two directions. We know from experience that crime gangs have their own eyes and ears both within the Met and in other forces. It is prudent therefore to minimise the number of officers who are aware of what we know.' She then passed over to Snow.

'Normally we are lucky to get even a whisper of a robbery in advance,' Snow said. 'This time, we have three sources. The first, let's call him Oscar, is an undercover officer who has been working for three years to penetrate a series of crime families in the Bermondsey area. The second, who is a serving prisoner, is Tango. Then there is Sierra.' Snow nodded at Gillard. 'Who rather fell into our lap.' The commander looked around at the officers present, and said, 'If we play this right, it will not only be a major crime prevented, but an enormous PR coup. As you know, the force has its share of critics, and we need a few high-profile victories to set against the inevitable miscarriages of justice and accusations of institutional this or that. Since the Sarah Everard case, the stakes have become very high.'

Snow then introduced Culshaw, who began a slide presentation.

'This is what we have been told. One, a high-value operation potentially worth half a billion pounds.'

'Half a billion? That's bigger than Brinks Mat, the Great Train Robbery and all the top ten combined!' said one grey-haired detective, who had been introduced as a DCS from the City of London Police.

'That's right, it could be huge. And it's imminent,' Culshaw said. 'To take place in the next few weeks. One source says on the Friday before Christmas, which is December eighteenth, another says merely in the run-up to Christmas. Two names have been mentioned. One is Mal Scattergood. Here he is.' The mugshot showed an apple-cheeked individual with a mass of wavy dark hair. 'He's known to his friends as Hobbit, partially because of his limited height. He works as a shopfitter for one of the big firms and has only a small-time criminal record.

But don't be fooled. Scattergood comes from good criminal stock. His father Les was a big wheel in some of the robberies of the 1970s and 80s. The family forte was melting down gold and silver, disposing of jewellery and gems.'

Culshaw moved on to the next slide. 'And here we have Scattergood's uncle, big Jackie Norris, whom I am sure needs no introduction.' This was no mugshot, but an up-to-date publicity pic from the Swallowtail Hotel website. Norris was big-built, with a thatch of white hair, a ruddy face, and a smile full of bleached teeth. Culshaw then went through Norris' extensive crime history and his public rehabilitation. 'I have to tell you, I was a little bit surprised to hear that Norris might be involved. He's been straight, or appeared to be, for many years. Become a bit of a national treasure, what with the ITV series and the establishment girlfriend, now his second wife. The big question to me was this: why would he need the money, seeing as he's already running a successful business empire? However, I've got some of my financial colleagues to do a bit of digging, and it seems our Mr Norris is up to his ears in debt, some of which comes due very soon. He needs a big win. Now Damian Norris hasn't got the prison record to match his dad, only a couple of years for some cannabis dealing back in 2007. But he's a bit flash, fancies himself with the ladies. Always been in his dad's shadow.'

'What would his role be, do you think?' Digby Snow asked.

'We are not aware of any particular technical skills,' Culshaw said. 'I do have to confess that it seems a little bit out of his league. It might well be that he is acting simply as a gopher on behalf of his father.'

The next slide was simply a question mark on a white background. 'This is only a partial cast list, of course, and we need much more to know who is actually going to be doing the dirty work. But the biggest question mark is, what is the job? It's clearly old school, based on the participants, but where exactly could such a large robbery take place? Up until yesterday afternoon, I had merely started whittling down the possibilities of where such value might be stored. But then we got this.' Culshaw clicked on a button, and there was a crackly recording of one voice saying in a marked south London accent: 'Righto then, see you at Oxford Circus at 8.15 a.m. on the day.'

'Where did that recording come from?' Gillard asked.

'Courtesy of Oscar, and the voice you hear is Mal Scattergood.'

The assistant commissioner intervened. 'This is good, but we need more. Some corroboration, and some more names.' She was in her fifties, slightly built, with a helmet of silver hair and gold-rimmed glasses. Gillard heard that she'd come in from the City of London Economic Crime Unit. Some had, unkindly, said she'd never got her hands dirty. But much police work was cerebral now, and no one doubted the power of her mind.

'I agree, ma'am,' said Snow. 'But for operational reasons you can't get informants to tell you more than they know. Questions raise suspicion—'

'—To be blunt, ma'am, grasses risk their lives just to give us the barest whispers,' Culshaw said. 'They all have their own motives, but have to be treated with delicacy.'

'I do understand that,' she said. 'But I want to know where it is, and soon. We simply don't have the resources to stake out every bank deposit facility or diamond jeweller, even if we know what day it is happening.' She picked up her papers and tapped them on the desk before sliding them into her briefcase. The meeting was clearly over.

–

Culshaw guided Gillard down to the incident room being set up for Operation Santa Claus. It wasn't a big room, but it boasted a great view over the River Thames, with Westminster Bridge just to the right. There were just three detectives allocated so far under DI Florence Latimer, plus a few phones and a couple of whiteboards.

'This is DC Brendan Musgrove, codenamed Oscar.' Gillard shook hands with the man, a sharp-featured individual with long greasy hair, ripped jeans and nicotine-stained fingers on which were half a dozen bulky rings. 'Brendan's greatest asset is that no one thinks he is a cop.'

'Not even my son,' Musgrove said with a strong Geordie accent. 'I disappeared for three months undercover, and he thought I'd genuinely been sent to prison.'

'Or had been on tour with Motörhead,' Gillard said, noting the extensive tattoos that ran up each side of Musgrove's neck. He'd have needed special permission for that, but Gillard could see why he'd got it. You can't go undercover if you don't look the part.

Latimer then introduced financial specialist DC Stacey Daines, a slender woman in her thirties with fair hair in a ponytail, and DC Jason Hart, technical specialist. Young and skinny, with a narrow face, he looked right for the part of the office anorak.

'Right,' Culshaw said, sitting on the edge of Daines' desk. 'Stacey here has done some solid work on where the job could be. What have you got, Stace?'

'Given the date, I was thinking about what the targets could be that are worth half a billion.' She got up and pointed to a large map of central London hanging on the wall next to her desk. 'The classic target for an old-style blag would be somewhere in Hatton Garden with all its diamond merchants, any major bank with safety deposit boxes, or possibly an airport. But to be honest I was struggling to come up with anything worth quite that much.'

Culshaw laughed. 'A bit of exaggeration in the criminal fraternity isn't unknown. If they want to recruit, especially. I'm sure that's the main reason we've heard about it, because everyone is shocked by the size of the job.'

'The timing, just before Christmas, makes sense. Offices will be closed, there will be fewer people about—' Daines said.

'That would make sense if it was actually Christmas Day or Boxing Day,' Gillard said. 'But not the Friday before Christmas. That would be a really busy shopping day, one of the most frantic of the year. Maybe it's something where a lot of pedestrians would mask the activity. Hence the Oxford Circus mention.'

'I'm not sure about that,' Culshaw said. 'It's not going to be actually at Oxford Circus. That's probably just the most convenient place to meet up.'

'Not in a vehicle, and they would be bound to be driving, wouldn't they?' Gillard insisted.

Culshaw shrugged. 'Someone is bound to be driving, yes, but they might just be picking up a couple of others at Oxford Circus, or somewhere nearby. Look, I don't want to get too hung up on details at this stage. We're juggling a lot of variables, and not all of them will be right. It's like the assistant commissioner said, we need more information.'

'Stacey's done a lot of work on picking out potential targets near Oxford Circus,' DI Latimer said. 'There's the Sharps Pixley Bullion and Safe Deposit near Piccadilly, and on Park Lane there is IVB International Vaults. There's Metropolitan safe deposits in Belgravia—'

'Have you contacted any of these places to ask about valuations?' Gillard asked.

'No, no. That's not the way it's going to work,' Culshaw replied. 'First off, there's a good chance there's an insider in this job. If you contact the banks or whatever, there's a pretty good chance it will be like stirring a stick in an ants' nest. Whoever is on the inside will see all the fuss and get the hint, and the job might be called off. I want to emphasise that I do *not* want this job to be called off, I want to catch the bastards in the act.'

'You wouldn't be able to get a valuation, either, in most cases,' Daines said to Gillard. 'The whole attraction of safety deposit boxes is that you don't have to let anyone know what's inside.'

'Which means there's bound to be a lot of criminal money,' Musgrove said.

'And that's another reason why it's good to make sure the blag goes ahead,' Culshaw said. 'We might end up retrieving an awful lot of stolen property.'

'So are you thinking gold, considering that Scattergood is involved?' Gillard asked. 'Something he can melt down just like his old man used to do?'

'Maybe,' Culshaw said.

'What's the price of gold at the moment?' Gillard asked, taking a spare seat and pulling out his notebook and pen.

'Roughly $1,800 an ounce,' Daines said, waggling a pen back and forth between her fingers. 'I've already done this calculation. If you are thinking about how much gold for half a billion, it's 27,700 ounces, which is a bit less than a ton. It would all be manageable in a single big vanload. But if it was silver, half a billion's worth would be a freight train full, about six hundred tons.'

'Right, what about other precious metals?'

'Platinum, palladium and rhodium are probably the ones you're thinking of,' Daines said. 'Rhodium is typically ten times the price of gold, the others just a bit more than gold. But I don't think you'll find any of them in a sufficiently concentrated form.'

'Catalytic converters,' said Musgrove. 'They have the biggest use of these metals, to absorb pollution. That's why everyone's nicking them.'

Gillard was aware of this too. Surrey Police had recently undertaken a big operation to stop catalytic converter thefts. The soaring value of the precious metals funded a crime where the devices were either stripped down and the metals extracted as a powder, or the stolen converters sold online.

'I don't think we're going to be talking about a half billion pound catalytic converter heist,' Gillard said.

'No, I agree,' Culshaw said. 'And I think we're getting off the point. Just because Scattergood's dad used to melt down stolen precious metals doesn't mean to say that's the route that young Mal is taking.'

'So what's the next step?' Gillard asked.

'We've just got a warrant for surveillance at the Railway Tavern in Bermondsey, which seems to be the epicentre of all the activity. Mal Scattergood doesn't live there, but it seems to be where he met Damian Norris.'

'I'd love to see how you can get a bug in there,' Gillard said.

'That will be down to me,' Musgrove said, 'this evening, because I'm in the darts team that is playing there. Do you fancy coming along?'

'Won't they sniff me out as a cop?' Gillard said.

'You'll be fine as long as you stay in the lounge. There's no end of office workers who go in there. The back bar is a private members' club; you've got to be signed in. That's the place where your face has to fit. And that's where I'll be.'

–

The Railway Tavern was only about half a mile from where Keith Sutton lived, down a narrow street of which a few parts were still cobbled. As Gillard approached on foot from the main road, he saw that the whole area was a collision between two different communities: the redeveloped offices where bearded hipsters sat in large-windowed open-plan offices at their laptops, and the 1930s brick-built blocks of social housing from whose long-stained walkways youths and the elderly stared down. Two railway viaducts muscled their way through, the main lines to parts of Kent shouldered on Victorian brick arches the colour and texture of fruitcake. The pub was wedged into the cleft where the two railway lines converged. It advertised Sky Sports, live music and every Sunday lunchtime, adult entertainment. There were two street doors, one marked lounge, the other members' club. Gillard took the former, as instructed. It led into a classic London wood panelled bar with bevel-edged mirrors and a fine original ceiling, nicotine coated over the original white.

Half a dozen drinkers were there, a couple of them like him wearing a suit, most of them transfixed by the muted music videos playing on a wall mounted screen. Two doors led out of the lounge, one marked to the toilets and the other private.

Gillard made his way up to the bar and ordered a lime and soda from a matronly barmaid, most of whom was squeezed into a low-cut leopard skin blouse. Behind her, he could see the longer bar that served the members' club, a much larger space, from which he could hear the clack of pool. He could see no sign of Mal Scattergood nor Damian Norris. Taking his drink, he sat down at a table in the corner and pretended to play with his phone.

Even here in the lounge, there was an atmosphere. A big guy, shaven head protruding through the top of his leather jacket, was playing the fruit machines with an apparently endless supply of tokens, and pints lined up on the bar. But he was clocking Gillard. It was clever, but the angle of a framed Guinness mirror next to the machine allowed him to see the whole lounge. Gillard soaked up details in his peripheral vision. Chunky gold wrist chain, oil-stained jeans, engineer boots, nicotine-stained fingers. He had stubbly creases in the back of his head that rolled up and down as he chewed gum. The dark eyes, beady as a sewer rat, moved to the mirror again. Gillard felt his flesh crawl, as if he was sweating cop DNA that everyone here could smell.

It seemed an endless fifteen minutes later when Gillard heard Musgrove's cheery tones greeting someone on the other side. Culshaw had told Gillard the story of how Musgrove had over the period of a year or two inveigled his way into the Railway Tavern darts team. Being trusted had taken a while, but the fact that he was a talented player helped smooth the process. In the meantime, he'd had to put up with a torrent of jovial insults aimed at his Geordie origins.

Gillard's own job was simple enough. It was to visit the gents, the only place where club members and ordinary front lounge customers might run into each other, and plant the tiny bug that Musgrove had given him. The object was no bigger than his thumbnail, with a magnetic base designed to attach to the fitting of a fluorescent tube. It was a ten-second job but carried some risk in case he was disturbed. Musgrove, who had invested three years in his undercover role, could not take such a chance, but a random customer like Gillard could.

He picked his moment, made his way in and saw that the fitting in question was above one of the cubicles. That would work perfectly because he could do it with the door locked. However, when he went inside, he found the lock was broken and the cubicle wouldn't stay shut. While he was there, someone came in and urinated noisily into the gulley. He waited, sitting on the closed toilet lid, a foot braced against the door to stop it drifting open. He waited until the man had finished and left, then lifted the lid and stood on the toilet to reach up and fit the bug. It looked perfect, even down to a slight yellowing and corrosion on the mounting, which made it look like it had been there for years.

Now all he had to do was keep his eyes and ears open. At a quarter past seven, the darts match began, and he could occasionally hear Musgrove's voice above that of others. He admired the undercover officer for the risks he was taking. He had told Gillard that he was planning to plant the other listening device on the underside of the pool table, not only the kind of place where no one would be able to look, but fairly central within the bar. Crouching down to put coins in the push tray would give him the few seconds cover he needed to reach underneath. The biggest practical problems of course were likely to be extraneous noises, not only the conversations of those nearby, but the thud and rattle of pocketed balls. Still, it was worth a go. His own device was even less likely to catch anything incriminating. Gillard drained the dregs of his drink, stood up, and called a cheery good evening to the barmaid. Fruit machine man turned and growled: 'You take care.' It was clearly intended as advice.

'Catch you later,' Gillard warned.

The man glanced at his watch, then grinned. 'Then I'll be shooting off too.' His hand strayed to his inside jacket pocket. Gillard extruded a thin smile, decided the threatening repartee had gone far enough, and made his way out onto the street. Just as he did so, he saw Keith Sutton being helped from a car by his daughter. She recognised him and smiled.

'Didn't think you lived round this neck of the woods,' she said.

'I don't. But I just thought I'd pop in for a quick half to remind myself what the place was like thirty years ago.'

Keith Sutton scowled up at him from the handles of his walking frame, which Dawn had just given him. 'You don't want to be coming round here,' he growled.

'It's all right, Dad, he can drink where he likes.'

'Get off out of it,' he said, waving Gillard away.

Dawn exchanged an exasperated glance with Gillard. 'I think it's the medication. Don't take no notice.'

Gillard knew exactly what Sutton meant. He said his goodbyes and hurried away. He glanced behind him after a few yards to check that fruit machine man wasn't following. Instead he saw Dawn was helping her father into the private club entrance. It seemed to be clear that all the intelligence the police had was coming from the same tightly guarded den of thieves. That might be okay if it was accurate, but it lacked genuine corroboration.

Chapter Six

Tuesday 8th December

It was four a.m. when a stolen VW Golf emerged from the fog on the A281 and coasted alongside the Rising Sun pub and restaurant. This was the main Guildford to Horsham road, but there would be little traffic for a couple of hours. The car passed the pub and pulled over in a farm gate entrance fifty yards beyond. A large male figure in dark clothing and a hooded top emerged from the car, wearing a rucksack and carrying a small toolbox. He made his way into the pub car park, walking along the grassy edge and avoiding the gravel. He passed through a small garden laid out with wooden picnic tables, and approached the covered dining room at the rear of the main building. The rear proximity light, which he had sabotaged the previous night, had not been repaired, and he worked in the light of his own head torch. The door was a substantial five lever mortice, bolted at top and bottom. However, the adjacent window was a tired wooden single-pane frame, with cracked putty and flaking paint. It was the work of only two minutes to slice out enough of the putty to dislodge the pane, using rubber suckers to ease it out. He lowered the glass to the ground and eased one leg and then the other through the gap, sliding his substantial body through. He was now standing in the rear dining room, its dozen or so tables decked with plastic menu cards. He made his way stealthily towards the next door into the pub proper. This was a simpler lock. He worked on it as silently as possible, and found that one of the fifteen keys he brought with him for a basic mortice turned the tumblers. He sprayed a quick blast of WD-40 on the hinges before he eased it open. Nothing worse than a squeak.

The door opened silently. He could see the bar, with its rows of bottles, and the till beyond. He took out a cordless drill battery from the rucksack and fitted it to the electrical connection for the till. As long as the till was in the usual printer mode, this would work. The drawer duly popped open, and he grabbed the few notes still in there. There was almost certainly more upstairs, but he wasn't going there. This was risky enough as it was. He reached up to the top shelf behind the bar. He grabbed what unopened spirits he could, and stuffed them in cardboard sleeves and into the rucksack, before heading for the exit. He stowed his haul in the boot of the car and headed off, easing the car gently onto the deserted road. Complete turnaround eight minutes. That was good.

Chapter Seven

It was a raw wet morning, wrapped in mist and winter darkness, as Gillard made his way through Byfleet and New Haw, suppressing a yawn as he did so. The car clock showed 6.43 a.m. and though the heater made the Vauxhall's interior cosy, he had to direct the blowers to the windscreen to stop them misting. It would be cold outside, just one of the things waiting to chill him.

There were reports of a body found floating in a canal. He'd been the duty overnight detective, so it was down to him. He found the place and turned left off Byfleet Road into a lane. It ran between railings into some woods, much abused for fly-tipping, in the roaring and rumbling shadow of the M25. He parked behind a couple of patrol cars, their flashing blues giving the nearby trees an eerie hue. They were fifty yards from the flyover. He emerged from the car, wrapped his coat around him, and picked up his grab bag from the boot. A female officer standing by the crime tape greeted him, made a note of his name on a clipboard, and pointed him towards the CSI van which was right by the canal. This particular spot was an extraordinary confluence of routes: a motorway, lined by pylons on both sides, crossing two canals and a railway line, all within a hundred metres of each other. On the far side of the waterway was an enormous electricity substation, with a metal-encased cable bridge which crossed over the canal, under the flyover, before disappearing underground. Every available vertical space on the M25's pillars had been daubed with graffiti.

It was a hellish final resting place: giant scarred pillars marching away into the gloom, filthy dark waters and an unending overhead soundtrack rendered in thunderous timpani.

As he made his way along the muddy path, his route was illuminated by repeated camera flashes. In the deep shadow of the flyover, crime scene investigators were active under arc lights. He recognised CSI chief Yaz Quoroshi, already dressed in his white Tyvek suit, talking to a man in a red fleece which marked him as a National Trust ranger. Gillard looked over the lip of the canal edge. The body was easy enough to see, lying face down, wearing dark clothing except for pristine white trainers. Male, youngish, well-built. Quoroshi took more photographs. Kirsty Mockett was busy putting up a rectangular white tent across the towpath.

'There are cycle tracks here,' Gillard said to her, pointing to tyre marks on the grassy edge near the canal. 'Look like fresh ones to me.'

'Ah, I better move the tent then.' She began to move the structure a little further away from the water.

'Where is the witness?' Gillard asked Quoroshi.

'Over there. A dog walker as usual.' Gillard followed his directions to a patrol car, where a middle-aged man with an aged border terrier was talking to a couple of uniformed officers. Gillard rubbed the dog's warm head as he exchanged greetings with the man. One of the female PCs had already taken a statement, and Gillard glanced through her notebook. The man had spotted the body at 6.15 a.m.

'So this is your usual route?' Gillard asked the man.

'Mornings and evenings, yes. A mile each way up and down, and I park the car just there, on the edge of the lane.'

'Did you hear anything? If you can, above the noise of the traffic.'

'As I told your colleague, there was just the rumble of the motorway above.'

'Were there any other vehicles parked nearby?'

'Not that I noticed. You can't get the car this far up, normally, because the gates there are locked across the lane.'

Gillard followed his line of sight. The nearest parking was maybe sixty yards from the water. The ranger had presumably been called out to allow CSI access right to the water.

'Is it busy along here?'

'Sometimes, in the evenings, when the weather is good. There are plenty of joggers and cyclists. Not so much this time of year. And in the early mornings it's often deserted, except for the occasional fisherman. It was raining yesterday evening so it was pretty quiet. But I'm sure someone would have spotted him if he'd been there yesterday.'

Gillard smiled. 'You're getting ahead of me there.' He thanked him, and then went up to the ranger, a burly man in his mid-fifties. He confirmed the details the dog walker had given Gillard.

'I can see you sometimes have problems with fly-tipping?'

'Yes. There's no one on site. They normally just dump it by the gates.'

'Any other problems, typically?'

'Most mornings there's a fresh collection of pizza boxes, McDonald's wrappers and drinks cans, used dog poo bags. And of course used condoms lobbed in the bushes by courting couples.'

'Revolting.'

'That's the great British public,' he said with a smile.

'There's no easier vehicle access to the canal round here, is there?'

'No.' He scratched his head. 'It always used to be blocked off right at the road because of the fly-tipping. That's the only way for a car. The River Wey Navigation joins the Basingstoke Canal, just down there near where the London railway line crosses.' He then turned around and pointed in the opposite direction. 'The canal goes under the A318 half a mile north, at New Haw Lock, that might be easier.'

'Ever had a body in the canal before?'

'Not in my time. I think we had a car that fell of the motorway once, years ago, before they put the side-screens up on the carriageway.'

Gillard thanked him. Maybe this death would turn out to be a suicide or an accident. But if it wasn't, this location made sense. If you wanted to dump a body, it was ideal: vehicle accessible right to within fifty yards of the water, hardly anyone around if you picked your moment, and plenty of traffic noise to mask the splash.

–

By the time Gillard returned to the canal edge, the body had been retrieved from the water with the aid of boat hooks and ropes. It was now resting on a piece of polythene sheeting inside the CSI tent, with Kirsty Mockett taking photographs. The Black or mixed-race ethnicity of the dead man was now clear. His skin had taken on a bluish tinge, and was wrinkled on hands and neck, but there were no obvious signs of injury or bloodstains. Gillard slid on a pair of neoprene gloves and lifted the drenched sweatshirt to reveal the man's torso.

'No evidence of a stab wound,' Gillard said. 'I suppose it could be suicide.'

'Or accidental,' Quoroshi said. 'Off his face on something, and just fell in.' The CSI chief took a cotton bud from the packet in his pocket and inserted it slowly up one nostril of the victim. It came back with a brownish-white fluid. 'Looks to be frothy. Kirsty, can we have a picture of this before I bag it? It could be evidence of drowning.' The CSI technician duly took close-up photographs of the bud.

Carefully, Gillard slipped his gloved hand into the victim's bulging trouser pocket. He retrieved a thin wallet and set it down for Kirsty to photograph, front and rear, before opening it. Two bank cards, one debit, one credit, in the name Jordan Idris, plus a student discount card with a photo. No address, no driving licence. He set the cards down on the plastic for Kirsty to photograph. 'I'll get one of the PCs to trace the address through the bank cards.' He stood up and looked at the body from head to toe. 'We need to get him to Dr Delahaye as soon as possible.'

Gillard emerged from the CSI tent to see that there were now quite a lot of rubberneckers on the towpath. Dog walkers, cyclists, joggers; all had taken a break from their early morning activities to have a gawp at what was going on. They were kept back fifty yards in each direction by the blue crime scene tape, but were still photographing what the police were doing outside the tent. Gillard crouched down and looked again at the cycle tracks, which he was disappointed to see had been almost obliterated by the movement backwards and forwards of constabulary boots. Amongst them was an impression of a smooth wheel, without tread, and a partial parallel track, obliterated by a car tyre, which had left the hard surface of the lane and ran for four feet across the muddy grass before reaching the towpath.

Kirsty Mockett came up as Gillard was photographing the tracks on his phone. 'I think we need to get a diver in,' he told her. 'Just in case there's any other evidence. Like a bike, for example.'

'I'll get on to it,' she said.

'Did you record these parallel tracks?' he asked, pointing at the ground.

'Not initially,' she said. 'They'd already been damaged by the CSI van by the time I saw them.'

Gillard shook his head. 'You're supposed to uncover evidence, not destroy it.'

'I wasn't driving,' she said by way of apology.

'Have a think about what could have left those tracks,' he said, and walked away.

—

It was ten o'clock when Gillard pulled up next to two police patrol cars in Addlestone Road, one of the rougher streets in Staines. The ground-floor flat they were interested in was in the middle of a row of Victorian terraced houses, a couple of which were boarded up. Their short front gardens were covered in wheelie bins, old settees and the occasional off-street parking space. Uniforms had already reported no reply at the address that corresponded with the bank cards found in Jordan Idris' wallet. There was no reply from the doorbell to the upstairs flat either. Idris had a small-time criminal record, though no recent convictions. No phone had been found on the body, and if it was in the canal, it would take a diver to extricate it.

Those same uniformed officers had established that Idris had been on a college course in Reading a year ago, but had dropped out before the end of the first term. The search was now on for his mother, whose last address was in the same town. In the meantime, they had secured a warrant to enter Idris' flat. Gillard and the two uniformed officers watched as the locksmith drilled into the door. Their first comment had been that the lock was so flimsy, they didn't really need him. Still, Gillard preferred to go by the book.

The door opened easily enough, revealing a grubby carpeted hall and the smell of stale food. Gillard slipped on plastic booties and gloves and made his way inside, followed by a male PC. The lounge opened to the left, and revealed a giant TV, a faux leather settee, and an enormous pair of speakers connected to a hi-fi. A glass coffee table was stacked with unwashed plates and plastic cutlery, and a few pizza boxes. No bills, ID or other paperwork. He re-emerged into the hall and then took the next door, which opened into a bedroom strewn with clothes and rubbish. A wardrobe was half open and inside it were a dozen boxes of brand-new white Nike trainers. On a bedside table was a half-smoked joint in an ashtray, and an RSPCA charity box in the shape of a plastic dog, complete with chain. The base had been levered open.

'Clearly differently moraled,' the PC said drily as he looked at the charity box. Gillard picked up the box and saw on the base a label which gave the address of the pub from which it had been taken. He opened a couple of drawers and found dumb phones still in their blister packs, and one that looked to have been used. There was also a sheaf of stolen bank cards in a variety of names. Gillard photographed the drawer and its contents before sealing the bank cards and phone in separate evidence bags. He took them with him while he gave the kitchen a once-over, and peeked into the adjoining bathroom. The shower curtain had been ripped from its rail, and appeared to have a smear of diluted and now dried blood on it. He retreated to the hall where the PC was looking expectantly at him.

'I want this treated as a crime scene until we're sure that the death is non-suspicious. I'm going to call CSI, though I'd be surprised if they get round to it today. I'm taking the bank cards and used phone. Let's make sure it's well locked up and someone is posted on the door.'

'I'll see to it, sir,' he said.

Gillard flicked through the bank cards again. One was in the name of Mrs Deirdre Robinson.

'It's a small world,' he said to himself. Too small, sometimes. Claustrophobic. This was now getting close to home. If he remembered rightly, Deirdre Robinson was the woman that Sam had seen pickpocketed in M&S. If so, it seemed likely that this dead body was of the man who had stolen her phone. An associate of the woman that just a week or so ago had tried to murder Gillard's wife.

—

Back at Mount Browne, Gillard spotted DI John Perry eating a lunchtime sandwich at his desk, and went over to him. 'John, the body we found in the canal today belongs to Jordan Idris. Is that one of the possibles for the associate of Lydia Marasova?'

Perry nodded and chewed as he looked up at Gillard. The triangular M&S plastic packet by his keyboard was labelled chicken and avocado. 'We still don't have any good photographs from the shopping centre, but he is known to be active in the area. We found a few associates but the trouble is, nobody is talking.' Perry wiped his fingers on a paper napkin, then worked the keyboard to pull up a mugshot. 'Is that him?'

'He doesn't look quite so good now, but yes. He's the right height.'

'How did he die?' Perry asked.

'Not sure yet. It might be drowning. Can't see it being suicide, somehow. No obvious stab or gunshot wounds. There was no obvious reason for him to be out on a rural stretch of canal that far from home, unless it was to meet a fence. And there's no car.'

'Idris has no current connections that we know of to the drug trade. If he did, that would be a good motive for someone killing him. A turf war, something like that.'

Gillard handed Perry the evidence bag containing the bank cards. 'I'm assuming these stolen cards are more relevant to your inquiry than mine. It would be good to know where he was for any transactions you find on them. Likewise, we know he's on a three-year driving ban, but I'd like to know what car he was driving. He won't be insured of course.'

Perry nodded. 'I'll find out everything I can.'

'If he does turn out to be the one who assaulted Sam, then I'm going to have to step back from the investigation into his death, so it will fall to you.'

'Understood. I don't think we'll know that for sure until we find Marasova.'

'Yeah, I wonder where the hell she is?' Gillard asked.

'Who knows? Maybe she's dead too,' Perry said, turning his hangdog expression to Gillard. 'Or maybe she killed him.'

Gillard inclined his head in doubt. 'He'd have taken some killing, and would have been a big weight to drag fifty yards from car boot to canal. Still, I've seen tracks at the scene which may indicate how she could have done it. We already know she is very dangerous.'

Chapter Eight

Dr David Delahaye unzipped the body bag and turned on the overhead extractor to maximum. The naked body of Jordan Idris was exposed. 'I'm sorry I wasn't able to see him in situ. I won't have time to do the full post-mortem until late this afternoon, but I thought you'd appreciate some initial observations.'

Gillard nodded. 'At this stage I just want to know if it was accidental or deliberate. I've got enough on my plate as it is.'

'Understood. Well, on the face of it, it does indeed appear that he drowned. There is fluid in the lungs, and considerable surviving mucosal froth in the deep airways. The body is quite fresh, which helps, and it does not appear that he was in the water for more than a few hours. The toxicology test will be important because if he'd been drinking heavily, or taken an overdose of drugs, that would help explain how he ended up in the water.'

'It's more than eight miles from where he lives and there's no sign of a vehicle.'

'I can't help on that side of things,' Delahaye said, looking owlishly at Gillard. 'However, I've given him a rudimentary physical examination and there are some unexplained contusions.' Delahaye called over the lab technician who assisted with turning the corpse over. The back of the head appeared to have some scrapes in the scalp. 'There are three or four pairs of grazes with a marked semicircular appearance. They broke the skin, but not deeply.' Delahaye pointed to them with a scalpel. 'It's particularly interesting that the pairing is quite exact: eighty-seven millimetres apart in each case.'

'Could that be from something in the canal?'

'Well, I'm not inclined to believe the body suffered a lot of damage once in the water, because there are none of the expected ancillary tears on clothing at knees and ankles present, or damage to elbows that one might expect had there been a strong flow of water, for example. I understand he was a long way from the nearest lock.'

'Then could we be talking about a weapon?'

'Yes, that's a distinct possibility, though I can't immediately think what it might be. However, some things we can be more certain of,' Delahaye said, fixing Gillard with a stare. 'Just here, there is a patch of petechiae,' he said, pointing to the back of Idris' neck, which clearly showed a coin-sized area of broken blood vessels. 'And here on the other side, there is a slightly smaller one.'

Gillard lowered his hand as if to touch the two areas. If he'd had larger hands, the two marks would have matched his index finger and thumb. 'Is that what you're thinking?' he asked.

'Yes. It's not the only explanation of course, but it is... interesting, wouldn't you say?'

'So, someone half strangled him and chucked him in the water?'

'It's a possibility.'

'And if he'd shouted his head off, no one would have heard him over the traffic. Still, he was a big fit bloke, he wouldn't have been easy to overpower.'

'All absolutely reasonable points. And of course there may be perfectly logical explanations for the injuries.'

'We're getting divers in later today, so we should be able to see anything in there that might have caused those bruises,' Gillard said.

—

Gillard returned to the canal to find an even bigger crowd beyond the blue tape, observing the divers at work. They were chest-deep in murky water at the edge, and periodically completely submerged at the centre. An enormous collection of old junk had been dumped on a tarpaulin on the edge: a mangled bicycle, some footwear, tin cans and bottles and decomposed clothing. A waist-high plastic screen masked the public view of these items. Kirsty Mockett was still hard at work, photographing evidence as it was laid out.

'Where's Yaz?' Gillard asked.

'Leading a team at the flat in Staines. What was it you were hoping to find here?' she asked him.

'A bicycle, perhaps, a bit newer than that one. Anything that might prop up the idea that he came out here of his own volition, and that this was an accidental death.'

'So do you doubt it?'

'I'm increasingly doubting it,' Gillard said. 'Delahaye has found some bruises on Idris' neck which makes it look like someone had their hands around the back of his throat.'

'So he didn't drown?'

'Ah. The indications are that he did. But if there was some kind of fight, here at least, there's a chance someone would have heard.'

'I'm baffled, sir.'

'Join the club, Kirsty.' Gillard looked around and squinted into the failing late afternoon light. 'I just can't think of any reason why an urban criminal like Jordan Idris would be round here unless he'd arranged to meet somebody. And if he had, where is his car? If he cycled down, okay, that's about eight miles, roughly half an hour. But where's the bike?'

'Byfleet and New Haw railway station is only a half mile south,' Kirsty said, indicating with a thumb over her shoulder.

'Yeah, but you have to go halfway into London to get here from Staines. He is unlikely to have come here by train, especially at the sparrow's fart time in the morning he'd have been here.' At the same time, Gillard thought that he would get someone to check the station CCTV just in case.

The remaining diver was being helped up out of the lock. 'I think we're pretty much done here now,' Kirsty said, making it quite clear that she thought they were wasting their time.

'If you say so,' Gillard said. To his mind, there were still plenty of unanswered questions, but he had already formulated a theory about how Jordan Idris had ended up in the canal. He just needed to check a few things.

–

Gillard's next stop was back at the flat in Addlestone Road. It was already getting dark and the CSI van outside was being loaded with the tent as Gillard arrived. He slipped into a Tyvek suit and fresh disposable gloves and booties before going inside to find Yaz Quoroshi standing in the hall.

'What have you got?' Gillard asked.

'Not too much,' Quoroshi replied. 'We've taken a sample of that blood smear in the shower, though there could be innocent explanations. We've not seen anything else in there. The bedroom was the most interesting. A fair amount of illicit drugs, tablets as well as marijuana. Stolen footwear. It's all packed up for analysis. I sent the phone off to Rob Townsend.'

'Good. I'll look forward to the results,' Gillard said. DC Townsend led a team of technicians who specialised in analysing the contents of phones and computers.

'I don't see anything here to indicate foul play,' Quoroshi said.

Gillard shrugged, and walked past him into the kitchen, and then into the bathroom. There was a linoleum floor, tatty at the edges, and it was clear that someone in CSI had lifted it earlier. Good, they were being thorough. The shower curtain had been draped over the bath, its fittings still attached, and a small section cut out where the bloodstain had been. He crouched down and looked under the lip of the tub where it joined the side panel. The mastic seemed to be in reasonable condition, bar the odd bit of black mould. He put his head into the tub itself and stared closely at the drain plug and then at the taps, which were of an old style, from a single mounting. Standing up, he then carefully inspected the ceiling and its polystyrene tiles, and saw more black mould on the paintwork by the extractor fan. He looked carefully at the cord pull, and gripping it away from the plastic weight, tugged it. The fan and light went on simultaneously. He brought out a tape measure from his pocket, and took a few measurements, jotting them down in his notebook. Satisfied, he nodded and then made his way out. Once outside, he looked around the house, checked the alleyway outside, and took a couple of additional measurements.

'You seem to still have a few questions,' Quoroshi said.

'I did, but now they have been answered. I think we're looking at a murder.'

'What on earth makes you think that?'

'I'd rather keep that to myself until I've spoken to Delahaye.' Gillard swiped open his phone and checked his messages. Nothing yet from him. The Home Office forensic pathologist wouldn't take calls while he was undertaking a post-mortem, and didn't take kindly when he was interrupted with stupid questions. He'd already extended Gillard the courtesy of giving him an initial overview, and to ask for more before the full report was ready would be chancing his arm. But he desperately wanted to confirm his theory. The key to determining whether this was an accident or murder would come down to diatoms. The tiny algal particles present in most sources of water would be able to tell him exactly what happened. He just wanted to make sure that Delahaye would send a sample for testing. Having been criticised over expensive tests by the police bean counters in the past, it wasn't something the pathologist would normally do. Not if he thought he was just dealing with an accidental death. But Gillard was now convinced this was a murder, and this test could be a crucial piece of evidence to prove it.

–

Gillard was back at Mount Browne by six and still hadn't had notification from Delahaye that he had finished the post-mortem. He was walking along the CID corridor looking at his phone when he ran into Chief Constable Alison Rigby.

'Craig, I understand that you think Idris is a murder case.' Rigby, a striking six foot one, had clearly been looking for him. On her rare forays into CID, she always had a purpose. Unlike many senior cops, she had a glittering track record on the front line. The drug squad in Hull was one of the toughest beats going, and she had excelled before going on to lead the National Crime Agency.

'I have a theory, yes. But I won't know for sure until we get the results back from the lab.'

Her bright blue eyes lasered in on him. 'Yes. I am a little concerned that if Jordan Idris turns out to be one of the assailants who attacked your wife, I'll have to remove you from the case. Conflict of interest. And I suppose I would have to merge the two cases.'

'I did consider that, ma'am. However, I was the duty detective when the body was found, and I'd like to be SIO up until the point where conflict is proven.'

'It might be prudent not to wait that long. I've asked DI Mulholland to be joint SIO with you for now, so that there won't be any catching up to do if you have to step back.'

Claire was Gillard's best friend in the force, and Rigby knew it. 'I appreciate that, ma'am.' At least it wouldn't be Perry. Gillard had been slightly disappointed that it was DI Perry who was looking after the investigation into the assault on his wife. He liked John, but he was more diligent than imaginative, and lacked the front-line experience of some others who had worked their way up the ranks. If he was put in charge of the Idris investigation too, Gillard thought it might be too much for him. But appointing Claire, that was great news.

'I know you work very well together. And we do need results. I'm still extremely concerned that we haven't found Lydia Marasova. It's my job to think the unthinkable. If she is dead too, that is going to look a little awkward from a public relations perspective.'

'I see what you mean,' he said.

'This isn't Brazil, of course, and you and I know that we don't have police hit squads. But simply the fact that of two people who assaulted your wife, one might be dead and the other missing could cause certain questions to be raised, especially if you were presiding over the investigation. We live in an age where conspiracy theories easily take root. So if we get to the stage where we have press conferences, it's going to be Claire not you who is in front of the cameras.'

Gillard nodded. He had to hand it to Rigby, she was very good on the big picture. 'I understand.'

'In the meantime, I have every faith in you. If you need to get urgent tests, make sure that you have the budgetary approvals.'

'Much appreciated, ma'am.'

He went down to the refectory and ordered cottage pie and cabbage with a glass of orange juice. The cottage pie was always reliable, and the cabbage survived extended cooking better than the carrots or broccoli. After he had paid and grabbed his tray, he saw Claire and newly promoted DS Carrie 'Rainy' Macintosh sharing a table. He headed in their direction and got a greeting from both of them.

'Welcome aboard a very tricky case,' Gillard said to Claire.

'Rigby has only just messaged me,' she said, holding up a phone.

'I heard two minutes ago.'

'How is Sam doing now?' Claire asked.

'Much better, thank you. She had a scan and the baby is fine. Her arm is very bruised though, where she was dangling from it.'

'You cannae believe it when a wee bit of Christmas shopping turns into such a nightmare,' Rainy said. 'The poor wee hen.'

'The only fatality was a coffeemaker that Sam threw at her assailant,' Gillard said. 'It fell a good hundred feet onto the ground floor. So much for that Christmas gift.'

Claire's laughter was interrupted by Gillard grabbing his phone. The pathologist had just texted him to say he'd finished the post-mortem. 'Excuse me a moment,' Gillard said. He pulled up Delahaye's number and tapped it.

The pathologist replied immediately. 'I guessed you would be calling with more questions. You're like a dog with a bone on this one.'

'I think he was murdered,' Gillard said.

'CSI picked something up at his flat, did they?'

'No. I don't think they knew what they were looking for. I just measured the distance between the hot and cold bath taps in his flat. Exactly eighty-seven millimetres.'

Delahaye didn't answer for a moment. 'You think he banged the back of his head on the taps?'

'No. Somebody else drowned him in his own bath. Those marks on the scalp were made as he struggled to get his head out of the water, while at least one other person was pushing him down into it.'

'That would have been quite a fight,' Delahaye said. 'Drowning victims exhibit almost superhuman strength, and I'd imagine he was pretty strong to begin with.'

'I'm willing to bet that he was drugged first. How long before tox tests come back?'

'Three days, I'm afraid. I didn't think they were urgent.'

'Did you send a sample for diatom testing?'

'Now, Craig, you're *really* trying to tell me how to do my job. As it happens, I did. And I've arranged for a sample of the canal water to be tested alongside it. If the diatom profile of the water in his lungs doesn't match that of the canal water, you'll have proved your point.' The forensic pathologist hung up.

'Well, that's told me,' Gillard said to Claire and Rainy.

'Och, never get on the wrong side of a pathologist,' Rainy said. 'I knew one in Glasgow who kept a severed hand in one of those big brown medical jars, and used it to terrify medical students.' Rainy, escaping a terrible marriage, had swapped being a junior hospital doctor in Scotland for a career in the police. She insisted the hours were shorter, there were fewer drunks to deal with than at A&E, and there was a lot less blood.

'Has Perry made any progress on the girl who attacked Sam?' Claire asked.

'We have a name, Lydia Marasova, but she's gone to ground. Rigby fears that the only reason no one can find her is that she's dead. That would be a terrible development.'

The two female detectives exchanged a glance.

'Aye, everyone would think you'd done it, sir,' Rainy said. 'A vengeful cop from a TV series.'

'That, broadly speaking, was what Rigby said to me.'

'So, to bring me up to date, who do you think did kill Jordan Idris?'

'I have absolutely no idea,' Gillard replied. 'But I tell you something, whoever it was showed some forensic awareness to take the trouble to drown him in one place, and lug the body eight miles and toss him in a canal as if it was an accident.'

'From what I've read of Idris' background, he was a small-time crook,' Claire said. 'When scores are settled at that level, they don't normally go to any trouble to conceal that it was intentional.'

'County lines drug gang was it?' Rainy asked.

'No, there's no evidence of gang connections,' Gillard said. 'But Claire is right, concealment of the intention of the killing leads us to the idea that someone fears being identified as having a motive.'

'You mean like the wife who poisons the millionaire husband to inherit, that kind of idea?'

Gillard laughed. 'A version of that, maybe. If we can dig up any of Idris' associates, perhaps we can ask them.'

–

That evening, Gillard sat down with Sam at the kitchen table just after eight. The remains of a shop-bought lasagne lay congealing on her plate. She seemed tired, and uncommunicative after a busy day. He was aware she had increasing difficulty sleeping because of the baby's movement, and could only sleep on one side because of her strained and bruised arm. All that didn't combine well with the shift system at the control room. Tomorrow was an early, so she had to be up before six. He made some small talk and then picked his moment.

'We fished a body out of a canal first thing this morning, not far from Byfleet and New Haw station.'

'I heard about that. Anyone we know?' She managed a weak smile.

'Actually, it could be somebody you know. He resembles the male pickpocket.'

'Gosh. How did he die?'

'He drowned.'

'So it was an accident?'

'I don't think so, but I can't prove it yet.'

She was silent for a moment, and then prodded the cold lasagne with a fork. 'I've got an alibi,' she said brightly. 'I was here in bed with my husband.'

He grinned and kissed her on the forehead. 'Good to see you thinking like a guilty woman.'

Chapter Nine

Thursday 10th December

Trainee PC Nita Basu pulled up in her patrol car outside the Rising Sun, then turned into the car park. She got out and took with her a plastic dog charity box. It was 10.15 a.m. and the pub didn't open until noon, but the lights were on. The licensee name over the door was Pearl Moses. Quite a name, that. She wrote it down in her notebook, then rang the doorbell and waited. A seventyish woman with sharp features and a highly retro beehive hairdo opened the door.

'Are you Mrs Moses?'

'I am, if it's any business of yours.' She folded her arms and glared at the policewoman.

PC Basu lifted up the charity box and said: 'I've come to return some of your property.' She showed the landlady the address label on the bottom of the box.

'Oh,' said the woman, visibly softening. 'That was nicked.'

'I couldn't find a record of it being reported,' the PC said.

A large presence loomed behind Mrs Moses. 'What's all this about then?' boomed a man in a strong London accent. The same age, he resembled a retired nightclub bouncer.

'The old bill found the RSPCA box and brung it back,' Pearl said.

'When exactly was it stolen?' the PC asked.

'It was Monday night, wasn't it?' Pearl said, turning to him.

'Are you Mr Moses?'

'Yes, for my sins, love.' He grinned at her, revealing a jumble of yellowing teeth. 'Can we offer you a drink for your trouble?'

'I don't drink, and couldn't accept anything on duty, but thank you.' She handed them a couple of leaflets. 'Please do report anything like this. We are a community police service, and it is very important for us to build up an accurate pattern of crime across the area, so that we can concentrate our resources where they are required.'

'Maybe we will, next time.' They took the proffered plastic dog but still showed no signs of inviting her in.

'So, just for our records, do you know what time it was stolen? Did anyone see it disappear?' She got out her notebook and smiled brightly at them again.

'Come on, Tel, she might as well know,' Pearl said.

'We was burgled during the small hours last Monday, which I 'spose makes it Tuesday,' he said. 'It's not the first time, but it's been a few years. We didn't think that much was taken. There's only a small amount in the till, and just a couple of bottles of spirits taken. But what a bastard to take the charity box, eh?'

'I couldn't agree more,' said the constable, as she wrote down the details.

'So where did you find it then?' he asked.

'It was found together with some other stolen goods in a property in the county during the course of an invest-igation.'

'Whose property?' Moses asked.

'I don't know the details.' She was still writing.

'Scum, people like that. Snatching money that should go to looking after stray dogs. It's cruel, that's what is.'

'Can you show me where they got in?'

'All right.' He showed her into the bar and the back door. He walked with a stiff gait. 'They come in here, must've picked the lock.' He opened the door and led her through to the rear dining area. 'And they cut out the glass next to that door.'

'Why didn't you report it?'

He turned and put his hands on his hips and looked at the young PC. 'I can tell you're just out of training, love. The police aren't interested in tackling this kind of crime. They're busier lining their own pockets, and persecuting law-abiding folk...'

'Now come on, Tel. She's only trying to help.' Pearl turned to the constable. 'My 'usband is a bit cynical. Look. We do appreciate your gesture, and if you'd like a cup of coffee, any time, just pop in.'

'Thank you, that's very kind.'

They closed the door gently, and as she turned away, PC Basu wondered why on earth they didn't report the burglary.

–

It was later that morning, a day after the body had been found, when Gillard convened the inaugural incident room meeting at Mount Browne. It had taken only twenty-four hours for what appeared initially to have been an accidental death to be ramped up to a full-blown murder case. There was a good attendance too, considering the short notice. DI Claire Mulholland, DI John

84

Perry, DS Rainy Macintosh, plus DCs Carl Hoskins and Michelle Tsu. Only Rob Townsend, head of the technical team, had given his apologies because of a heavy workload elsewhere.

'All right people, we've got a lot to do,' Gillard said, pointing to the whiteboard on which a mugshot of Jordan Idris took centre space. 'You've all seen his criminal record. This picture is three years old, from his last incarceration. What we know for certain is that Jordan Idris was found floating in the canal first thing on Tuesday morning. Cause of death was drowning. We've now got the full autopsy report, minus a few outstanding tests.'

'I've had a quick flick through this,' Hoskins said, looking at his screen. 'What makes you think he was killed?'

'The injuries on the back of his head exactly match the bath taps in his flat,' Gillard said. 'I believe he was drugged there, by someone he let in, then drowned in his own bath, before being taken out and dumped in the canal. Test results we have just got back show he had both cannabis and ketamine in his system.' He turned to the others. 'For those of you who don't know, ketamine is a powerful and quick-acting anaesthetic. It's abused for its narcotic effect but also sometimes used as a date rape drug, because of the speed of its effect. In lower doses, it makes you feel remote and disassociated from events. It can either be snorted in powder form, taken as a tablet or in some cases injected.'

He wrote the word 'ketamine' on the whiteboard and circled it, drawing an arrow back towards the central picture. Then he pinned up a photograph of a wheelie bin.

'Is that the suspect?' Hoskins asked.

'In a way,' Gillard replied. 'A green bin like this is missing from the Addlestone Road flat. The neighbours all have one. The wheels of the neighbours' corresponding bins are 561 millimetres apart, exactly matching a short track I found by the canal. The impression I measured at twelve millimetres deep, which I reckon indicates a heavy load.'

'A body,' Michelle whispered to Rainy.

'It's the logical way to remove a sodden, heavy body from the scene of the crime and get it to the disposal site. But you need a reasonable-sized vehicle to accommodate it.'

'So who killed him?' Hoskins asked.

'We don't know. There's not much to go on,' Gillard said. He then wrote 'associates' on the whiteboard and drew a box around it. 'John, how are you doing finding known associates?'

'It's been an uphill struggle, frankly,' Perry said. 'We found two minor criminals previously convicted with him in the Reading area, but neither claim to have seen him recently. As far as his family is concerned, his mother is a substance abuser, and is currently sectioned in a mental health unit in Reading. The news has been broken to her, but she is in no condition to be interviewed. There is a half-brother, but he's not at the last address we have for him. No father on record.'

'And still no sign of Lydia Marasova?' Gillard asked.

Perry shook his head. 'We are very concerned about her welfare.'

'Maybe she killed him,' Hoskins asked. 'Seeing as she had a good go at chucking your wife off the top of the shopping centre.'

There was a ripple of nervous laughter around the room. 'Yes, thank you for that Carl. It's not been ruled out. She would have been in a good position to administer a drug, but she would surely have needed help to remove the body, even if it was in a wheelie bin.'

'Good point,' Hoskins said. Gillard noticed that the department's largest detective was looking quite a bit slimmer these days, the result of a change of diet following a diabetes diagnosis.

'Michelle, over to you,' Gillard said.

'I've been collating all the evidence from the crime scene at his flat,' she said. 'We found plenty of his DNA, and some of Lydia Marasova's, as well as that of two others, neither of whom are on the database. Idris' DNA was also found at her flat. So the connection between them looks pretty robust.'

'I didn't notice any wet carpet in the flat on my visit,' Gillard said. 'Did the CSI people mention it?'

'No. I can't say I noticed. Maybe the body was left to drain in the bath for a couple of hours. It could have been wrapped in towels before being moved.'

'This is all quite a lot of trouble to go to,' Perry said, shaking his head. 'To disguise it as an accident.'

'John, what about the bank cards?' Gillard asked.

'He made extensive use of the contactless facility in Woking, Hersham and Reading to buy boxes of trainers and mobile phones on the cards he stole. The card records show he also bought jewellery, perfume and other high-value items to the tune of £1,250 or so. As for his own card, he hasn't used it since two days before his death. The financial records we've been forwarded from his account show little abnormal activity, although there are some substantial payments from eBay and Vinted a few months ago.'

'That's probably the sale of stolen goods,' Gillard said. 'We'll be able to confirm it once we find his phone. At the moment we only have a dumb phone, which we assume is a burner, and we are waiting for Rob's team to finish with it.' He looked around at the assembled group. 'Is there anything else?'

There were no questions.

'All right, seeing as we now have a firm forensic connection between Lydia Marasova and Jordan Idris, I'm going to be stepping back from the SIO role because of my conflict of interest over the attack on my wife. DI Mulholland will take over.' He indicated his friend and colleague with a smile. 'I'd still like to sit in on the meetings though.'

With that, he sat down and Claire took over.

—

As soon as the meeting was wrapped up, Gillard printed off the best pictures they had of Jordan Idris and headed downstairs to the control room where Sam worked. He stood by the glass door, staring in at the rows of people handling operational calls across the county, the first line in the connection to the public in the fight against crime. Sam was at the far end by the window, and due a break about now. He didn't have to wait long, and spotting him by the door, she gave him a cheery wave as she picked up her jacket. Once they were outside in the corridor, Gillard showed her the pictures. 'This is him?'

'Looks like him, but I can't be sure,' Sam said. 'His hood was drawn down; I didn't get a very good look at his face.'

Gillard nodded. 'Well, he roughly matches the description and we have now got some good forensic links through DNA to show that Jordan Idris and Lydia Marasova spent a lot of time together. And as a result of that, I've got to withdraw from the case, because of the conflict of interest.'

'So has she still not been seen?'

'No.'

'Do you think she's dead?'

'I've no way of knowing. Only when we know why Idris was killed can we take a view on that.'

–

While Gillard was still in the meeting, Research Intelligence Officer Rob Townsend looked at the day's workload sitting in a plastic box on his desk, and rubbed his hand over his short and still itchy beard. Seventeen mobiles in clear plastic evidence bags, labelled with name and case number, to examine for evidence. All of them had been through the forensic data kiosk, a desktop device which allowed non-specialist staff to quickly extract photographs, text messages and call logs. That was just some of the various types of data that could be stored on a mobile phone. It was a huge time saver for him and his team to only have to deal with the more difficult work. Like looking for deleted information that had to be retrieved from the server of the service provider. Rob flicked through the case numbers. Eight of the cases concerned rape allegations, and he put them to one side for later in the day. He dreaded these because they had to be exhaustive and robust to survive any court cross-examination. Far too often the work would not lead to a conviction. He'd lost count of the times that he'd spent a week or more reconstructing the exchange of messages between victim and accused, only to find that the more evidence of an association, friendship or sexual relations he uncovered, the less the Crown Prosecution Service felt like pursuing the case. It almost felt like he was doing the defendant's job. It was an intrinsic problem with rape cases: most of the time there was only ever the woman's word that consent had not been given on a particular occasion, while the mobile phone data gave a circumstantial but extensive context in which apparent consent had on previous occasions been offered and accepted.

As he put the final phone back in the box, he thought about his old girlfriend Kirsty Mockett, with whom he'd often discussed these issues. A rising star in crime scene investigation, now apparently dating some slimy Flying Squad detective called Culshaw. They had broken up a month or two before, but it still irritated him that she had already effortlessly fallen into another relationship while he was still nursing his hurt feelings. He saw her in the CID building from time to time, and she would always give him a cheery wave. He'd obviously meant less to her than she had to him.

Searching for distractions, he picked up the next phone in its plastic bag. That was more like it. A basic Samsung burner phone. No photos, no videos, just call records and some texts. A nice simple job to do before Gillard's incident room meeting finished. This one had been found in the flat of Jordan Idris, who he recalled had been found dead in a canal. Townsend called up the record from the kiosk, and Gillard's terse note attached to it. *Look to see if anyone threatened him, or evidence of a dispute. CG.*

Townsend smiled to himself as he pulled up the list of texts. There weren't many and they didn't seem to make much sense.

> green lite mate for bm job, as of now

> when?

> dec 20

> Y not Dec 18?

> ezr to get the jcb in tel

The owner of this phone was either being addressed as Tel, a London shorthand for Terry, or it was a mis-typed reference to intel, intelligence. Which wouldn't make sense, for a criminal. Maybe this wasn't Idris' phone at all. He looked for stored voice messages, but none were indicated. There was no sign of deletions. He double-checked the evidence bag against the case number. It was accurate. He looked on the case record and couldn't find any mention of fingerprints or DNA linking this phone to Jordan Idris.

Still, mention of a JCB and security. BM job. It sounded like the description of a robbery. Maybe Idris had stolen the phone. If so, it could be a lucky break. He picked up the phone and rang Gillard.

–

Gillard sat with Townsend and looked at the texts. 'It certainly could be interpreted as a robbery being planned.'

'One with a JCB involved,' Townsend said, scratching his beard.

'Leave it with me.' Gillard got up and returned to his office. He shut the door, and peered out through the glass at the rest of the CID crew, working away as normal. He wasn't about to tell Townsend, but it was the date change that was really chiming with him. December eighteenth, the Friday before Christmas this year, matched up with what Keith Sutton had told him. If this was the same blag, it sounded like the date was being put back by two days. Either way, Townsend's suspicion that the phone didn't belong to Idris seemed well-founded. Idris had never been in a deal bigger than a few thousand pounds, and certainly nothing involving a JCB. What Sutton had told him about half a billion would put it way out of his league. So of all the pockets he'd picked, Idris had managed to find a phone with explicit details of a robbery. Quite a coincidence, but stranger things had happened.

He picked up the phone to Culshaw. The Flying Squad detective would certainly be interested in this. It was definitely a stroke of luck. For all that, what was the chances of a phone with such crucial details on it falling into police hands? Either way, they had just over a week to find out exactly what this job was, and where.

Chapter Ten

Nita Basu had not been in the CID office at Mount Browne before. Being summoned to a meeting with the famous DCI Craig Gillard made her anxious. What if she had done something wrong? As she made her way through the large open-plan office with its dozens of detectives, she recognised the pull inside that had made her want to become a police officer in the first place. The desire to pit her brains and wits against those of the criminal fraternity, the search for hidden clues, and the thrill of the chase. Her training had done a good job of knocking that romantic view of policing out of her head; the course tutor had said that the average detective, like the average employee anywhere, spends 90 per cent of their time behind a screen. In the CID it was looking through CCTV, preparing paperwork for the Crown Prosecution Service, or on pure admin. At least as a uniformed officer, she spent half of her time in the community.

She recognised Gillard, standing outside his glass-walled office. He was a solidly built man of rugged appearance, with quite a bit of grey showing through his dark hair, and was talking to a short and rather overweight female officer who had a pronounced Scottish accent. He looked up and saw her approach.

'PC Basu? Do come in.' He showed her into the office and closed the door, then offered her a seat. 'I want to pick your brains.'

'If you can find any,' she said with a nervous laugh.

Gillard smiled and sat opposite. 'I understand you took it upon yourself to return a stolen RSPCA charity box to the Rising Sun pub in Glissingbourne.'

'Yes, did I do wrong?'

'No, in fact quite the contrary. You've drawn our attention to something potentially very important.'

'Oh, really?'

'Yes. Can I ask if you met the licensee or her husband?'

'I did. They didn't seem that fond of the police.'

Gillard laughed. 'No, they wouldn't be. Terry Moses has got a criminal record as long as your arm. It's all a long time ago, but he was an armed robber, who specialised in security vans and building society raids. A real old-fashioned south London gangster.'

'Oh, good grief!'

'Don't worry, he's retired. Well at least officially he is. Your witness statement from them makes no mention of anything else being taken apart from the charity box, about thirty pounds cash and two bottles of spirits.'

'That's right.'

'No mention of a phone being stolen?'

'No. They seemed reluctant to even give me the details. His wife, Pearl, is a piece of work as well. I could see she didn't like me.'

'Well, nobody joined the police because they wanted to be liked. But at least now you know why.'

'I had assumed it was race. So have you found a phone belonging to him?'

'We found a phone, which does indeed have some of Terry Moses' DNA on. As well as some fingerprints from the man who stole it.'

'How exciting. So can I interview the thief? Or at least be in on the interview?'

Gillard laughed gently. 'How are your séance skills? I'm afraid our thief is dead.'

'Oh dear.'

'His body was found in a canal—'

'Oh, you mean near Byfleet? I saw the reports. So do you think he was murdered?' She tried to suppress her excitement, but it was clear from Gillard's expression that he had noticed it.

'It's one of the lines of enquiry,' he said cagily.

'Maybe this Terry Moses tracked him down and killed him for breaking into the pub. It's a really good motive, isn't it?'

Gillard smiled. 'Terry Moses was certainly a nasty piece of work back in the day. But I think his days of settling scores personally are probably over.'

'He could have got one of his gangland cronies to do it, couldn't he?'

'Well, it's possible, but only just. He would have to have been very efficient. If, as he said, the burglary took place in the early hours of Tuesday morning, and our supposed burglar was found dead in the water first thing on Wednesday, that's about twenty-four hours to discover you'd been burgled, find out who did it, learn where he lived, contract somebody of the required toughness, and who could do the job pretty much immediately with a reasonable amount of forensic awareness, and finally lug this big guy eight miles from his home to chuck him in the canal.'

'I see what you mean.'

'Now of course it is possible that Terry and Pearl Moses lied to you about the date of the burglary,' Gillard said. 'All of this would be possible if it had happened a week earlier. It would be easy to check. Any of the regulars would notice if the charity box was missing, and you can be sure that Moses would have moaned to them about it being stolen.'

'Do you want me to go back and ask some regulars?'

'Hold your horses.' He smiled again. 'Incognito might be better, don't you think? I've got a detective over there, Carl Hoskins, who looks like he was born in a pub. I'll send him over one lunchtime to ask a few questions.' PC Basu followed Gillard's gaze, and saw that indeed Hoskins would be a natural propping up the bar anywhere in the country.

Gillard thanked her for her enthusiasm and initiative. 'If we get a breakthrough on this, it will be partly down to your work.'

Grinning all over her face, Nita Basu made her way out of the building. Perhaps she would apply to be a detective after all when she finished all her training.

–

Gillard watched the young constable leave, with a big smile on his face. They needed more like her, full of fresh ideas and enthusiasm. In fact, he remembered when he was like that himself, before the big meat grinder of police officialdom, CPS inertia, and worldly cynicism knocked it out of him.

He turned back to his work. No longer SIO for the murder of Jordan Idris, he still planned to attend the incident room meeting at ten. An hour later, he had been booked a video conference on Operation Santa Claus. He got up and stretched, before making his way over to Carl Hoskins' desk. For once there was no sign of food there.

'How's the diet going, Carl?' he asked.

'I'm down to fifteen and a half stone. One and a half gone, two more to go.'

'That's very impressive. Are you feeling fitter with it?' Hoskins had been the classical sedentary male for as long as Gillard had known him. It hadn't mattered much when he had uncomplainingly sat through hour upon hour of CCTV, which was unpopular with other officers. But Gillard really wanted to make sure that nobody on the team was that unfit.

'I am. I'm going to the gym and started swimming. Of course the first time I went to the pool, a bunch of people from Greenpeace tried to refloat me.'

It was an old joke, but it showed that Hoskins' self-image must be improving. He'd always had a good sense of humour.

'Got a job for you, Carl. I need you to go for a lunch-time drink at the Rising Sun in Glissingbourne. Can you make it today after the incident room meeting?'

'A pint during work time? Are you winding me up, boss?'

'No. Want you to hang around long enough to hear if any of the locals talk about the theft of the RSPCA box.'

'A charity box?'

'Don't worry Carl, it's not as trivial as it sounds.'

'That's Terry Moses' boozer, isn't it?'

'Very good. He doesn't know you, does he? You being a Croydon boy.'

'Nah. I've never met him, but he's got quite a reputation. So you think he's up to something?'

'Not sure. His charity box was found at the flat of our dead thief Jordan Idris.'

'Blimey. Nobody would have dared do that to him twenty years ago. He'd have had them fitted with a concrete overcoat.'

'Maybe he did, or at least arranged for it to be done. He wouldn't have had enough time unless the burglary took place at least a few days earlier than he said. Idris was dead within twenty-four hours, and that just seems too quick.'

He wasn't going to tell Carl about the phone or the messages. Hoskins had in the past shown a little poor judgement, and leaked information. Mainly, but not exclusively, to journalists. Gillard wasn't going to take any chances on Operation Santa Claus. The stakes were too high.

–

The Idris murder incident room meeting was run jointly by detective inspectors Claire Mulholland and John Perry. Claire was the SIO, and now had a very well-populated whiteboard, with Idris' mugshot at the centre of it, and a series of arrows going in various directions. As well as Sam's name as the victim of an attempted murder, there was a box around Lydia Marasova, and a strong line connecting her to Idris.

'All right everybody,' Claire said. 'First a forensic update. We've now had the results of the diatom analysis, which proves conclusively that the water in Idris' lungs does not match the canal water. Another one of DCI

Gillard's hunches has proved correct. Idris was drowned in his bath at home, and then transported in a wheelie bin, eight miles to the canal where he was dumped.' She clicked on a slide viewer, which showed a series of photographs of wheeled tracks, with a tape measure set between them.

'CSI has re-examined the crime scene, enlarging it by a hundred yards in each direction, and discovered the remnants of identical tracks near the gates which would have been locked at the time of the crime. They match the width of a typical council wheelie bin, which would probably have been used to transport the body the sixty yards from the nearest parking place to the canal.'

'Aye, ma'am. We searched at Idris' flat, and the bin is definitely missing,' Rainy Macintosh said. 'CSI didn't find one in the canal, which is a wee bit of a surprise because they found a bit of everything else.'

'Have you made any more progress on the DNA traces?' Gillard asked.

'No. We can place Idris and Marasova in the flat, and one other, not known to the police.' Claire turned back to the meeting. 'So to summarise, we think Jordan Idris opened the door to his killer. He may have known him, and if he didn't, he must have been expecting him. There is no sign of a struggle, and he would not have been a pushover. The discovery of ketamine in his bloodstream indicates that he was sedated by the time the drowning took place. Toxicology tests on the carpet show minute traces of ketamine powder. The chances are it was snorted, though it may be the victim didn't know that it was ketamine.

'But at this stage, I think we have enough of the "how" he was killed. We have made much less progress on the "why" and the "who". Fortunately, that might be about to change. We have made contact with a former girlfriend of Idris' from Reading. Her name is Sharissa Day, and I'm going over this afternoon to Reading Police Station to interview her.'

–

Claire Mulholland peered between the venetian blinds and through the internal window of the rape suite where Sharissa Day was waiting. The interviewee, a substantially built woman dressed in sweatshirt and jeans, was sprawled across the settee, reading one of the women's magazines, looking quite at home. If she was upset about the death of her former boyfriend, it wasn't showing. Before going in, Claire quickly scanned through the background details. Sharissa had a minor criminal record, all spent convictions for shoplifting and cannabis possession from before she was fifteen. She was now twenty-two, and worked at a nail bar. She had impractically long green nails, which contrasted nicely with the dark skin of her hands.

Claire pushed open the door and greeted the woman, who hastily pulled herself up to a formal seated position as if the headmistress had walked in at school.

'Thank you for agreeing to help us. We are trying to piece together Jordan's movements in the days and weeks running up to his death.'

'I ain't seen him,' she said. 'We broke up four months ago.'

'Do you still have his phone number? We didn't find his mobile, and if you've got the number, we can trace it.'

Sharissa got out her phone from her jeans pocket and worked it rapidly. Claire was impressed that she could do this despite the length of her nails. She then showed Claire the number on the screen, which she wrote down in her notebook.

'When was the last time you exchanged messages?'

'Two or three weeks ago maybe.'

Claire wanted to get the woman's permission to borrow her phone, but this was almost always a contentious request. To people of Sharissa's age, it was like asking to camp in their bedroom. Every secret, every love affair, every argument, all there for the world to see.

'Could you show me some of them?' Claire asked.

'Why? I didn't kill him.'

'We might be able to tell his state of mind from the tone of his messages.'

'You should ask his Romanian bitch.'

'Who's that?' Claire guessed that this was Lydia Marasova, but wanted confirmation.

'Hideous Lydia. He was spending all his time with her, doing drugs together. He'd always had his troubled side, but I made it better and she made it worse, you know what I'm saying?'

'I understand.'

Tears were slowly crawling down Sharissa's face, and she wiped them away angrily with her arm. 'You don't understand, none of you understand. His mum couldn't cope, he didn't know who his dad was, and his brother hasn't spoken to him for three years. And now he's dead.'

'Did he ever mention to you being frightened of someone—'

'He was never frightened of anyone, at least he never told me. Except of course he really was frightened of himself, his dark side, like.'

'No enemies?'

'I don't know. He never told me about any. Because that would mean admitting fear, and he always reckoned he was fearless.'

This certainly didn't feel like a breakthrough. Sharissa was the most promising of the half-dozen of Idris' friends and mates that Thames Valley Police had managed to track down. She was seemingly the closest to him, the only one who had cared about him.

'Did you ever go to his flat in Staines?'

Sharissa looked puzzled. 'I didn't know he had a flat in Staines. He lived in Reading.'

'He was living in Staines most recently. Okay. I'd just like to take a cheek swab, so that we can eliminate you from the various DNA traces we have found.'

She gave Claire a stony stare, but finally said, 'Okay then.'

'Could I borrow your phone for just half an hour? It could be really important to finding out why he died.'

'You can't have my phone. You'll learn nothing about him, everything on there with him is old.'

'I'm really sorry that you're taking that attitude, Sharissa,' Claire said. She knew she could apply for a warrant, and depending on the magistrate could get it granted. But in fact, now she finally had the number of Idris' smartphone, she could get the service provider to give her the contents and location data.

'You be better off finding hideous Lydia. She is the one who tried to murder that woman in the shopping centre. She probably killed him.'

'What makes you say that?'

'Stands to reason. She was more on drugs than he was, and she has this vicious temper.'

'Have you met her?'

'No fear. She's fucking mental. He did tell me that. And she deliberately got herself pregnant to blackmail him to stay with her.'

'She's pregnant?'

'Yeah. That's what he told me. He wasn't happy about it.'

This added a new facet to the investigation. 'Do you have an address for her?'

'No. If I had I would have said, wouldn't I?'

–

'Terry Moses, well well.' DCI Culshaw was as intrigued as Gillard had predicted by yet another snippet of information which might be relevant to the supposed half billion pound robbery. 'I haven't heard that name in a long time.'

'He runs a pub called the Rising Sun in Glissingbourne, right out in the sticks.' Gillard was calling from his own office with the door shut. He didn't want this information too widely spread.

'And this is Terry's phone you've got?'

'Yes, seems to be. We found his DNA on it, and it's clearly a burner because there are hardly any messages or other activity.'

'What are the chances of that, eh?' Culshaw said with a chuckle.

'It's certainly a stroke of luck.'

'And the bloke who stole it is dead?'

'Yes, drowned in his own bath then lugged eight miles to a canal and dropped in, to make it look like an accident. He'd been drugged with ketamine.'

'Not your usual gangland revenge killing. Sophisticated, and an attempt to conceal the act.' Culshaw sounded absolutely intrigued. 'Moses' main period of criminal activity was well before my time, but the JCB mention does sound right up his street. You know he was implicated in the Millennium Dome diamond robbery? A Mr Big that was never caught.'

'And I seem to recall there was a JCB involved there, too,' Gillard said. The attempted robbery in November 2000 involved half a dozen criminals armed with ammonia, smoke bombs and a nail gun, attempting to use the digger to smash through the armoured glass protecting the diamond collection including the flawless Millennium Star, which alone was valued at £200 million. Sixty Flying Squad detectives were waiting for them when they arrived. 'He's obviously a man for the big time.'

'There is one snag,' Culshaw said. 'If big Jackie Norris and his son Damian are involved in this, it can't be Terry Moses. Because they hate each other, have done for years.'

'Maybe they've mended their bridges in pursuit of a bigger prize.'

'Anything's possible,' Culshaw said. 'But that would be very surprising. Norris personally cut up Moses' brother Alf so bad he never walked again. It would be nice to talk to him, but he died in the first wave of Covid.'

'Well, the Millennium Dome job was foiled through good surveillance. Maybe we can do the same with this.'

'If they have put it back two days, that might make it easier. But we've still got no bloody idea what the target is, and not much more than a week to figure it out.'

'The message to Moses called it the BM job. Does BM mean anything to you?' Gillard asked.

'Bank something, I s'pose.'

'Haven't you learned anything from the bugs?'

'Nah. The one under the pool table that Musgrove fitted just seems to get us a load of racket, with the odd rumble of pool balls. The one in the gents, at least you can tell what they're saying, but it's mainly football. I'd have been surprised had we learned much from that.'

'We've still got seven days, though.'

'It's not much time. We have another name though. Colin Lamb.'

'Means nothing to me,' Gillard said.

'Nor me. He is a mate and cousin of Scattergood's. Did a bit of time for receiving stolen property, but that was years ago.'

'So maybe he's the fence.'

'Could be. He seems to have been straight for a good fifteen years. Worked as a guard on the Northern Line, years ago. Then in a bus depot. Now admin. Of course, none of that stops him working as a fence. He lives quite close to the Railway Tavern, in one of those 1930s council blocks.'

'I think I know the one. It might be hard to get surveillance in there.'

'I get the impression he's not a big player. Fencing any kind of stuff that costs half a billion quid would be well beyond his experience, surely,' Culshaw said.

Chapter Eleven

The Swallowtail Hotel and Spa was a classic eighteenth-century manor house, set in 200 acres of parkland, draped in ivy, with a large Victorian-style glass extension. As Gillard and Sam turned into the grand drive, he brought the car to a halt to allow a gaggle of well-heeled golfers, all diamond pattern pullovers and baggy white trousers, to cross. It was only 9.30, and the car park was half full. None of the vehicles were more than three years old, and Gillard slid his old Ford Focus between a Rolls-Royce and a top of the range Lexus.

They got out of the car, and took in the surroundings. It was a clear day but very cold. He felt slightly overdressed in work suit and tie, but then this was Sam's treat for him. She was wearing a cream trouser suit, matching heels, and the rather fine sapphire earrings he had bought for her birthday. Her long dark hair was artfully piled up. It looked great, but he couldn't understand why she had gone to the trouble of having her hair done just yesterday when she was about to have a massage. His own first thought had been to dress casually in loose T-shirt and trainers, until Sam had reminded him about the lunch afterwards.

They were greeted at reception by a courteous and efficient woman, who checked their details, and then offered to show them some of the facilities. Gillard trailed along behind as she led them through into a large glass extension. There was a sizeable heated pool, with nobody in it, a couple of Jacuzzis and a connected plunge pool, and then just outside the window she pointed out the vitality pool, which to his eye looked like a pond screened by high and carefully trimmed *leylandii* bushes.

'What's a vitality pool?'

'It's unheated, Craig,' Sam whispered.

'Wild swimming is *en vogue*, of course,' the guide said. 'This morning's session is for those who prefer to swim *au natural.*'

'Right,' said Gillard looking more closely to see if anyone was in it. He could see nobody, which given the chilly weather didn't surprise him at all.

Sam was led into the spa treatment centre, while Gillard was left sitting at a small glass bar near the side of the main swimming pool, where a tiny Thai woman offered him a complimentary smoothie. He couldn't quite follow her heavily accented description and picked one at random. She disappeared into a small kitchen behind, and after some heavy-duty blitzing noises, reappeared with a glass of something thick and green. He thanked her, and as she turned her back to return to the kitchen, he sniffed it suspiciously. Could it be greengage? A slight sip brought a taste more akin to Brussels sprouts with ginger. Something to go easy on, he thought.

Looking round the place, Gillard could hardly believe that Norris was behind all this. Emerging from a life of crime as long as his with your sanity intact would be enough of an achievement. But Jackie Norris hadn't just done that; he'd retained, or to be more charitable, made, plenty of money. Millions. He'd crossed the invisible social threshold into acceptability. Gillard swigged his smoothie, and wondered why Jackie Norris would be mad enough to jeopardise all this for one last big blag. It just didn't make sense. Not unless those debts were very pressing.

The door behind him opened, and a statuesque young woman in a short silvery kimono approached him. 'I'm Astrid, your masseuse.' She was the same height as Gillard in her bare feet, and she had huge pale green eyes. He followed her into a hot and humid corridor. She pointed out a changing room. 'Down to underwear?' Gillard asked.

'You might as well take everything off, otherwise it will only get soaked in oil,' she said. 'You're going for the hot stones, yes?'

'No. Just a massage.'

'Full body, yes?'

'Yes.'

'You'll find a bathrobe and towel in there. Come into the room opposite when you're ready.'

Feeling slightly nervous, Gillard undressed in the changing room, using a locker to hang up his clothes. He slipped on a thick light-blue bathrobe, with a towel round his waist underneath. He padded across the corridor and pushed open the hardwood door. The room was lit with scented candles, and suffused in gentle rainforest sounds: parrot calls and piping frogs plus the patter of rain. Astrid was standing at the very far end of the room at the head of the massage table. She called him forward and asked him to lie face down. He slipped off the robe and lay on the table in his towel. She covered his shoulders and back with fresh heated towels, and then exposed one of his legs. She had warm oiled hands and worked her way up from ankle to thigh. He began to relax with her unhurried and gentle pressure, and was pleased that there was very little small talk. With his head protruding through a towel-lined hole in the table, he couldn't hear too much anyway. She worked away on the other leg, and then to his surprise, removed the towel covering his buttocks. She massaged there, pinpointing areas of tension, pressing and kneading the flesh. She knew exactly what she was doing. It was extremely pleasant. At this point she whispered to him: 'We've a discount on the lingam massage at the moment. It's an extra fifteen minutes. Would you like it?'

Gillard had been expecting something like this, and lifted his head to look at her.

Astrid continued: 'Do you know what it is? It's an intimate massage for men using Tantric techniques. It helps to rebalance the chakras at the centre of your body.'

'Does it indeed,' Gillard muttered. 'I'll pass for now, thank you.'

Dress it up any way you like, it was still a rub-and-tug shop. He wouldn't put it past Jackie Norris to have a secret camera in here, for a bit of Russian-style *kompromat* for any policeman or politician foolish enough to agree to 'extras'.

The massage continued, with some heavy-duty kneading on his back. The rainforest noises were quite soporific, and he felt himself drifting off to sleep. The masseuse was really putting some weight into it now, and Gillard lifted his head to ask her to go easy.

The person he saw was not who he had expected. A big man in his late sixties, with snowy hair, a craggy face, wearing white medical-type scrubs.

'What's this, a shift change?' Gillard muttered.

The man laughed. 'You're very tight in the deltoids, detective chief inspector,' he said with a south London accent. 'It must be all those years of putting villains away. You need someone who can really exert a bit of pressure.' He pressed a thumb very deep under his shoulder blade. Enough to make him wince. Gillard had never met Jackie Norris but he had no doubt that this was who was now massaging him. It certainly made him glad that he hadn't opted for the extras. 'So you keep your hand in on the front line do you?' Gillard said, rapidly losing any semblance of relaxation that the previous forty-five minutes had given him.

'Only for very special guests. And none come more special than you and your delightful wife.'

Gillard wondered what was happening to Sam at the moment. He'd rather have Jackie Norris here dealing with him than walking in on her. He'd calculated the risk of running into the retired crime boss as a result of a trip to the Swallowtail Hotel, and had assumed that it would come at its highest when he was sitting in the bar or at lunch. Not here, when he was at a total disadvantage, naked and vulnerable.

'All right, that's enough,' Gillard said, levering himself up to a seated position. Norris seemed to have possession of all the towels, including the one that had until the last moment been draped across his bottom and thighs.

'Did you enjoy it?' Norris asked, smirking and staring at Gillard's exposed groin.

'The first two thirds were pretty good, the last few minutes not so much.'

'In which case, it's on us. If you're not totally satisfied, we pay.'

Gillard laughed. 'I'm happy to pay.'

'Because it's on expenses?'

'No. I couldn't claim for this, obviously.'

'But you are here on a case, right?'

'No. I don't bring my wife with me to work.'

'I thought she worked in the control room at Mount Browne.'

'You seem to know a lot that you shouldn't.'

'She told her masseur. By the way, she might be a bit late. She's having the yoni massage.' His smirk was the size of the South Circular.

Gillard tried not to look troubled. 'Would you be good enough to pass me the bathrobe?' he asked.

Norris turned away and lifted the bathrobe from the hook on the back of the door and handed it to him. 'Showers are through there,' Norris said. He watched as Gillard slipped on the robe and tied the towelling sash around his waist.

'I know you're sniffing around here for something, I just don't know what,' Norris said.

'I had no idea you were associated with the place, to be honest.'

'Sure you didn't.'

Gillard took a hurried shower, and dressed rapidly, now as tense as if he'd been at work all day. His shift started at two p.m. He exited the changing room and made his way out of the corridor to the waiting area where he had earlier been served a smoothie. There was no sign of Sam. It was another twenty minutes before she emerged, looking rather flushed, her expensively coiffed hair hurriedly clipped up.

'How was your massage?' he asked.

'Fantastic,' she said. 'Really, really good. I decided to go for the full body.'

That was a lot of praise. He scrutinised her, trying to decide whether she had gone for the extras. Maybe she had. 'Mine started well, but while I was dozing off my masseuse slipped away to be replaced by big Jackie Norris himself.'

'Really? Attention from senior management.'

'Yes. When you booked in, did you use both of our names?'

'Yes, I didn't give it a second thought.'

'I should have said.' Gillard could see she was looking quizzically at him.

'Did you use the pool?' she asked.

'No, I didn't quite feel like it by the end.'

'I'm sorry Craig, this hasn't turned out how I wanted it to be.'

'It's not your fault.' They headed off to the dining room, where they had a pretty good lunch of mussels in a cream sauce with herb bread and steamed vegetables. Just as they were on the dessert, a handsome man with a blond ponytail wandered past, and he and Sam exchanged a smile.

'Who's that?' Gillard asked.

'Lee, my masseur.'

Gillard looked at the broad-shouldered and upright body receding across the dining room. 'Did you go for the extras?' he asked her.

'Extras?'

'Norris said you chose the yoni massage.'

'I did not. Tempting though it was.'

Gillard slid his hand over hers. 'I'm glad to hear it. Not only because it would make me jealous, but because we don't want to let some former crime boss have a hold over us. I'm presuming they have cameras in the massage rooms, for just that purpose.'

'Eugh. I never even considered that.'

'You always should. Having a suspicious mind isn't a bad thing.'

'In relationships, it most certainly is. And I thought today was for us, not for work.' She looked upset.

Chapter Twelve

Sunday night darts match, back bar at the Railway Tavern. Packed as usual, noisy, football on the back TV. The half of them he didn't know were probably with the other team, the Greyhound at Peckham. Brendan Musgrove stood by the mark, and held up the first dart. He needed 157 to finish. Treble nineteen, treble twenty, double top. He held his dart in an open fist in front of his face, little finger cocked, as if sewing an invisible stitch. Thwack. First one was comfortably in, suppressed shout of 'yeah' from Mal Scattergood, who would go next if he failed. The treble twenty, the shot he practised a hundred times a day. In his peripheral vision, he saw a big man that he recognised. The man he'd been looking for. Different specs now, but definitely him.

Thwack.

A single twenty, just below the line. There was a groan behind him. He couldn't finish now, but a treble twenty would bring it down for Mal, if the next player from the dog didn't win in the interim. The dart flew to the mark, sixty points, now leaving Mal to get a double ten to finish.

Musgrove walked to the board and retrieved his darts. Someone had already chalked up his score. He returned to his table, and drew deeply on his pint, lager shandy. Hated the stuff, gassy and sweet. But everyone there downed half a dozen pints over the course of an evening, Carling normally, Guinness some of them. All right for them. He had to keep his wits while they lost theirs.

He'd been on this gig for three years. Working his way in with the lads, the locals who'd been here a lifetime. *Sarf Landan*, as they called it. Being good at darts was the breakthrough for a Geordie like him. Welcomed him to the team, gave him guest membership. Took the piss out of his accent, but his legend was cast iron. Shipbuilding until the yards closed, then welding freelance. *Auf Wiedersehn, pet*, they used to say at the end of the night. Because he looked a bit like Jimmy Nail. But they couldn't fault him. He'd had plenty of questions about it. Given jobs on the side, to weld a trailer for Mal. Watched by his mates who would know a good gas mix from a bad one, to see if it was neat or whether it would be a 'pigeon shit' messy join. But you couldn't fault him. His dad had been everything he now pretended to be, and he had learned when he was young to do everything that he needed now. Fucking bulletproof, his back story. Just omitted the bit where he went to university, dropped out after a term, and joined the police. No mention of that.

You could feel the criminality here, absorb it through the pores in your skin, see it hanging in the air, like fag smoke used to. Ran through their blood like Brighton through a stick of rock. The women as much as the men. Hardened girls, shrewd eyes, dyed hair mostly. Some good lookers amongst the youngsters, but tired by the age of forty. Exhausted, in a way that only city people can be. Suffering behind the make-up, caught in the expectations of extended families that were woven together, cousins, nieces, uncles. Every other one, male and female, had done time. And these days they were on the defensive. They'd surrendered the lounge, a front bar for the office workers, the trendy youngsters with their neat beards, bright eyes and earrings. Vera had drawn the line at 'fucking gnocchi', as she had told him. 'I serve good English grub, and a roast on Sunday. That's what people round here like.' She used to deride the menu at the Lamb and Flag across towards the main road. 'A trio of fucking filo pastry parcels, my arse,' she had told him one time when pulling him a pint. 'Over my dead body.'

In the back bar she had a warming cabinet of bangers. Sausages, onions and finger rolls for a fiver. Not hot dogs, she wouldn't have that. A proper British sausage. Warmed, re-warmed, re-re-warmed again, as far as he could see. In the last hour before closing time people couldn't resist them. It was probably a place like this where the plague started.

Where was he? Musgrove scanned the crowd. He was there at the bar, a massive bloke with beard and glasses, who seemed to have an extra dimension of solidity beyond that bestowed simply by his height and breadth. It must be Horace Mower. He'd seen the file, months ago. Always tried to memorise the mugshots. This was a name to make your balls shrink, to try and hide back up in your body where they dropped down from all those years ago. The way the man grasped the pint was like he was trying to strangle it. Straight down in two pulls. Back of the big tattooed hand wiped across his mouth, a satisfied sigh, and a slight twist of the big torso as he called across the bar for another.

There was a slight movement behind Musgrove. He turned to see Mal Scattergood was up next. Crap darts player, actually. Double ten finish, and what did he do?

A single six. The worst result, because it left the awkward double seven on the bottom left of the board. Easiest ways to checkout were either the double top, which everyone practised, or the right-hand doubles strip of thirteen, six or ten. Missing vertically was more common than horizontally, and you get more vertical leeway on these. The right-hand edge also matched the curve of the wrist for right-handed players like him and Mal. His dad taught him that, too. But now Scattergood was stuck with double seven. Musgrove could see he was going to miss, and sure enough Scattergood was outside with the second dart, and bust on a single sixteen with the third.

'Tough darts, Mal,' Musgrove said as his teammate came over after retrieving his darts.

'The dog will go out on that one,' Scattergood said, taking a gulp of his pint. The next player, wearing a white T-shirt with *The Greyhound, Peckham* written on it, above an emblem of a sprinting dog, leaned up to the mark. The darts flew in, treble twenty, twice, double ten. Finished. One of the other players, similarly attired, walked up to Scattergood and handed him a small Jiffy bag. 'There you are, mate, as promised.'

'Thanks, Col,' Scattergood said, hurriedly stuffing the padded envelope into his jeans pocket.

'Were you running the odds on this one?' Musgrove said.

Scattergood blinked a couple of times. 'Er, no, nothing like that.' He suddenly seemed a little nervous. Musgrove watched as his eyes flitted towards Mower. 'He ain't got much of a tan, 'as he?' Scattergood said. 'Spends most of the time at his villa.'

'Whereabouts?' Musgrove said.

'Torremolinos, maybe fucking Billericay,' Scattergood said with a laugh. Musgrove could see why they called him hobbit, with his youthful crown of curly hair that seems somehow wrong on a bloke pushing fifty. And of course, he was a short arse. Five-five, five-six maybe.

'I'm going on holiday myself,' Scattergood said, pausing only briefly for the cheer when the dog's player won the pool competition. 'Christmas away. Away from the rain and the cold, eh?'

'Even Spain can be chilly over Christmas, like,' Musgrove replied.

'Not facking Spain,' Scattergood said, shaking his head as if Musgrove had suggested kipping down at Battersea Dogs Home for the festivities. 'Bali, mate. Fantastic. Unspoiled beaches. Aussie birds.' He cupped imaginary breasts and scrunched his face up for emphasis.

'That's a bit out my budget, like.' Musgrove was enjoying this, spooling in the loose-lipped drunk. What serious criminal outfit would want this guy in with them?

'Crypto, that's the thing. It's going up and up. When you're in the know,' and at this point he tapped the side of his nose, 'anything is possible.'

'So you've got enough money in crypto for a holiday in Bali?'

'And the fucking rest,' Scattergood said. 'A long holiday.'

'Which is the best then? Is it Bitcoin or one of them others?'

'Personally, I'm going with—'

The looming figure of Horace Mower stood over them. 'Who's this then?' Mower demanded of Scattergood, his big finger pointing at Musgrove.

'That's our Geordie darts star,' Scattergood said.

'Brendan, glad to meet you.' Musgrove offered his hand which was swallowed up to the wrist in the huge paw of Mower.

'Didn't do us much good tonight, did yer?' he laughed in Musgrove's face. He almost expected to be scorched by the heat of his breath.

'Well…'

'He's all right 'Orace.' Scattergood gave a nervous laugh.

'Whedjalivethen?' *Where do you live then?* Mower was asking Musgrove, and he intended to get an answer.

'Londonderry Court, just over the back.' It was true. He lived the lie so completely he kept a flat that fitted it. An untidy, Geordie man-flat complete with Newcastle United paraphernalia, and some welding gear. He slept at the bedsit three or four nights a week.

'Past your bedtime, don't you think?' He glared at Musgrove, who could see a vein throbbing on Mower's head.

Musgrove broke his gaze and picked up his pint. His hand was shaking slightly as he drained it. Christ, he hoped he hadn't been rumbled.

''Orace, it's only half nine,' Scattergood squeaked.

'Nah, I'll see you next time,' Musgrove said. Under Mower's watchful gaze, Musgrove tossed goodbyes to the other members of the team, and made his way out of the pub. Every part of him, from the back of his head to the back of his knees, was trying to watch to see if Mower was going to follow. It had been years since he'd had to run for his life, and it took all of his self-control not to do so the moment he was out of the pub. He forced himself to walk slowly along the street, under the railway bridge, and round the corner. He heard no sound of heavy boots following. He gave a shuddering sigh and headed for the bedsit. There were only nine flats in Londonderry court, and his had a Newcastle United sticker in the kitchen window. If Mower was intent on doing something, he'd know which flat to find him in.

Change of plan. He would pick up an overnight bag and go back to his real life for tonight. Muswell Hill, long-suffering Liz and his little boy. Gary. The one he did it all for. Nights like this, he hated his job. Living like a dosser for no thanks and the chance of ending up dead in the Thames, with a knife in his back.

Stuff it. He wanted out.

Chapter Thirteen

Monday 14th December

Gillard was sitting in an almost empty carriage on an early train heading into London. It was a bright, crisp December morning, and he'd left from home, catching the Victoria train and leaving the car at Banstead. He didn't mind being dragged into an early incident room meeting, so long as there was some progress to discuss. Culshaw had promised there would be. Operation Santa Claus's search to narrow down the location of a half billion pound robbery was getting increasingly urgent. The original intelligence suggested a job taking place on the Friday before Christmas, now five days away. If it had been put back two days, as the message on Terry Moses' phone seemed to indicate, it would take place on a Sunday. That still only left a week.

He stared out of the window as the train pulled into Clapham Junction. He emerged and joined a small crowd on the platform for the Waterloo service. After the train departed, trundling alongside a line of tower blocks in Vauxhall, he could just see, in the gaps between them, the gleaming glass tips of the various skyscrapers and the curved arc of the London Eye. Somewhere amongst that lot was half a billion worth of something: gold, silver, jewels. Something that could be readily turned into cash.

But what? He had been too busy with the Jordan Idris murder to really think about what it could be. The trouble was it was such an old-fashioned idea. A bunch of mainly old white men, with a hundred years of jail time between them, risking all by going for one big last job. Michael Caine and his merry men, a made-for-TV plot. In some ways it didn't make sense. The names he'd heard just didn't seem to fit together. Old enemies Terry Moses and Jackie Norris. At least either of them were credible organisers considering the size of the operation, if not together. But Mal Scattergood? Colin Lamb? Small-time operators with no unique skills. Even if they pulled off the job, they weren't going to get away with it. London had a million CCTV cameras, and almost every electronic device could be tracked. It wasn't as if you could just flee abroad easily, either. The days when the train robber Ronnie Biggs could live an open and glamorous life in Brazil, thumbing his nose at the British police, were long gone. Britain had extradition treaties with the vast majority of the world's countries, even Libya and Cuba. There were exceptions of course: Israel, China, Russia, Zimbabwe, Saudi Arabia, Myanmar. He couldn't imagine either Moses or Norris being at home in any of those places.

There was clearly something going on. But what was it?

He picked up a free newspaper from the previous day and flicked through it as the train made its grindingly slow approach into Waterloo station. On one of the pages near the back, he saw something that made him do a double-take. Of course! Why hadn't he thought of that before? He took out his phone and rang DC Rob Townsend. He wanted to make sure.

A bigger room had been co-opted for the Operation Santa Claus incident room meeting. As well as DCI Culshaw, DI Latimer and their small team of detectives, they had found space for Assistant Commissioner Kay Thompson and Commander Digby Snow. Gillard was the only external officer involved.

Culshaw began his presentation. 'Given the compressed timescales, we have implemented a limited surveillance operation on the Railway Tavern in Bermondsey and, with the assistance of Surrey Police, at the pub run by Terry Moses in Glissingbourne. I have to confess that we've gleaned little extra intelligence to either confirm or deny that a major robbery is taking place. However, it is fair to say that radio silence, so to speak, amongst the principal conspirators could well be evidence that the plan is going ahead—'

The assistant commissioner interrupted: 'It could equally be evidence that it never was going to go ahead, don't you think? I don't think we can use this information either way.'

'That's certainly a point of view, ma'am,' Culshaw said.

'So how many targets do we have on our list, Culshaw?' Snow asked.

Culshaw looked down at his list. 'We have sixteen banks and safety deposit locations in central London, of which four are in close proximity to Oxford Circus.'

'How important is this Oxford Circus element?' the AC asked.

'It's come up from two separate sources, ma'am. One from Tango—'

'That's the serving prisoner, yes?'

'Yes, and the other is courtesy of Oscar, our undercover officer, who recorded a phone conversation involving Mal Scattergood.'

'So we've got two independent sources. What other input do we have?'

'The most interesting new development is the burner phone conversation which has fallen into DCI Gillard's hands.' Culshaw looked to Gillard for support.

'Yes, ma'am. We found the phone in the flat of a known criminal—'

'Jordan Idris, found drowned in a canal not far from Byfleet and New Haw station. I do read my briefing papers, detective chief inspector.'

'I'm sure you do, ma'am. There is forensic evidence that this phone belonged to Terry Moses and was stolen from his pub in a burglary in the small hours of last Tuesday. Idris was found dead a day later.'

'I've read the text messages, and they mention a JCB.'

'Yes, ma'am.'

'What is BM then? As in "the BM job"?'

Gillard looked to Culshaw.

'Bank Metropolitan, possibly,' Culshaw said. 'It's not too close to Oxford Circus, but they do have safe deposit boxes. There's also Bullion Metals Ltd, but that's a couple of miles away up the Edgware Road. We've got a couple of MBs nearer, but no BMs.'

'Sounds to me like you're grasping at straws,' she said, fixing Culshaw with a glare. 'One other thing. If I was Terry Moses and had just lost a phone with such important details on it, I'm not sure I would go ahead with the robbery.'

'With all due respect ma'am, I suspect you are a more cautious and less greedy person than the average bank robber.'

She gave him a wintry smile. 'Indeed. But all the same, it is taking a risk.'

'I agree.'

She turned to Gillard. 'And you are undertaking surveillance of Moses, I gather?'

'Yes, ma'am. It's been a bit of a rush job, given the timescales, but we have tapped the pub's landline and Internet connection from the nearest BT telegraph pole. We're also getting copied in on the two registered mobile phones for that address. We've got an undercover team making a note of every vehicle which stops at the pub, and every car movement by Moses himself.'

'Anything suspicious?' she asked.

'Not so far. He seems to be carrying on as normal. But this close to the main event, most of the key decisions and arrangements have probably already been made.'

'Does Moses actually possess a JCB?'

'Not that we are aware of. We are going through his web traffic to see if there's any evidence of him having arranged to rent one. We haven't found anything so far.'

'We're really not getting very far, are we? I remain far from convinced this robbery is actually going to happen.'

'Major criminals are not stupid, and unlikely to exchange vital information through any channel that the police could easily tap,' Culshaw said.

'I detect arse-covering here,' the AC said, fixing Culshaw and Gillard with a stare. 'Get me a firm location by Wednesday evening at the latest and I can get you the resources by Friday. That's three full days. I want results.'

She stood up and left the meeting, closing the door quietly behind her. The combined exhalation of a dozen detectives could be heard. Commander Digby Snow looked at Culshaw and said: 'I've backed you on this, so get me some convincing details.'

It was clear to Gillard that there were two sorts of possible failure now. One was going full-on Keystone Cop mode, then standing there like a Nelly when nothing happened. The other was failing to have the courage of your own convictions, and not acting when one of the biggest heists in history took place. He wasn't sure which of the two possible screw-ups was more likely.

Culshaw turned back to his whiteboards. 'Okay, everyone. Let's start with the conspirators. Big Jackie Norris, career criminal turned national treasure.' He pointed to a picture on the board, showing Norris in a dinner jacket and bow tie with his glamorous second wife Sally Winchester. 'He, I think, is the Mr Big. His son Damian, a bit of a flash Harry, would be the head of operations. Mal Scattergood, who is Norris' nephew, is apparently the driver.' Culshaw pointed to the two pictures. 'Now we've got three other possible participants. One is Colin Lamb.' There was no mugshot of Lamb, only a surveillance picture taken in the street from a distance. Gillard had never seen someone who looked less like a career criminal. Lamb had a doughy face, a greasy combover and a body which resembled a pre-diet Carl Hoskins. 'We are struggling to be honest to see how he fits in, skill-wise. But he is a long-time friend and drinking partner of Mal Scattergood, and passed him a Jiffy bag on Sunday right under the nose of our under-cover officer. The second guy we don't have a name for, but is purportedly on the finance side. This snippet came from our serving prisoner.'

'They're not exactly the magnificent seven,' said Gillard to some laughter around the room. 'More like a bunch of superannuated small-time criminals. Jackie Norris and Terry Moses excepted.'

'I think the AC is right, it ain't gonna happen,' said DC Hart, the technical specialist.

'Just a bit of fantasy by some old lags down the pub,' said another.

Gillard had been looking at his phone, having received a text back from Rob Townsend. Good, it was possible. He got out the free newspaper he'd picked up on the train and waved it at them. 'It might be nothing, but the world's most expensive painting is coming to Britain on Thursday.' He opened the paper and read the story. 'The *Salvator Mundi*, painted by Leonardo da Vinci, is on its way to the Guggenheim Gallery in New York for a six-month loan, but by special arrangement with the National Gallery, it will be displayed here to the public for ten days over the Christmas holidays. It was auctioned in 2017 for $450 million, and bought by a prince from Abu Dhabi, thought to be acting on behalf of the de facto ruler of Saudi Arabia, Mohammed bin Salman.'

Jaws dropped around the room.

'There's your current value, right there,' Gillard said. 'Half a billion, if not more.'

'You could do no end of damage to a painting with a JCB,' said Hart. There was some laughter.

'It's an intriguing idea,' Culshaw said. 'It doesn't obviously fit in with "BM job", and Oxford Circus is not the nearest tube.'

'None of our conspirators have any experience in fencing artwork,' DI Latimer pointed out. 'And I can't see how you could sell something like that anyway.'

'I accept all that,' Gillard said. 'There's a lot of boxes it doesn't tick. But cell tower triangulation proves that whoever texted Terry Moses to give the green light for the BM job was standing in the north-east corner of Trafalgar Square at the time. And guess what? That's right next to the National Gallery. My hunch is that he'd just done a reconnaissance.'

Chapter Fourteen

No Leonardo painting has been more controversial than Salvator Mundi. Just twenty-six inches by nineteen, the oil on walnut panel painting shows Christ in a blue Renaissance robe, making the sign of the cross with his right hand, and holding a transparent, non-refracting crystal orb in his left, which signals his role as saviour of the world and represents the 'celestial sphere' of the heavens. Around thirty copies or variations of the work by Leonardo's pupils and followers have been identified, giving some idea of the difficulty facing art experts in establishing its authenticity. As recently as this year, one renowned expert dismissed the possibility that Leonardo would have painted anyone where the eyes are not level, and where there was not a single reflection from the orb. Nevertheless, what are said to be preparatory chalk and ink drawings of the drapery by Leonardo are held in the British Royal Collection.

In 2005, the very same painting, described as 'after Leonardo da Vinci', was listed in a U.S. auction catalogue at $1,200–$1,800.

Yet despite a significant minority of experts still doubting its authenticity it was sold at auction just twelve years later for U.S. $450.3 million in 2017 by Christie's in New York. The buyer, Prince Badr bin Abdullah, set a new record for the most expensive painting ever sold at public auction. Prince Badr allegedly made the purchase on behalf of Abu Dhabi's Department of Culture and Tourism, but it has been suggested that he may have been a stand-in bidder for his close ally, the Saudi Arabian crown prince Mohammed bin Salman. The current location of the painting has been reported as unknown, but a report in June 2019 stated that it was being stored on bin Salman's yacht. The National Gallery last exhibited the painting in 2011, and is not surprisingly delighted to get the opportunity to display it again, albeit briefly.

(London Evening Standard)

–

Culshaw closed the newspaper and handed it back to Gillard. The meeting had ended half an hour ago, and they were now standing in Trafalgar Square with their backs to Nelson's Column, looking at the broad neoclassical façade of the National Gallery to their north. There were three huge banners fluttering in the stiff breeze advertising an exhibition of Leonardo's *Salvator Mundi*. The square was thronged with tourists; the most Gillard had seen since before the start of lockdown. Many of them were visiting the European-style Christmas market at the bottom of the steps. They looked around them, at the High Commission of Canada to their left and the church of St Martin-in-the-Fields to their right.

'They've moved the main entrance from the Charing Cross end round to the Sainsbury's wing of the gallery,' Culshaw said, pointing to the left of the main façade. They headed across the square towards Pall Mall East and looked at the entrance.

'No steps,' Gillard said. 'That would make it easier for the JCB.'

'Yeah, but they are bound to put the picture in one of the central galleries.'

'I don't think they're going to wait until the picture is installed,' Gillard said. 'If the JCB idea is correct, they would probably use it to intercept the painting on arrival. Remember the text said "easier to get the JCB in".'

Culshaw nodded. 'The exhibition starts on Sunday the twenty-first, then runs up until Christmas Eve, resuming the day after Boxing Day. I presume they would need a few days to set it up beforehand, so either the Friday before Christmas or the Sunday are tenable dates.'

'Shall we?' Gillard said, indicating the entrance. The two detectives entered the gallery, and followed the directions up a series of steps and long corridors, until they were in the main part of the building. The huge galleries, hung with paintings from all over the world from the thirteenth to the nineteenth century, echoed to the sound of schoolchildren and the many organised trips. Gillard approached one of the attendants and asked where *Salvator Mundi* would be displayed. He was directed towards a central gallery, currently closed off by plastic sheeting and official noticeboards.

After half an hour, they retreated to the cafe to consider what they'd seen. 'I think you're right,' Culshaw said. 'It would be pretty difficult to steal from that central gallery. There would be no access for a JCB and no role for it. Besides, it would take you at least five minutes to get out.'

Gillard nodded. 'A lot about this doesn't make any sense. It's a junior crew for a job of this size, and even if there is a specialist art thief involved that we don't know about, you still can't imagine managing to sell the work.'

'It would be utterly brazen to grab it in the street on arrival, and your best chance of getting it out through London's traffic would surely be on a motorbike. I don't know if Scattergood was planning to use his van or not.'

'We need more information,' Gillard said ruefully. 'I'm going to have a last try to see if I can get anything more from my own source.'

Culshaw sighed, and rubbed his forehead. 'I really don't think we can ask any more of Tango. If you're inside, and called in to see official visitors more than once in a blue moon, word gets around. Not just from other inmates – there's always someone on staff spilling the beans. We might be able to get some more from Oscar, but we've only got two days—'

'Hold on,' Gillard said, staring over Culshaw's shoulder at someone who had just walked into the cafe, clocked them, and walked right out again.

'What is it?' Culshaw asked.

'I could have sworn that was Horace Mower.'

Culshaw turned to look, but the man had gone. 'Oscar reckons he saw him yesterday in the Railway Tavern,' Culshaw whispered. 'I was dubious. From all we'd heard he was on the Costa del Crime, keeping his head down.'

'I never forget a face,' Gillard said, standing up. 'Especially one as ugly as that.' The two detectives abandoned their expensive coffees, and made their way out of the cafe. If Gillard was right, he knew this was a significant moment. Horace Mower had been a notorious hard man, used by gangland bosses for settling scores in the 1990s. He'd disappeared from view about ten years ago and had been thought to be living under an alias. Gillard had only come across him once when the body parts of a drug dealer were found in bin bags in Redhill in 2006. He had only been a detective sergeant then, and his boss had suspected Mower.

By the time they had exited the cafe, the man was nowhere to be seen.

'What on earth would Mower be doing in the National Gallery, eh Craig?'

'I can't imagine him having an interest in fine art.'

Culshaw chuckled. 'Somewhere, in an evidence bag, there is reputed to be a business card from years ago saying: "Mower. I cut grasses."'

'I think he might have recognised me,' Gillard said. 'That was a decisive U-turn, which only makes me more certain it was him.'

'We could ask to see the CCTV at the entrances?'

'We could, but it might risk tipping off the insider, assuming there is one.'

'Not if we say it was a pickpocket, or something. They get those kind of minor queries every day.'

'But not from officers of our rank,' Gillard said. 'Let's get a plod to do it, but sharpish. We need those images quickly.'

Culshaw worked his phone to contact the office.

By the time the two detectives had returned to New Scotland Yard, DI Latimer and her team had made considerable progress.

'We got a PC from Charing Cross to visit the gallery and ask for a CCTV disc. Unfortunately, they can't do downloads. We've also got requests in at the cameras to all the nearest three tube stations,' she said. 'I'm not sure we have enough time or resources to find him in the crowds before Wednesday night.'

'That's all right,' Culshaw said. 'If Mower is involved, I think the AC might finally be convinced that we're on to something.'

DC Stacey Daines had pulled up a Google Street View map on her screen. 'There's a goods entrance to the National Gallery opposite St Martin's Place, which also serves the National Portrait Gallery, which is currently closed. There are plenty of overlooking offices that we could use. Oh, and we just heard from Oscar that he has attached a tracking device to the underside of Mal Scattergood's van, so wherever it is we will know.'

'That's brilliant, Stacey. Even if we don't know where the job is, all we have to do is follow the van.'

While the incident room was buzzing with activity, Gillard tried Keith Sutton's landline. He had tried it earlier and there been no reply, so this time he left a message. He was reluctant to press Sutton for more details, or about who he'd got his information from, but it was vital to firm up as much as possible about the job. They now had two possible dates, 18 or 20 December, a slightly odd mention of Oxford Circus which didn't sit perfectly with the National Gallery location, and the idea of a JCB. One thing Gillard also wanted to ask Sutton was whether he had seen Horace Mower about in the last few years. As Mower had apparently made an appearance at the Railway Tavern, that might be a confirming factor. Of course, assuming Sutton knew of Mower's reputation, he would be terrified.

Gillard had just finished leaving a message when his phone rang. It was Carl Hoskins.

'Got some interesting news for you, boss,' Hoskins said. 'The burglary at the Rising Sun definitely took place in the early hours of Tuesday, because the regulars here recall Terry Moses was in a right state about it Tuesday lunchtime. He was particularly aggrieved about the theft of the charity box.'

From the traffic noise Gillard could hear, the detective constable was no longer in the pub.

'There's another thing, sir. The Rising Sun has karaoke on the Friday and a quiz on Sunday night.'

It took a moment for Gillard to realise what the detective constable was telling him. 'You mean Terry will be busy?'

'Yeah. He runs the karaoke and is the quizmaster on Sunday. Just saying.'

'Well, it's a good alibi I suppose. Of course it depends what time on the day in question the raid takes place.'

Hoskins laughed. 'Well, if I'd just knocked off a half billion job during the day, I'd be on the first plane to Rio, not standing around asking regulars when Bristol Rovers last won the FA Cup.'

'I take your point, Carl. One other thing, are you aware of whether Terry Moses ever worked with Horace Mower?'

'I'm not sure. Isn't Mower on the run in Spain?'

'He's been seen in London,' Gillard said.

'That's interesting,' Hoskins said. 'I know that Mower used to do the dirty work for big Jackie Norris. But that was more than twenty years ago.'

'Anything new on the Idris killing?' Gillard asked.

'Nothing forensically. I was in the incident meeting this morning, and we haven't got any further. And there's no sign of Lydia Marasova either.'

Gillard thanked him and hung up. He was increasingly worried about the woman. Whoever took care of a difficult victim like Idris would make short work of her.

It was late afternoon when Gillard finally got to Waterloo station to return home. He'd already told Sam that he would be home at a reasonable time. She had promised to make a meal for them both. He felt pretty good. The incident room meetings had gone well. Some good colour CCTV had turned up from the gallery entrance showing that it definitely was Horace Mower. Well over fifty now, Mower still had the build of the proverbial brick shithouse. And though the hair was now a fuzz of grey instead of the dark crewcut, the bent nose and lantern jaw were a giveaway, even with a light beard. He still favoured tinted spectacles, but these days oval framed instead of square. Mower was normally a purveyor of unmitigated violence, working on the quiet, with surprise on his side, and a fair degree of forensic awareness. He'd never gone down for murder, despite all the suspicion, but he had done time for GBH. How he fitted into a half billion pound robbery was far from clear. Maybe he would actually be there to grab the painting, with a cosh in his hand. Still, with three big names from the past coming up together, there was clearly some major operation going on. Culshaw's team had checked with the Border Force, and Mower had not crossed any UK borders to their knowledge in the last ten years. He must be using a forged passport.

There was a train waiting to leave on the platform, absolutely packed, and on the opposite platform one was just arriving. Gillard thought he could spare the few minutes to let that one empty out and ensure he got a seat. While the arriving commuters were streaming past him, his phone rang. It was a female officer from Peckham Police Station, but he didn't catch her name in the racket of public announcements.

'We found a message from this number on the phone of a Mr Keith Sutton. Are you a family member?'

'No, I'm not. I'm Craig Gillard, a detective chief inspector from Surrey Police. What's happened to him?'

'Ah. Well, I'm sorry to tell you, sir, that we and paramedics were in attendance early today at Mr Sutton's home address, and have to tell you that Mr Sutton has sadly passed away.'

'I'm very sorry to hear that,' Gillard said. And he really was, for all sorts of reasons. 'Did it look like natural causes?'

'Yes. We had to break in. His daughter was frantic with worry, because she hadn't heard from him, and couldn't raise him on the phone. We found him sitting on the toilet. Can I ask what Surrey Police's interest was in him, sir?'

'You'll be aware of his criminal record. I knew him from years ago, that's all,' Gillard said. 'Nothing more than that.' He had no idea who this woman was, though from the cumbersome way she passed on the news of Sutton's death, she clearly was a serving officer, not an imposter. Gillard put one hand over his ear so he had a fighting chance to hear what she was saying. When he finally had a moment of clarity, he took the officer's name. He'd make a note of her superior officer, and send a message to make sure there was a full post-mortem.

As he got on the train, he thought it through. Mower was about, and there was already one dead grass, one dead pickpocket and a missing girl. He just hoped Oscar, a.k.a. DC Brendan Musgrove, was being careful.

–

'If this horrible murderer Mower is back in Britain can't you just arrest him?' Sam asked as they shared a meal. It was roast chicken with slices of chorizo slid under the skin of the breast, a recipe she got from her Jamie Oliver book. She had served it with asparagus, baked potatoes and gravy. It was delicious.

'It's not as simple as that,' Gillard said. 'We're expecting this big robbery at the end of the week, either Friday or Sunday, depending on which grass you believe. Culshaw wants to catch them in the act, and it would be a huge coup if we did. But if we arrested Mower now, and he *was* involved, then the job wouldn't take place and all the preparations would have been spoiled.'

'I see what you mean. So did he kill the man that was found in the canal?' she asked as she speared a piece of asparagus.

'It's entirely possible, and it was just the kind of neat and well-disguised job that he used to do. If it was him, it would almost certainly mean that Idris had already upset somebody powerful, even before burgling Terry Moses' pub.'

'You've lost me there.'

Gillard thoughtfully chewed a piece of chicken. 'Idris breaks in and steals an RSPCA charity box from the Rising Sun in Glissingbourne in the early hours of last Tuesday morning. By the early hours of Wednesday morning, he is already dead. Even Mower is not that efficient. So that means Moses is not in the frame for contracting the killing, unless the burglary was somehow just the latest bit of a long-running feud between Idris and him.'

'I see what you mean. So where does Jackie Norris fit in?'

'We're not sure. Norris and Moses hate each other, supposedly. It would seem unlikely that they would join forces even for a job as big as this. The more money there is the more a basic level of trust is essential – that's how the criminal underworld works, and that's why families are so important. We know that Norris has used Mower in the past, but were less sure about Moses using him.' He sighed, and cut up a chunk of baked potato. 'Now, on top of it all, my informant has just died.' Sam's look was blank. 'You know, Keith Sutton. I went to see him in his tower block in Bermondsey.'

'Oh yes I remember.'

'Poor old sod. Couldn't have been much of a life. The fags were going to get him in the end, and his poor daughter running from pillar to post.'

His mobile rang, and he picked it up. 'Sorry, that's probably her now from his landline. I better take this.' He stood up and walked out into the hall, and answered the call.

–

'It was terrible, honest. The police broke the door down before I could get back from work with the spare key, and there he was sitting on the bog with his trousers down, and his face was horrible and grey, and his gob was open, his dentures was on the floor. It was terrible. The paramedics said he'd been dead a while. And I feel shit for not being there for 'im. But I had overtime on Sunday because I need the money, and I do need the money.' She began to cry, great sobs turning into crackles on the phone.

'I'm so sorry,' Gillard said. As far as she knew, he was just Craig Roberts, her father's old probation officer. 'If there's anything I can do—'

'Well now there's his funeral, and me sister in Australia to tell, and I tell you it's come at the worst possible time. I got Covid didn't I, and felt shit for a month, and still can't taste nothing. I've got bills up to here because the cladding on my own flat is a fire risk and I don't know where to turn to, I rang the social an' I couldn't get through, and me credit ran out. You know, I should never have bought the bloody place, and I'm in overdraft up to here and behind on the mortgage, that's why I'm working every hour God sends.'

Gillard inserted small sounds of sympathy into the breathless monologue, and eventually Dawn calmed down. 'If there's anything I can do, let me know,' he said.

'I don't know what to do about the benefits he was on, and all that. I have to cancel them don't I, or I get prosecuted?'

'Eventually you would. You can look up how to cancel online, but if you are confused, the best thing is to go to your local Citizens Advice Bureau. They have a helpline too.'

She cried a bit more, then thanked him profusely and said she would let him know when the funeral was, before hanging up. He felt for her, trying to hold it all together on her own. But the last thing he wanted to do was spend more time with her. She wasn't stupid, and she might eventually figure out that he wasn't a former probation officer after all. He had seen her at the Railway Tavern with her father, and presumed there was a chance she might run into some of the same dodgy characters in the back bar that her father had overheard. She clearly had a tale of woe to tell for anybody who would listen, and just in passing could easily blow his cover. Some of the old lags in there might well remember who Sutton's real probation officer was back in the 1990s.

He walked back into the dining room, and saw that Sam had finished her meal. His own had grown cold, and he took it back into the kitchen to microwave.

'I could hear her crying from here,' Sam called through to him. 'Poor woman.'

'Yeah, there's lots of people out there only just holding it together.'

'So he just died, he wasn't murdered?' Sam called through.

'Seemingly not.' The microwave pinged and he pulled out the plate, which was now almost too hot to hold, the remnants of the meal sizzling. He brought it through, grasped in a tea towel, and soon wished he had taken the time to find the proper oven glove.

'Wow, you've turned into a smoking tandoori dish,' she said, laughing, as her husband hurriedly dropped the plate onto his table mat.

Gillard speared a piece of chicken, and held it close to his mouth. 'Still too hot.'

'Obviously.' She was grinning at him.

'Can't take any chances,' he said, blowing on the morsel. 'I'm going to make sure there's a proper post-mortem on Sutton. Just in case.'

Chapter Fifteen

That same evening Assistant Commissioner Kay Thompson was in a taxi heading for a royal charity gala night in the Metropolitan London Hotel for the benefit of Syrian refugees. It was a glittering black-tie occasion, attended by the great and the good, and studded with celebrities who had been willing to pay at least £500 each for the chance to hear Elton John play a few numbers, and listen to some well-known raconteurs and comedians. She had been offered the ticket at short notice because her boss had not been able to go. It was only when the taxi was stuck in traffic on Park Lane that her husband John turned to her and said: 'You know who's giving the after-dinner speech don't you?'

'Surprise me.'

'Jackie Norris, the former bank robber.'

'You're kidding me.'

'Listen to this. "Mr Norris, now a bestselling author and a tireless worker for charity, will take you back to the streets of south London and the old days of crime".'

'Anyone would think there wasn't any crime now,' she said. It all made sense now. No wonder the commissioner had decided she had a more pressing engagement. The last thing she would have wanted to see was the man she arrested back in the 1990s parading his rehabilitation.

Norris had been interviewed on the BBC in a documentary about steering youngsters away from crime, and was popping up here there and everywhere, aided by the coolly glamorous Sally Winchester.

When they arrived, they mingled with others in the grand foyer. She noticed the Mayor of London, with whom she had crossed swords on a number of occasions, and the leaders of a couple of London borough councils, as well as the comedian Lenny Henry. While she exchanged pleasantries, John was peering at the seating plan pinned on a noticeboard.

'Did you know you were on the top table?'

'I'm not surprised, that's where they would have put the gaffer, had she been able to come.'

'Well, you are seated next to big Jackie himself.'

'Oh, for goodness sake! They're just trying to embarrass me.'

'I doubt it. The social planners no doubt thought you could have a good conversation. That's their job after all. Remember, our Mr Norris is now embraced to the public bosom.'

'Well, I'd rather he wasn't that close to mine.'

He chuckled and looked at her from under heavy eyebrows. 'And I'm next to his charming wife Sally.'

After each being offered a glass of champagne, they were shown to their tables. Sally Winchester made a beeline for her. She was slim, blonde and stylish. 'I'm so glad you came,' she said. 'I've put you next to Jackie. He is very keen to meet you!'

Kay smiled and sprinkled her conversation with small talk. She was aware that Sally had continued in her role at the *Sunday Times*, and wondered if that included contact with the crime reporters. She wouldn't be surprised if from somewhere within the great creaking, leaky Metropolitan Police organisation, hints of a half billion pound robbery in the offing might not have reached the ears of the more diligent reporters.

She saw Norris in the distance, in a well-tailored white evening jacket, chatting animatedly with someone from *Dragons' Den*, and one of the judges from *Strictly*. John had spotted Stephen Fry too. They were already sitting down, about to begin their hors d'oeuvres, when Norris came to take his place.

'Delighted to meecha,' Norris said, his south London accent as thick as ever. He offered her his hand, which she smiled and took in hers.

'It looks like it's going to be a fascinating evening,' she said. In fact, she thought it was going to be an ordeal. She had been looking forward to having a glass or two of wine; now she realised that in reality, she was at work and had to keep her wits about her.

The first half an hour passed pleasantly enough. A presentation from a Syrian refugee who had become a surgeon in the NHS brought a hearty round of applause. Then there was a medley of songs from Elton John at the piano, against a heartrending projection of suffering on the screens behind him. Charity fundraisers moved between tables, collecting details for donations. She noticed Norris pluck a bundle of £50 notes from his pocket, count them out as if he was buying a used car, and drop them in one of the collection boxes. It was over £1,000, she was certain of that.

'Still a big user of cash, then?' she asked.

'Oh yes, always have been, always will be. Besides, refugees need cash for food, cash for rent, all that.' He asked a few questions about her career in the Met, and then said, 'It's nice we're all on the same side now, isn't it?'

'Yes. If your influence can help keep youngsters out of jail that would be a real positive,' she said.

'Would you like a signed copy of my book?' he asked. When she hesitated, he said: 'Come on love, put your hand in your pocket. All the profits go to refugees.'

Bristling, she said: 'I've already read it, Mr Norris. And I've already contributed to the charity.'

'Have it your own way,' he said, turning round to one of the waiters. 'Oi, garcon,' Norris said to a male waiter. 'This lady is a bit uptight, could you top up her wine to relax her?'

'No thank you,' she said, putting a hand firmly on top of her glass.

Norris continued to address the waiter. 'Go on. Might help loosen her up a bit. If the contents don't work, we could always use the bottle, eh!' He cackled. One of the other guests on the table, a frail-looking aristocratic woman who might have been transported from *Downton Abbey*, looked on in mute horror. Kay turned to her right, where a small dark-haired man of Middle Eastern appearance started to engage her in conversation.

'Maybe he'll get bored and leave you alone,' he said.

'Thank you. He is an insufferable man,' she muttered.

The waiter pulled back, realising he had been used as a pawn. Hoping for reinforcements of a different kind, Kay glanced across at her husband. He was deep in conversation with Sally Winchester, who was telling some animated tale, which apparently required her fingers to rest on the back of his hand. He was lapping it up. Meanwhile Norris was staring at her. She could feel his proximity.

The hairs on the back of her neck rose as his lips almost brushed her ear.

'Tell me, Kay, what's all this I hear about someone going to steal that Leonardo painting from the National Gallery?' he whispered.

She stiffened and moved her head away, before turning back. 'I'm afraid I don't know what you're talking about. I don't get involved in operational matters.'

Norris seemed to find this quite funny, and chuckled to himself. 'That would look nice in the Swallowtail Hotel lounge. *Salvator Mundi*, saviour of the world. Be a nice little earner for someone, wouldn't it?'

'I couldn't possibly comment,' she said, feeling more uncomfortable all the time. The main course arrived, a vegetarian risotto for her, and a crown of lamb for him, each of the tiny bones decorated with a paper hat. She tried not to watch as her neighbour, after making short work of the meat, snapped the bones from the assembly one by one, and gnawed them.

'You know why I can get away with this, Kay?' he muttered, gravy running down his chin.

She made no reply, hating the fact he was using her name like a tool, a false intimacy to prise her open and get to her, as if she was an oyster.

'I can do this because I'm a national treasure, see. A bad boy made good, reminding everyone where I come from, confirming all you lot in your moral superiority. I'm a bit like one of them handbag dogs that sits on your lap and then charmingly licks its balls.'

'I think you've had too much to drink.'

'And I think you haven't had enough, missus, not nearly enough.'

She made her excuses, and headed off to the ladies. She was incandescent with rage. At the mirror, her hands shook as she reapplied her lipstick. Her face was pale. She had never been treated in this way. She waited a few minutes before re-emerging, and was pleased to see that the seat next to her was now vacant.

Norris, however, was on the stage with a mic in hand, just about to start his speech.

'Ladies and gentlemen, we'll just wait for the lady to take her seat. Don't stare, we will all soon reach the age when our bladders are not completely reliable.'

Of course everybody immediately turned to look at her. Except her husband, who was still staring into the eyes of Sally Winchester. *John, I need you to take me home.* She tried to beam the thought into his head, but as she sat at her seat, she saw that he had twisted round in his to watch Norris.

'Ladies and gentlemen, lords and ladies, I want to take you back in time, and over the other side of the Thames into south London. Imagine, if you will, flying over darkened streets, before a single high-rise tower block had ever been built, and then down past the Elephant and Castle into Bermondsey proper. There, in a terraced house on a soot-streaked street called Omdurman Terrace, under the shadow of the chimney from the bomb-damaged Hallway leather works, and opposite Sarson's vinegar factory, a little boy was born in the outside toilet, his mother screaming blue murder for help. There was no hot water, and no towels, like you always hear the midwife wants. There was no midwife either, just the lady from next door, and two copies of the *Radio Times* hung up in strips in the khazi, normally used as toilet paper, to wipe up the mess. It was 1947, and that little boy was me. I arrived a few weeks early, probably the only time in my life I ever was.' He paused for some gentle laughter from the audience, whom he clearly already had in the palm of his hands.

'Just down the road from me, there was a pub that was eventually bought by some East End brothers, from the other side of the river. Where I grew up, they had a reputation as softies, cry-babies. I think they were called the Krays. And round the corner was the Richardson family, soon to make themselves a big name in scrap metal. So you could say I was born with a sawn-off shotgun in my hands.'

Kay finally managed to attract her husband's attention, and tapped her watch, indicating they should leave. John's face contorted in disagreement, and his thumb indicating towards Norris showed that he would prefer to stay and listen. Still fuming, but unwilling to leave on her own, she sat through another half hour of folksy reminiscence, which covered his time in prison, and his gradual rehabilitation. Looking around, she could see that everyone but her was lapping it up. Sally Winchester gazed up at him adoringly.

When they finally left, Kay's anger had been forged into a cold fury, to which her husband was the first bewildered victim, savaged in a five-minute row in the taxi on the way home.

'I'm sorry, Kay, but what is this all about?' he responded, after she had berated him for his inattention to her difficulties, and his doe-eyed focus on Norris' wife. Once they had sunk back into silence, and the taxi, curiously enough, wound its way past the Elephant and Castle down to their home in Dulwich, she mused to herself: who said crime doesn't pay?

Chapter Sixteen

It was 9.15 a.m. and Gillard was running late. Traffic had been held up by roadworks, then he'd been buttonholed in the corridor by Chief Constable Alison Rigby, wondering if he really needed to spend so much time on a London-based case. He hadn't even got to his desk when DCI Matt Culshaw rang him on his mobile. It was awkward, as the Idris case incident room meeting was due to start in five minutes. He went into his glass box and shut the door. 'All right Matt, I've only got a minute or so, what's up?'

'The coroner is going to approve my request for a post-mortem, once I mention that Sutton was an informer. I asked the hospital pathologist at the mortuary to give Keith Sutton the once-over, because there is likely to be a day or so delay for the Home Office forensic pathologist, because of Covid.'

'Righto, did he come up with anything?'

'Yes. A broken hyoid bone in the throat, and those little blood spots in the eyeballs.'

'Petechiae, that's what they're called. Indicative of asphyxiation.'

'Yeah, that's what he said. He couldn't commit himself, but said he would make note of his observations for when the full PM takes place,' Culshaw said.

'If the paramedics tried to revive him, that could have broken the hyoid,' Gillard said. 'I'm not sure about the petechiae.'

'Shit, I wish we had more time,' Culshaw said.

'I know what you mean,' Gillard said as he watched Rainy Macintosh, Carl Hoskins and Michelle Tsu heading off to the meeting room.

'If there is clear evidence of murder, a dead informant, that's extra ammunition to get the AC on our side,' Culshaw said.

'Does Musgrove know?' Gillard asked.

'Yes. I think he is going to make himself scarce, having seen that Horace Mower is about. By the way, the name Mower was caught by the bug you put in the gents of the Railway Tavern last night. I'll email the transcript, and a digital file to listen to.'

'I look forward to it. I've got to go now,' Gillard said, seeing DI Mulholland beckoning him through the glass. 'I'll call you later.'

–

The incident room meeting had already begun. Claire Mulholland was detailing the latest round of interviews with contacts of Idris, none of whom had given any useful information. 'We've interviewed nine so far, and we are no closer to discovering his movements on the last day of his life. Now onto CCTV, Carl.'

DC Hoskins stood up and made his way over to the whiteboard. 'We've broadened the search for camera footage anywhere near Idris' flat in Staines. Unfortunately, there isn't too much in the area. Two of the local authority anti-crime cameras aren't working, and a third is for some reason pointing at the sky. The nearest usable one we have is at the southern end of the street where he lived, but the more well-connected northern end doesn't have anything. We've asked for dashcam footage on the dates concerned, and once that's examined that's about all we have. Not only are we looking for Idris' own movements, but those of any vehicle which might have been used to take his body from Staines to the canal.'

'Have you identified the vehicle, Carl?' Gillard asked.

'Unfortunately not. The nearest ANPR camera to the canal is three miles away, and wouldn't be on the most favoured route from Staines. We do have a few hundred hits from it on vehicles that passed in the twelve hours up until his body was found, but the actual vehicle used may not be among them. We have found forty vehicles so far that tripped both this camera, and at least one of the cameras in Staines.'

'Have there been any more forensic discoveries?' Gillard asked Mulholland.

'We still have one DNA trace in the room that remains unidentified,' she replied. 'Nothing else to report.'

'I take it nothing matched Horace Mower,' Gillard asked.

'He is on file, so no. I did check after you mentioned it.'

'Okay,' Gillard said, his eyes flicking to the wall clock. 'Look, I've got a little job to do now in London. It looks like I've got another murder to look at.'

'Who?'

'A retired bank robber who used to slip me the odd tip-off when I was a young detective up there.'

'Isn't that up to the Met?'

'Not if you don't want the criminal underworld to hear about it. This has got to be kept completely secret.'

'Can you give me a lift to the station, sir?' Rainy asked, as Gillard stood to leave. 'I'm off to Glasgow for the next couple of days.'

'Yes, of course.' Once they were in the car, he asked about her trip. 'Is it something to do with the divorce?'

'Aye, it is,' she sighed. 'Ross is contesting Ewan's residence with me, and trying to vary the terms of the contact order we agreed. He's being a right bastard, actually. So we're in court tomorrow.'

'I'm sorry to hear that,' he said. He knew that Rainy had made several previous trips all the way back for court hearings, which had seemed to go on and on. Her ex-husband, a paediatric consultant, had abused her during the marriage, and was now dragging his feet about providing for his fifteen-year-old son. Gillard dropped her off at Clapham Junction, and watched her making her way in the drizzle into the station. She was a tough cookie, and he admired her for her resilience to all this domestic stress on top of the inevitable pressures of work.

–

Gillard parked well away from Thamesway Tower and walked in the drizzle to the base of the building. The usual crowd of ne'er-do-wells were hanging around the entrance, but took a look at Gillard in his suit, with briefcase and false lanyard, and probably thought: social worker. Certainly that is what he hoped. The lift was working, and no one shared the ride with him. That was a definite plus point. Looking around Keith Sutton's flat was a bit of a high-risk activity. As far as the family and neighbours were concerned, he'd died of natural causes. If a vanload of crime scene investigators had turned up word would be out in no time, and they didn't want to tip off anyone at the Railway Tavern that they had suspicions. Culshaw was adamant that nothing must prejudice preparations for the big robbery, even the suspicion of a murder. DI Florence Latimer had borrowed the key to the police padlock that secured the flat from the desk sergeant at Peckham Police Station and offered Gillard the chance to look around with her. As arranged, she had just called him from inside the flat. He got out at the sixteenth floor and made his way quietly along the corridor. She let him in without him having to knock. The place smelled worse than stale, just what you expect when someone had died there.

'Good to see you,' she said quietly, in her Caribbean lilt.

'I really appreciate being in on this,' he responded.

Her disguise was impeccable. Grey trouser suit, unfashionable shoes, and her usual prominent crucifix. Maybe a social worker or some other official, possibly even a Jehovah's Witness. Certainly she was unlikely to face awkward questions on the way in. The moment she had closed the door behind him, they rapidly donned booties and gloves. Gillard took a camera, a fingerprint kit and some cotton buds for DNA from his briefcase.

'You did check the daughter is at work today?' he asked. 'If Dawn sees me, it would be a disaster.'

Florence's wide face twisted slightly. 'I'd hoped she'd be going into work, but she's at home. Compassionate leave. Her flat's a good mile away, and I've got an officer in a car within sight of the entrance here who will ring us if he sees her. We gave her a key to the padlock.'

They concentrated on the bathroom door handle, the toilet flush handle, and on the edges of the adjacent bath. 'We'll have to get elimination samples from the paramedics,' Gillard said.

'It's in hand,' Florence replied. 'I've already got the elimination record for the female officer who found the body.'

'Whoever did it must've been known to him, to be let in. I'm not sure if Sutton even knew Horace Mower, but he's my favourite.'

'The neighbours on the corridor came out when the door was knocked in yesterday morning,' Florence said. 'None of them said anything about there being a racket, according to the PC.'

'There may not have been much noise,' Gillard said. 'Last time I saw Sutton, he was on oxygen. He could hardly breathe as it was. Mower wouldn't have had any trouble. Plastic bag over the head, twisted round the neck, that's all it would have taken. Two-minute job, tops. Then lifted onto the toilet and his trousers pulled down.'

'So let's look at the bedroom,' Florence said. They moved carefully, not touching the door handle. The bed was piled high with clothes, and some of them had already been stashed into plastic bags.

'She's not wasting any time is she?' Gillard said.

'Sometimes when you suffer a shock, you just need to do something. To clean, to make tidy, any kind of routine behaviour to postpone the grief.'

Gillard looked at her again with appreciation. 'That's true.'

'I was a family liaison officer for three years. I've seen it all. Sometimes they leave all the victim's stuff untouched for years, like a shrine, some others it's gone and in bin bags in ten minutes.'

He carefully removed some of the clothing and bags and sniffed at the duvet cover. 'This is clean.' He looked at it. There were still crisp creases in places from where it had been folded up. 'I don't think anyone slept here since the linen was changed.'

'As you said, she's been busy.' She looked around at the old man's bedroom. Faded wallpaper, a few photographs in frames on the wall, with Keith and his two daughters. With her gloved hand, she carefully opened the drawer of the bedside table. It was stuffed with old paperwork, some of it very old, including a marriage certificate.

'I'd quite like to find the dirty linen,' Gillard said. He watched as his colleague knelt down on hands and knees to look under the bed. The material of her trouser suit stretched over her sizeable bum. He looked away and banished the maverick male thoughts that always galloped into his head at such moments.

She pulled out an old and dusty suitcase. 'What's this, I wonder?' She lifted it onto the bed and undid the old-fashioned metal spring catches. Inside was a stack of fading paperwork. Newspapers, cuttings, and a scrapbook.

Gillard peered over her shoulder. 'Press accounts of his exploits,' he said. And it was true, there were breathless newspaper accounts of bank and building society raids from the 1970s and 1980s. Florence Latimer seemed fascinated, and flicked through several pages, reading out small sections.

'To be honest, Florence, I think this is beyond the scope of our inquiry here.' He felt uncomfortable at the intrusion, which was purely to determine whether Keith Sutton had met his end from natural causes or not.

He stepped outside the room and looked for a laundry basket. He found one in a small utility room adjoining the kitchen, which had a male shirt, some Y-fronts and a pair of trousers, but no bed linen. He crouched down to look at the washer dryer, which was still flashing to show the end of a cycle. Peering through the small glass door of the front loader, it seemed the machine was empty. He pulled open the door and checked around the drum with his hand.

'What are you doing?' Florence asked. She was standing behind him now, maybe looking at his bum, who knows.

'I want to see if we can find any of the bed linen or any clothing that Keith Sutton was wearing at this time of death.'

'They'd have cut it off him in the mortuary,' she said.

'They would, but remember he was found with his trousers round his ankles. They might have pulled them off him, rather than pull them up. Anyway, there's no sign of them.'

'What's this then?' She was pointing out of the utility room window.

Gillard clambered to his feet, and peered out of the aluminium sliding door. There was a very narrow balcony beyond, barely two feet deep and six long, glass panelled to waist height with a caged exterior above but open to the elements. Within it was a washing line, and there was bed linen still hanging on it.

'I think your quest for forensic evidence is at an end,' Florence said with a chuckle.

They were interrupted by a noise in the corridor, and the sound of the front door opening.

'On the balcony,' Florence hissed, stripping off gloves and booties. 'I'll deal with this.'

Gillard slid open the glass and stepped onto the balcony, which ran alongside the utility room and the main lounge. He heard Florence slide the door shut. He stripped off his gloves and booties, then stood with his back to the three feet of wall which separated the two sets of windows. The bed linen was strung in front of him at chest height, but below it there was a drop of a couple of hundred feet to the communal grass. He stared out over a huge expanse of south-east London, a distant hazy sun picking out the graceful quicksilver curves of railway lines. The drone of traffic and the grind and squeal of slow-moving trains made it impossible to hear what was being said inside the flat. Florence could pass herself off as any number of officials from the local authority, though he could imagine that Dawn would be furious with any of them for not being told.

A minute passed, then two, then five. He heard the click of the catch on the door he had just exited. Florence protecting him from casual intrusion? Or Dawn locking up? He didn't dare peer in, just in case. With impeccable timing, it began to rain, a fierce shower that first drenched the bed linen, and then him. Ten minutes. He took out his phone and texted Florence. Two more minutes and no reply.

He looked down through the gaps in the balcony's glass panelling. From the sixteenth floor you'd take about five seconds to hit the ground. He wasn't scared of heights, he'd done plenty of rock walls in Wales and the Lake District of at least this height. But for some people this would be terrifying. The traffic looked like toys, manoeuvring in the streets around the base of the tower. The rain had stopped by the time his text was returned.

'Ring me in a minute,' it said.

He did so. 'What's happening?'

'I'm right down the hallway out of earshot. Dawn Sutton's son, Adam, is here with a workman.'

'Her son?'

'Yes, I didn't know about him either. He's fifteen.'

'Shouldn't he be at school?'

'Probably. I told them I was from social services, doing an assessment for health and safety following the death, and had borrowed the key for the police padlock. I actually do have a social services lanyard. The kid just shrugged.'

'How long before he finishes?'

She laughed. 'I was hoping for a jobsworth, but this guy is a craftsman. Huge toolbox, promised the boy he'd make the place like Fort Knox. It could be an hour or two, but I'm hoping to persuade the guy to take a lunch break, so I can let you out.'

'What about the boy?'

'He's rung his mum, and after he passed the phone to me, she gave me an earful. Says she wants me out of her dad's flat.'

'Is she coming round?'

'Almost certainly, from the way she was talking.'

'Shit. I could be stuck here.'

'The boy and the locksmith have been talking about football. I can probably let you in, but you'd have to hide under the bed or something.'

'None of it will help if I'm locked in.'

'It's either that or brazen it out, claim you were here with me all along. Whatever it is, you'd better be quick, because Dawn is on her way.'

Gillard craned his head out through the bars and looked upwards. 'I could probably climb to the floor above.'

'What? Are you crazy?'

'I'm just saying it's an option. Not one I prefer. It's four floors up to the roof, and that might be a bit too tricky even for me. Especially wearing work shoes.'

'Ah, I see the workman, he's got toolbox in hand so he may have finished. I'll unlatch the window, and then give me one minute to see if I can distract the boy in the lounge.' She hung up.

It was exactly three minutes later when he heard the click, and after the minute, he slid the window back and gingerly stepped in. He was still pretty wet, and took a moment to wipe the utility room floor with a cloth. He could hear Florence speaking to the boy.

'…now these windows need maintenance to make them suitable for an elderly person. Would you write that down, please? And at the top of the pelmets here, there is some evidence of spot mould. I'll be speaking to the council myself about this…'

Gillard tiptoed past the half closed door to the lounge, and exited the flat. He walked as briskly as he could along the corridor to the lift and summoned it. It was already on its way up. Something made him decide to back up the stairs towards the higher floor, so he was out of view. The lift doors juddered open, and someone got out. He heard the sound of female heels, and just a few seconds later, a yell down the corridor. 'What the hell has been going on here?' The voice was Dawn's. He made his way down the stairs, pressed the call button, and when the lift doors reopened, slipped inside. He didn't think she'd seen him.

–

Gillard returned to New Scotland Yard, handed in the forensic evidence from the flat at the CSI front desk then, having heard that DI Latimer had returned, went up to a debrief with Culshaw in his office.

'You're looking a bit damp,' Culshaw said as Gillard sat down gingerly on a chair opposite Culshaw's desk. 'I heard you got caught in the rain.' He was smirking.

'Occupational hazard, Matt,' Gillard replied. He'd taken a couple of minutes in the gents to comb his hair, but his trousers were still sticking to his legs in places.

Florence joined them and perched on a desk, no longer wearing her social worker spectacles.

'That was an experience I don't want to repeat,' she said. 'Dawn Sutton had a right go at me. Swearing and shouting. Asked for my business card so she could make a formal complaint to my line manager. Of course, she won't have to do too much research to find out that social workers don't do risk assessments without making an appointment.'

'It's all right,' Culshaw said. 'If you can drag it out until the end of the week, it won't matter then if your cover is blown. We can make an apology to Dawn next week and come clean.'

'There's probably no reason for her to go to the Railway Tavern now that her dad has died,' Gillard said. 'She can't taste anything, as she said.'

'Should be a definite advantage there, from what I've heard,' Culshaw said.

Florence smiled. 'She is desperately short of money and has a teenage son to look after. I suppose we should cut her some slack.'

'She probably has no idea her father was a grass,' Culshaw said.

'So where are we with the raid preparation?' Gillard asked.

'Ah, a new piece of intelligence!' Culshaw said, leaning forward to pick up a piece of paper. 'Passed on by Crimestoppers. A member of the public said that somebody was going to try to steal the *Salvator Mundi* on Friday morning. It even gave a time, 8.45 a.m.'

'That's brilliant,' Florence said.

Gillard's brow was furrowed. 'I've always been very sceptical of Crimestoppers. Completely unverifiable.'

'Yes, but sometimes it's right,' Culshaw said.

'Yes, sometimes. I'd much prefer if we got insight into exactly *how* this painting is going to be turned into cash. If they hold it hostage, for example, they will only get a small fraction of the face value and any money paid will be traced.'

'Not if it's crypto,' Culshaw said.

'Well, it depends which crypto currency we're talking about,' Gillard said. 'The one great advantage of Bitcoin is the fact that it has an ineradicable audit trail built into the code.'

'I never went on the crypto course,' Florence admitted.

'Neither did I, but it doesn't matter,' Gillard said. 'It changes so fast that what we knew last week is already out of date.'

'Well, forget that for now,' Culshaw said. 'I've been able to establish that the painting is coming on a private Saudi jet flight from Riyadh to Heathrow that arrives at 6.10 on Friday morning. It will then be taken to the gallery by fine art logistics firm Hallam & Day in a three-vehicle convoy. It's a well-established legit firm, thoroughly vetted, and I felt able to contact the managing director Richard Hallam to ask about security. He in turn had to get my security vetted through the AC's office, which from his view is probably a good precaution. The upshot is that I've now been briefed that there is a decoy convoy, consisting of a marked Hallam & Day van with police motorcycle outriders and a patrol car. Five minutes later, the real painting will be conveyed in three unmarked white vans, in each of which there will be a Saudi security guard.'

'Armed?' Gillard asked.

'No. The Saudi government initially requested it, as the painting is being treated like a member of the Saudi royal family.'

'I wouldn't like the idea of British robbers clashing with armed foreign guards on London's streets,' Gillard said.

'That was exactly what the assistant commissioner said to me, and the Home Secretary agreed with her,' Culshaw replied. 'So she vetoed it, and the only armed close protection officers will be ours.'

'If the robbers know about the decoy, they must be very well-placed indeed,' Florence said.

'Too right,' Culshaw said. 'As of now, the only people who know about this plan are the MD of Hallam & Day, the head of the Met's diplomatic protection unit, which is providing the escort, plus AC Thompson. And us three.'

Gillard stroked his chin. 'What's the expected time of arrival at the National Gallery?'

'Roughly 8.45, depending on traffic.'

'So exactly the time we got from Crimestoppers,' Florence said.

'Yes.'

'I can't see them being able to pull this off,' Gillard said. 'The calibre of the crooks isn't high enough. Mal Scattergood, Colin Lamb, Horace Mower, Damian Norris, Terry Moses. It just doesn't add up.'

'I can see where you're coming from,' Florence said, turning to her boss. 'What about the tracker on Scattergood's van?'

'He seems to be going about his normal shopfitting business,' Culshaw said. 'He did go down the bottom of Charing Cross Road past the National Gallery yesterday, but didn't stop.'

'What about activity at the Railway Tavern?' Gillard asked.

'Mower has been seen,' Culshaw said. 'But they are keeping very quiet. As I mentioned, we got this from the bug in the gents last night. Apologies, Flo, for the tinkling in the background.' He clicked on a sound file. There was indeed the sound of urination, some coughing, a door squeaking. Then two men, clearly close to each other.

Fine job you done so far.

Yeah? Glad to keep the gaffer happy. So you're ready for the big day Friday?

Yeah. It all depends on Ian. He's testing and retesting the kit. Bit of a perfectionist, our Ian.

I hear your old man's giving the filth a bit of a runaround.

There was laughter, then the last bit of the conversation was lost in the sound of the hand dryer. 'Play it again,' Gillard asked. Culshaw did, and all three officers looked at each other. He still didn't catch the last bit.

'The first voice is definitely Damian Norris,' Culshaw said. 'The gaffer is presumably big Jackie. The second voice could be Horace Mower.'

'They said Friday, not Sunday,' Gillard said.

'Maybe the info on the phone is wrong,' Culshaw said. 'Terry Moses' phone had a message about Sunday.'

'And who's Ian?' Gillard asked. 'Could he be the financial specialist they referred to?'

'But testing and retesting the kit?' Florence said. 'Doesn't sound like financial work.'

'You're right,' Culshaw said, rubbing his chin. 'Mal Scattergood, Colin Lamb, Damian Norris, Jackie Norris, some guy called Ian, and the financial person. And no mention of Moses, except on the phone you found, Craig.'

'You think these could be two separate jobs?' Florence asked. 'Moses has got one on Sunday the twentieth and Norris' job is on Friday the eighteenth.'

'Maybe that's what they mean about giving us the runaround,' Gillard said. 'You think there's any chance that they know about the bug I planted, and are feeding us a line?'

'They're pretty good actors, if so,' said Florence. 'That conversation sounded totally natural to me.'

'From all your experience hanging about in male toilets?' Culshaw asked, and then grinned at her. She mimed slapping his face, and they both smiled. Gillard detected a trusting and informal relationship between the two. He just hoped it was nothing more, for the sake of

Kirsty Mockett. He glanced again at the large crucifix around Florence's neck. He could imagine Culshaw trying harder because of that. The kind of bloke who would boast about seducing a nun.

'I think she's right,' Gillard said. 'It was casual, two blokes who know each other really well. I'd wager the other guy was Horace Mower. It's beginning to make me doubt Moses' role.'

'Maybe Moses isn't involved at all,' Culshaw said. 'After all, there's no evidence of a JCB being booked either. Maybe everything on that phone is a red herring.'

'Well, someone standing outside the National Gallery did text Moses,' Gillard said 'Referring to a JCB. That's the entire basis for the idea that it is the *Salvator Mundi* that they're going to steal.'

'What if it's wrong?' Culshaw said. 'What if we're barking up the wrong tree entirely?'

'Back to Oxford Circus, a bank, and on Friday,' Florence said.

'We're going round in circles,' Culshaw said, leaning back, feet on his desk.

'No, we're not,' Gillard said. He found a fresh whiteboard and a marker pen and drew out a grid. 'Information sources down the side. One, Keith Sutton, two, our undercover officer, three the prisoner, four, Terry Moses phone, five what we just got from this bug, and six, Crimestoppers. Right, across the top we have the informational elements. One, the date of the job, two, Oxford Circus, three JCB, four *Salvator Mundi*, and so on.'

'Yeah, but we have got lots of items that are only mentioned once,' Culshaw said.

'True, but I'm interested in confirmations. For example, we've only got one mention of the job being deferred to Sunday. Everything else is consistent with Friday. We've got two mentions of Oxford Circus, one from the prisoner, the other overheard by Musgrove. As a confirmation I'm going to take it seriously, as a meeting place prior to the job. That doesn't exclude it being the National Gallery job. What I do want to exclude are entirely contradictory ideas.'

'Is this going to be enough for AC Thompson?' Florence said, pointing at the whiteboard.

'I doubt it,' Culshaw said. 'It's not even enough for us, is it?'

'Well, we have two sources confirming the National Gallery: one, the location of Moses' phone at the time of the texts, and the second on Crimestoppers. We haven't identified anywhere else that fits the bill. If we track Scattergood's van on Friday morning near the National Gallery, that would be enough.'

'Yeah, but the AC wants to be in the know ahead of time.'

'Let's concentrate on finding out who Ian is,' Gillard said. 'He's obviously a crucial member of the team. Once we know what his background is, we're halfway to knowing what the job is.'

'We can find out. What about middle names?' Culshaw asked. 'Prison nicknames? Any Ians amongst them? He's referred to in a kind of trusted way, "our Ian", as if he is well known, at least to Damian Norris.'

'I'll dig up the interview records for Horace Mower, to confirm that is his voice.'

'Right, I'm onto it,' Florence said, gathering up papers. 'I'll check all known associates and nicknames.'

'What about Damian Norris?' Culshaw asked Gillard. 'He spends most of his time in your patch.'

Gillard picked up his notes. 'Not much previous. Affray and assault as a minor, cannabis use and then a suspended sentence for low-level dealing. The prison time was 2007. Three months for being caught dealing once again. He was remanded to HMP Woodhill in Milton Keynes, then served the rest of the sentence in HMP Coldingley, a cat C establishment.'

'I'll check cellmates and associates there,' Florence said.

'And how's the surveillance going?' Culshaw continued.

'Not too bad given the limited resources.' Gillard walked to the whiteboard, and attached to it with a handful of small magnets a series of surveillance pictures of Norris junior. They showed a well-dressed and tanned man in his forties, with a trendy hairstyle, wearing designer glasses and a sharp suit. In some of the pictures he was accompanied by an attractive young blonde, expensively dressed. 'That is his girlfriend Holly, and this is where they live, near Leatherhead.'

Gillard added half a dozen more photographs. 'As you can see, a new build, big metal remote-control gates, a couple of three-foot-high cement dragons on the plinths either side of them. A large mock Tudor gable at the front, and extensive outbuildings. Mostly paved frontage, with plastic grass on the limited lawn edges, and quite a lot of expensive model trees in stone-filled planters, of the kind you see in front of restaurants. Lots of money in other words, but not an ounce of style.'

He admitted that the house had been watched off and on for only a few days, given there was no time to organise any more comprehensive surveillance. 'But we do know something about his movements. He's been to see his father on two occasions at the Swallowtail Hotel, and according to ANPR, to London just once in the last week. He has however spent a fair amount of time visiting Caffè Nero and Starbucks in Leatherhead itself.'

There was a solitary photograph of him entering a Starbucks with a briefcase in one hand, and what looked like a laptop in the other. 'As you know, this is a savvy way of avoiding electronic oversight of Internet activity. So what exactly he's been researching and who he's been emailing remain unknown.'

'Has anyone visited him?' Culshaw asked. 'Mower? Scattergood? Any of the others?'

'Anyone called Ian?' Florence added with a laugh.

'Not that we are aware of,' Gillard said. 'In the last day, we have made some progress on finding what phone he's using. Using cell site triangulation matched to the timings of surveillance, my research intelligence officer Rob Townsend had been able to isolate the unique electronic IDs of a number of phones which have been used in and around Norris junior's home, and two of them which on different occasions were with him in the car when he left. One is a burner phone, and we're hoping within twenty-four hours to have a copy of all texts and messages from it from the service provider.'

'Okay, good work everyone,' Culshaw said, gathering together his papers. 'We've got twenty-four hours before presenting to Thompson. We need a cast-iron case.'

–

Gillard had work to do back at Mount Browne, and as he drove through London's Tuesday evening rush-hour traffic, he used his hands-free phone to call colleagues there. His first call was to DI Mulholland. If he'd been hoping for a breakthrough on the Idris murder, he was disappointed. Claire told him that they hadn't been able to narrow down the vehicle that might have been used to dump the body. There were just too many possibilities. Likewise, Lydia Marasova hadn't turned up dead or alive. That wasn't necessarily bad news, but it wasn't good either. Claire confessed she had almost reached a dead end.

'All right, bear with me,' Gillard said. He hung up and punched out Culshaw's number.

'Matt, we didn't discuss this, but do you know what vehicle Mower might be driving?'

'Stacey Daines is looking at that. He's obviously using a false name so there's no chance of finding a rental in the name Mower.'

'What about the night he was seen at the Railway Tavern. Do we have a sighting of him in a car?'

'Unfortunately not. We are collecting all the numbers of vehicles seen in a half-mile area of the pub, which is being done manually and is far from exhaustive. We've got a couple of ANPR cameras on the main road, but there are other routes to get to the Railway Tavern.'

'Do me a favour,' Gillard said. 'Can you send me all the numbers you have for the day in question, which was what, Sunday?'

'Yes, it was Sunday.'

'Then I can get one of my people to match them against the number plates we have here at the time that Idris was killed. It's a long shot, but there may be an overlap.'

'Happy to do that, Craig. By the way, enjoyed your little logic grid. That seems a really good way to assemble all this disparate information. I don't mind admitting I learned something there.'

'Thank you.' Gillard hung up with a rather warm fuzzy feeling. In the often macho environment of the police, it wasn't very often that a fellow officer would admit to learning something. Colleagues in different units were more likely to be rivals, particularly for resources for an operation, and of course rivals for credit at the end. Culshaw had rather surprised him there.

As he drove, Gillard ran through a mental to-do list. Complex police operations are not like they are portrayed on TV. For every action-packed chase or raid, there were ten thousand emails, phone calls, checks on procedure, and the filling out of warrant or detention paperwork. It never ended. Now, he used the remaining minutes to make a few phone calls to other members of the team to see how they were getting on. The last was to Carl Hoskins, to get him to co-ordinate the two lists of number plates in the search for a vehicle that might have been used by Horace Mower, both near the London pub and near Idris' home. That kind of work was right up Hoskins' street.

He was almost within sight of Guildford when he remembered there was something else he had not done for a while. Routine, but now buried at the bottom of his list of urgent tasks. He dialled into his own desk answerphone and listened to the messages. He was surprised to discover he had not done it for four days, the perils of working mainly in London and away from his desk, and having two other mobile phones that he used more regularly.

The first few messages were routine and could be ignored. Then there was one on Saturday night from a familiar and breathless south London voice, now one from beyond the grave.

Gillard. Listen, I've had some terrible news. It's a disaster, and I don't know what to do. Give us a call soon as you can. You know the number.

He pulled over onto the hard shoulder and listened to it again. What could be the terrible news? And worse still, if he'd picked it up first thing Monday morning, might Keith Sutton still be alive? No, the female police officer who rang him said they broke in on Monday morning. Something terrible had happened that weekend and he had no idea what it could be. Was it about benefits? No, it sounded too apocalyptic for that. What kind of terrible news do people get? Sutton knew he was dying himself, so it wouldn't be that. In fact it didn't sound like he was scared for himself at all. Maybe he was scared for Dawn. A cancer diagnosis, something like that? No, he decided it must be related to the robbery, or he'd have found somebody else to talk to.

Whatever it was Keith Sutton so desperately wanted to tell him, he would never know.

Chapter Seventeen

Wednesday 16th December

Gillard was on his way into work when he took a call from DC Carl Hoskins.

'Got some good news, boss. I just ran a check on the forty vehicles which were pinged both in Staines and on the road near the canal against that monster list you sent me yesterday. And there is just one on all three.'

'And whose is that?'

'It's a long-wheelbase Renault van registered to a big shopfitting firm, the one that Scattergood works for.'

That was interesting. 'Well done, Carl. That's a result.' He thanked him and hung up. He didn't believe for a moment that a little hobbit like Scattergood could have overcome the fit six-three Jordan Idris, nor indeed have lugged his body out of the flat on his own. That would be where Horace Mower came in. It was either Mower alone, or with Scattergood as the driver.

Gillard rang Claire Mulholland and let her know his thinking.

'This sounds more and more like it's dovetailing with the job you're doing in London,' she said.

'Certainly does.' He brought her up to speed on everything that had happened in his last two days in London. 'I'm just surprised that we can't find a single piece of Mower's DNA in Idris' flat. I take it the unidentified sample didn't match Scattergood either.'

'It doesn't match anyone on the database.'

'That's weird. So we've got Lydia Marasova's trace, and this other one.'

'That's it,' she said.

'We can't move in on Mower yet, even if we knew where he was staying. It's got to be after Friday.'

'Ah yes, the infamous half billion pound job,' Claire said. 'There's a lot of chatter about it all round Mount Browne.'

'We've tried to keep it quiet, but I suppose it's inevitable. The trouble is we don't have clear evidence that it *is* happening, and though we have a pretty good grasp on who is behind it, we just don't know where, for sure.'

'That's not the usual problem. More where-done-it than whodunnit.' She laughed.

'Matt Culshaw and co of Flying Squad still have to convince Assistant Commissioner Kay Thompson, otherwise they don't get the resources for a stakeout.'

'And I'm told the current favourite location is the National Gallery, right?'

Gillard was appalled. 'It's supposed to be top secret.'

'The juicy stuff always is,' she said, and laughed. He was just about to hang up when he remembered something. 'Claire, can you do me a favour? I interviewed Horace Mower in 2006, in Redhill. Can you ask one of the team to look it up and see if we have still got the videotape? I want to hear what his voice sounds like.'

'I'll get Michelle to do it,' Claire said. 'I think they've been digitising the old records as they don't have space for all the cassettes. If not, we will definitely have the analogue evidence tape.'

An hour later, Gillard was sitting side-by-side with Claire and Michelle Tsu watching a digital copy of a scratchy interview. It showed Horace Mower sitting at a small table, looming over a tiny female lawyer, and opposite him Gillard, then a sergeant, and a female PC called Kirkpatrick. Mower had his arms folded, like two hams, over a tight T-shirt. Without the beard, his jutting jaw looked even more implacable. He hadn't been any prettier back then.

'You look so young, boss,' DC Tsu said with a chuckle.

'Well, I was in my late thirties,' Gillard said with an appreciative smile.

Mower didn't say much, but his gravelly voice was quite distinctive. It was definitely the same person he heard caught on the bug in the gents' toilet at the Railway Tavern on Sunday. Gillard had been asking him about the discovery of a body, found cut up in bin bags in a skip on an industrial estate.

'I don't know what you're talking about,' Mower said.

'It's your MO, Horace. Chopped into bits, for being a grass.'

Mower had even smiled at the accusation. As Gillard recalled, there wasn't a shred of forensic evidence to link him to the killing. And that's how it stayed. It would be great to get him now after all those years, if not for this killing then at least for the murder of Jordan Idris. Mower had led a charmed life, criminally speaking, for years. He had been linked to at least three murders, in terms of his MO and the kind of people he normally worked for. Yet none of them stuck. Lack of forensic connection, usually. A believable alibi on one occasion. His luck was bound to run out eventually. Maybe now would be that day.

Gillard returned to his office, closed the door to discourage interruption and flicked through the fifteen-page post-mortem report on Keith Sutton. The author was a top Home Office forensic pathologist by the name of K. B. Bartholomew, with a slew of letters after his name. It was a thorough job, no doubt, and it confirmed a number of observations that had been made by the hospital patho-logist. The broken hyoid bone, the petechiae in the eyes and the face, some cyanosis – a blueing of parts of the face indicative of asphyxia – and then something new: a sizeable contusion, a bruise essentially, in the middle of Sutton's back. The pathologist thought it matched the size of a patella. A knee bone. Someone had knelt on poor old Keith Sutton, forcing his head down on the bed or floor, probably at some point with a plastic bag over it.

It was murder, no doubt about it now.

There were some problems, though, in pinning the killing to Mower. Carl Hoskins had just spent his lunch-break looking through the CCTV records from the outside of Thamesway Tower for the three days prior to the discovery of the body. That covered from the Saturday, when the message had been left for Gillard, when clearly Sutton was very much alive, through to the time when he was discovered dead. Hoskins admitted to having watched the footage on fast-forward, but anyone the size of Horace Mower would have stood out. It was the only entrance and there was no sign of him.

Gillard stroked his chin. That left only two possibilities. One, the most likely one: somebody else had killed Keith Sutton. Second, and a real outside chance, Sutton wasn't at home when he was killed, and his body was taken back there. He hadn't asked Hoskins to look for anything else but the sizeable figure of Mower, but he thought that if someone had, for example, brought in a wheelie bin possibly with the body in it, he might have taken notice. He stood up and made his way across to Hoskins' desk.

'I'm sorry to have to ask you to do it, Carl, but you're going to have to look through all that CCTV again from Thamesway Tower. The post-mortem makes clear that Keith Sutton was murdered—'

Hoskins' face contorted in frustration. 'But ain't this a Met police job, sir? I've got shed loads of local work to do.'

'I know you have, Carl. Normally, as you say, this would fall to someone in Peckham. But the fact that this is a murder isn't being disclosed to them. Not yet, anyway. I would be very surprised if there aren't some south London coppers whispering into the ears of people like Terry Moses or big Jackie Norris. DCI Culshaw is asking us to look after this, at least for now—'

'—While the Flying Squad gets all the glory for the big National Gallery robbery,' Hoskins said.

'Trust me, Carl, the robbery investigation is finely balanced between triumph and disaster. The intelligence is all over the place. It's Culshaw's baby and I'm more than happy for it to stay that way.'

Hoskins sighed. 'All right, boss. What do you want me to look for?'

'One, any of the suspected conspirators to the robbery. I mean, Sutton was so unwell, even Mal Scattergood could have killed him.'

'Murdered by a hobbit, eh?' He jotted the various names down. 'Anyone else?'

'The time of death in the post-mortem is approximate. Any time from Friday night. That matches when his daughter last saw him alive. There's her son too, Adam, fifteen. Keep an eye out for them both, and anyone else who looks suspicious.'

Hoskins turned back to his terminal and called up the video file. 'Righto, off we go,' he said with another deep sigh.

–

Gillard was on the phone in his office when Hoskins came in. He put his hand over the receiver, and asked, 'Got something interesting?'

'Yes and no,' Hoskins said. 'Come and have a look with me when you got a moment.'

He finished up the phone call and went to join Hoskins at his desk. There was a plastic food box and the remains of a fruit salad within it. Gillard was impressed. Hoskins really was sticking to the diet he been given months ago. It wasn't what he'd predicted, but he was glad to be wrong.

Gillard grabbed a wheeled typist chair from another desk, sat on it and scooted it across next to Hoskins. The screen in front of the detective showed a view of the base of Thamesway Tower, frozen at 3.34 p.m. last Saturday, and a woman entering the building. 'Can you zoom in a bit, Carl?'

'It won't go much further.' When he zoomed in, the image unhelpfully pixelated, making it harder to recognise individuals. 'I could be wrong, but isn't that Keith Sutton's daughter?'

'Could be. Let's see a sequence.'

Hoskins clicked back a minute with his mouse, and they both watched the sizeable woman, in a distinctive red quilted jacket and a grey woolly hat, approaching the building with two shopping bags, and a small black leather backpack. It looked like Dawn, but then a lot of people looked a bit like her. Gillard hadn't seen her wearing the coat before.

'She said the last time she saw her father before he died was on Friday,' Gillard said. 'She said she'd been doing overtime at the weekend, that's why she felt guilty about not seeing him.'

'She stayed half an hour,' Hoskins said. He clicked on a later time which showed her leaving the building, with the rucksack but no bags.

'It's probably nothing, Carl,' Gillard said. 'There are hundreds of homes in that tower, and she might have been dropping something off for one of her dad's neighbours. Is this all you've got?'

Hoskins nodded. 'I couldn't find any of our target criminals entering or leaving during that time. Plenty of other dodgy-looking characters, mind, just not the ones you asked me to look for. There was no one leaving or entering with a wheelie bin or a coffin, or anything big enough to put a human inside.'

'Okay, thank you for that.'

That demolished the most unlikely possibility, that Sutton had been killed somewhere else and been brought home. He wasn't quite sure what to do with the information that Dawn, or someone very much like her, had visited the building when she claimed to be at work. She had been distraught at her father's death, and Gillard couldn't quite see that she could have had anything to do with it. Which left the much more likely possibility that someone other than their known conspirators had killed him. Okay, this was the kind of job that Mower could have done in his sleep. But with his distinctive frame, and the knowledge that there was CCTV, it might have been too much of a risk. So who was this killer?

The only named conspirator for whom they didn't have a picture was Ian. Who was Ian? Florence Latimer had pulled together a handy list of all the old school villains, contemporaries of Mower, Norris senior and Terry Moses, who had been involved in bank jobs in any way. They included Ian 'Gelly' Gibson, aged seventy-four, an explosives expert back in the day, diagnosed with Alzheimer's and living in a care home in Tunbridge Wells. No, surely not. Next, Ian Parkinson, fifty-four, close associate of Terry Moses. A bit of an engineering bent. He had been involved in at least two jobs where large industrial drills had been used to get through into bank vaults, but that was in the late 1990s. He'd only been out of jail for six months, and was living quietly in Colliers Wood, south London. The probation reports so far had been pristine, but he was definitely a possibility. The only other candidate was Iain McCallum, sixty-three, a hard man who had worked for big Jackie, and alongside Horace Mower, but whose last known address was in Glasgow. Iain McCallum could be the man, or it could be Ian Parkinson.

Gillard saw DC Michelle Tsu walking back into the office with a coffee. 'Got a little job for you, Michelle. Can you get me up-to-date pictures of Ian Parkinson and Iain McCallum, alongside the mugshots of when they first went down? When you do, can you take them across to Carl, and get him to check that Thamesway Tower CCTV again, to see whether either of them visited it? I'll ping you across their prisoner numbers and you can cross-reference it from there.'

'Okay, sir,' she said. She glanced sideways at Hoskins, who was staring at them both from his seat.

'You mean, I've got to go through it yet again, boss?'

'Sorry, Carl. Shouldn't take too long if you've already noted and timestamped the miscellaneous dodgy characters you mentioned.'

Hoskins groaned and turned back to his screen.

–

The latest email from Culshaw gave the lowdown on Colin Lamb. The minor criminal record Gillard already knew about, but the attachments were new. This was a bit of hurried surveillance by Musgrove who, now having given up going to the Railway Tavern, had been sitting in the back of an unmarked white van looking out of a peephole outside Colin Lamb's ground-floor council flat. There were photographs of Lamb leaving home to go to work, catching the bus, coming home with shopping, and doing some minor DIY work in his front garden. The only intelligence of any interest was a short piece of video which caught Lamb entering a greasy spoon cafe not far from his home. The subsequent still photos showed he sat in a booth with another individual who was in shadow. Musgrove had got the number plates of every car in the vicinity. One of them, a white Audi, belonged to Damian Norris. Sure enough, Norris left the cafe and drove off. Lamb left a little while later, and headed off to the local bookmakers.

Gillard sat back and thought about it. Lamb was overweight, clearly unfit from his waddling gait, and had absolutely nothing as far as he could see that a gang of professional criminals would need. He worked in a White City back office of Transport for London, kept regular hours, drank heavily, as Musgrove had witnessed, had no girlfriend and spent most of his time watching sport on TV. He did however gamble regularly, on the football results and a bit on the horses. Was there something there? Gillard couldn't think what it might be. What could have been in that package that he gave Scattergood? From the text of the email, it was clear that Culshaw wasn't exercising too much energy trying to figure out the answer to that question. Lamb was involved and that was that. But for Gillard it wasn't enough. What the assistant commissioner would make of this dog's breakfast he had no idea.

He looked at his watch, and headed off with his laptop to Mount Browne's smallest meeting room. He was due to participate in a final Zoom call with DI Matt Culshaw and his Flying Squad unit starting in five minutes. The call was to summarise and evaluate all the intelligence they had for Operation Santa Claus. When it was over, the assistant commissioner would give a final decision on whether to resource an operation to prevent a half billion pound robbery.

He tapped into the call and watched as the participating officers popped up one at a time. Commander Digby Snow, DI Florence Latimer, DC Stacey Daines, undercover officer Brendan Musgrove, and technical specialist DC Jason Hart. The last to appear was the decision-maker, Assistant Commissioner Kay Thompson. Culshaw began by quickly running through the targeted criminals: Jackie Norris, Damian Norris, Terry Moses, Horace Mower, Malcolm Scattergood, Colin Lamb and the two unknowns – the financial specialist and the mysterious Ian.

'Are we any closer to knowing whether it's Norris or Moses in charge?' Snow asked.

'Their names only occur once each on the intelligence we have,' Culshaw said. 'I do agree it is unlikely to be both. I don't think their mutual hatred has diminished.'

'If it's one or the other,' Thompson said, 'I'd choose Norris. As some of you know, I ran into Norris at a charity gala on Monday night. He's heard rumours of the robbery, and of it being at the National Gallery. He asked me what I thought.'

'I agree. In fact it could be a double bluff, ma'am,' Culshaw said. 'It might make him look in the clear, but he could still be involved if he's organising it remotely.'

'Frankly, it's an astonishing piece of arrogance on his part,' Snow said angrily. 'Leopards do not change their spots.'

Gillard was then asked to give his briefing on the state of play in the murders of Keith Sutton and Jordan Idris. The fact that they had now definitively linked Mal Scattergood's van to the Idris killing was warmly received. 'Unfortunately, it being dark, none of the ANPR cameras near the victim's home were able to catch an image of the occupants. But if you ask me, I'd say Scattergood was driving, and Mower did the dirty work.'

'And what about your late informant, Keith Sutton?' Thompson asked. 'Any progress there?'

'A considerable amount. The post-mortem found a broken hyoid bone and other evidence of asphyxia. There was no involvement in resuscitation by paramedics which would explain this. There is also bruising in the middle of the back consistent with a knee having been forced there. The most obvious explanation is that Sutton was overpowered and suffocated face down on a bed or floor, possibly with a plastic bag over his head.'

'But I understand we have no CCTV of any of the target criminals entering or leaving the tower block where he lived?' Thompson asked.

'No ma'am. There is one conspirator named but not identified, referred to as Ian. We don't know what he looks like, so it could be him.'

'Okay, now what about the location?' she asked. 'I'm not very convinced by this National Gallery idea, not least because Norris himself talked to me about it. I think he would be very happy for us to believe that a raid was going to take place on the National Gallery if it was actually planned somewhere else.'

'Or on a different day,' Stacey Daines said.

'I have my own pet theory,' Thompson said. 'Wasn't there a mention of BM, as in the BM job?'

'Yes, that's right, ma'am,' Culshaw said. 'It was mentioned in the text messages recovered from the phone which we believe belongs to Terry Moses.'

'Which also mentioned a JCB,' she said. 'Have you considered that this BM is not a bank at all, but the British Museum?'

'Is there anything there worth that much ready money, ma'am?' Culshaw asked.

'Well, they do have the Beng Melea rubies on loan there at the moment. They've been here for nearly a year. I went to see them last weekend. It's the last week before they are sent back to Cambodia. There are thousands of gems recovered from a lost city near Angkor Wat in the nineteenth century, but stolen before they were properly documented, and only rediscovered after World War II. Many of the finds are of raw and unpolished stones, and others are set in golden figurines, so their true international values can't really be estimated accurately. But I read on the various interpretation panels that the best rubies match diamonds for value.'

'How well are they guarded, ma'am?' Commander Snow asked.

'Oh, it's extraordinary. There are several dozen glass cases, all of which are inside an armoured glass cube. There are directable TV cameras, so that you can look more closely at any particular item.'

'Could you get in with a JCB?' asked Florence Latimer. 'That was in the same message.'

'I couldn't really say,' Thompson replied. 'I mean, not easily from the front because of all the steps. I've no idea if there is a back way.'

'It would be better suited to the gang than the theft of a painting,' Gillard said. 'While disposing of rubies might not be easy, it's got to be a lot easier than trying to flog a world-famous Leonardo.'

'My thoughts precisely,' Thompson said. 'What are we hearing from the Railway Tavern, Brendan?'

DC Brendan Musgrove shrugged into his screen. 'They seem to be keeping very quiet right now. I've had my own issues since Horace Mower showed up. He's made it clear he doesn't like me for some reason. I still go to the darts matches, but that's only once a week.'

'Well we don't want you taking any unnecessary risks,' she said. 'We know what Mower is capable of.'

The next half hour was spent analysing various ancillary information, until Thompson held up a hand and said, 'All right, that's quite enough. I've come to a decision.'

Everyone was silent for a moment.

'I've decided to throw the full weight of the Met's resources at this. Seeing as we are not sure of the location, I recommend a minimal plainclothes presence at the

National Gallery and the British Museum, and a much larger contingent of reserves in vans able to deploy to either of the two locations at short notice, and a couple of helicopters should you need them. They are after all less than a mile apart. I'll leave you to sort out the details, DCI Culshaw.'

She clicked off the call.

Chapter Eighteen

The Angkor civilisation, including all of Cambodia, south-eastern Thailand, and northern Vietnam, flowered between ad 800 to 1300. Although it is best known for one Khmer city, Angkor Wat, there are dozens of other less well-known temple complexes and towns, many of which were swallowed by jungle hundreds of years ago, and are yet to be excavated.

Khmer society was a cosmopolitan blend of Pali and Sanskrit from a fusion of Hindu and High Buddhist beliefs, and was for centuries connected in a trade system that encompassed India, China and even Rome, from before the time of Christ. At that time, Angkor and the other cities not only had hundreds of miles of roads big enough for columns of elephants, but also a sophistic-ated irrigation system to support agriculture. Temple inscriptions show that a wide range of commodities were traded between Khmer cities and China, including rare woods, elephant tusks, cardamom and other spices, wax, gold, silver, and silk. Tang Dynasty porcelain has been found at Angkor and

Song Dynasty white wares, such as Qinghai boxes, have been identified at several Angkor centres.

However, it was the expedition of French military officer Louis Delaporte in 1872 which uncovered the great treasure trove of grave goods in Beng Melea in what is now northern Cambodia. His private expedition, which followed an earlier Commission d'exploration du Mékong by Admiral Pierre-Paul de la Grandiere in 1866, found an astonishing collection of bracelets, headdresses, earrings, and costume jewellery, made of gold and silver and inlaid with lapis lazuli and rubies, some of prodigious size. Although Delaporte described his finds in great detail in his diary, the French public who had become quite excited by his daring exploits were destined to be disappointed. Delaporte's expedition, having just crossed a tributary of the Mekong, were robbed at gunpoint by a gang of what they took to be bandits, and the three survivors arrived home empty-handed.

For the next sixty years, the whereabouts of the horde remained a mystery, until a nationalist officer during the Chinese Civil War came upon them in a cave in the south-east of China. France purchased the items in exchange for weaponry to help Chiang Kai-shek defeat the Communists. However, the horde once again disappeared en route, only to turn up in Beijing in 1952, where it remained until the rapprochement of relations with Mao in the 1970s. Still, this British Museum exhibition marks the first time the entire collection has been assembled in one place since the French showed them in 1970 to mark the centennial of the founding of the Third Republic.

Modern examination of the horde has revealed that the rubies were mined in the Mogôk Valley, in what is now Myanmar, and the lapis lazuli in Afghanistan, further under-lining the trading reach of the Khmer empire. The British Museum is proud to have secured the rights to show this unique collection.

–

Gillard looked up from the information panel, and stared into the brightly lit armoured glass box, sitting in its own purpose-built and darkened exhibition space within the museum's famous central reading room. All around the edge and ceiling of the room, projected close-ups of the jewellery flashed like gems, staying a few seconds before winking out to be replaced by others. There were hundreds of visitors on this Thursday morning, many of them schoolchildren with their faces pressed against the glass. It was hard to get a good view. However, the sheer magnificence of the headdresses was quite extraordinary. The central helmet-cum-mask, supposedly worn by the chief priest of Beng Melea, sported one ruby the size of an egg, and a dozen more the size of marbles. Gillard swiped through his phone, back to the website of the Gem Society, which showed that rubies of the best, most intense colour could be worth $1.1 million per carat. He recalled that Sam's engagement ring was a diamond of half a carat, which had cost him several hundred pounds. He wondered how many of those would fit into this large central gem. Hundreds, possibly thousands. His googling had revealed that the largest ever ruby weighed over eight pounds, and was over 18,000 carats, though its colour was not of the highest quality. Could this lot be worth half a billion? He could imagine that some skilled gemsmith could cut those huge rubies into smaller, more saleable ones. Even as he speculated, he was aware that DC Stacey Daines back at New Scotland Yard was trying to get authoritative information on this collection and its value.

He looked around him, and then he thought about the criminal crew that they had identified. Once again, they didn't seem the right people for this kind of job. Okay, Mal Scattergood might well be able to melt down the gold and silver surrounds of these headdresses, but who was going to deal with the rubies and other gems? This was expert stuff. Imagining Horace Mower in here was the classic bull in a china shop scenario.

And what about the JCB? The Angkor horde had been placed in almost the exact centre of the British Museum, entirely inaccessible for any kind of heavy machinery, let alone something as big as a construction yard digger. He just couldn't imagine it. One of the messages intercepted referred to Jackie Norris giving police 'the runaround'. Gillard could think of no more convincing description of what Flying Squad was currently doing as they raced around like the proverbial blue-arsed flies from one possible robbery scene to another.

–

Less than a mile away in New Scotland Yard, DCI Matt Culshaw made the momentous decision to tip off the heads of security of each of the likeliest central London targets that they should keep their eyes peeled for a raid on Friday or over the pre-Christmas weekend.

Friday was tomorrow. There was so much that needed to be done.

Most banks and similar institutions employ retired police officers as security consultants, and Culshaw rang each of them in turn. In many cases he was speaking to people he had either heard of or used to work with, who understood why he could only give out minimal information. He said nothing about the suspected conspirators, and didn't share any of the detailed intelligence. He simply asked them to double-check their security systems, and watch out for any signs of insider involvement: staff asking for extra ID badges, unusual changes in shift patterns, employees found in secure areas they were not supposed to be in. He also asked them to think about suspicious customers or unusual visits, ones that did not lead to any business. Finally, he asked them to review their CCTV footage over the last month, and send him anything that they found suspicious, whether it was individuals inside the premises, or vehicles parked for long periods outside.

Having run through the contacts for a dozen banks, safety deposit facilities, and some of the biggest names in Hatton Garden's diamond district, Culshaw turned to the British Museum. He didn't know the head of security there but the man in question, a former detective chief superintendent called Norman Thornton from Special Branch, had heard of him.

'So what exactly do you expect to happen?' Thornton asked Culshaw.

'The information we have is pretty vague to be honest, but it does come from three different sources.'

'Mentioning the British Museum?'

'No. There is one mention in electronic intelligence of "the BM job".'

'That's funny, because I'd heard that it was going to be an attempt to steal the *Salvator Mundi* from the National Gallery,' Thornton said.

'Where did you hear that?' Culshaw asked.

'You know better than to ask that,' Thornton said with a chuckle. 'But don't worry, my underworld sources are all rusty. This came from an old friend with connections in New Scotland Yard. I like to be in the know. I heard that Jackie Norris is in the frame.'

Culshaw sighed. The police jungle telegraph seemed impossible to silence. If every retired police officer working in security in the private sector was party to even the most confidential information discussed at New Scotland Yard, then it was almost certain that some of the better placed criminals would also get to hear. It was a well-known fact that a small minority of retired cops were bent, and in the pay of crime bosses.

'So it's true, then,' Thornton said, taking his cue from Culshaw's discomfited silence. 'Look, I helped design the armoured glass box that the jewellery is in. It's even more secure than the display cases used for the millennium diamond exhibition. I also got put in place the budget to make replicas of the most valuable pieces. You can be sure that come close of play tonight, all the really valuable stuff will be safely in the vaults, and the copies will be out.'

'Well just make sure you have plenty of security around when you're moving them,' Culshaw said. 'That's when they're most vulnerable.'

'I shan't tell you how to do your job, young man. And you don't have to tell me how to do mine.' He cut the call.

Gillard arrived just as a clearly bad-tempered Culshaw was staring into his phone receiver.

'Patronising bastard,' Culshaw said.

'Which one?' Gillard asked.

Culshaw told him. 'I just have this horrible feeling it's all going to be called off, and we'll end up looking stupid.'

'Look, Matt. I know you've set your heart on catching these boys, but it's entirely possible that they've been giving us the runaround deliberately right from the beginning, feeding us obscure and contradictory information. Remember what Scattergood was heard to say to Norris junior in the gents at the Railway Tavern? Something about big Jackie giving the filth the runaround.'

'Yeah, of course, but why would you bother going to all that trouble unless there was an actual job that you wanted to steer us away from?' Culshaw asked.

'Well, it's not much effort for them to ring Crimestoppers, or drop a few hints in a pub if they know we're listening. Now, I do admit that the phone we found in Idris' possession is a bit more sophisticated. It's a bit too much effort, if you don't have a clear objective.'

'What objective could there be apart from disinformation to cloak a real crime?'

'I don't know,' Gillard said. 'Maybe to drop Terry Moses in it, by implicating him.'

'We looked at Moses, and apart from Horace Mower, no one's been mentioned that ever worked for him.' Culshaw sighed heavily. 'This is a make or break move for me, career wise. If I screw up, then the assistant commissioner and all the other bigwigs won't remember any of the good stuff I've done. You're only as good as your last operation.'

'That's always been true,' Gillard conceded.

'What are your plans tomorrow?' Culshaw asked him.

'I want to interview Sutton's daughter, Dawn. Some of the timings around her father's death don't seem to add up. She hasn't returned my calls. I know where she works, so I'll surprise her there.'

'If you had time to spend a couple of hours with us in the control room, I'd appreciate it.'

'All right, perhaps I'll go and see her now. It's only a few stops on the Circle Line. I'll be here at nine tomorrow.'

'Thank you.'

Gillard checked his watch. Even late afternoon was a good time for a Dawn raid.

–

Dawn Sutton worked in a gleaming glass office block sandwiched between the Westway to the north, the railway line to the south, and Paddington Basin to the east. The ten-storey building at Sheldon Square was packed with the offices of financial services companies, like a mini City of London. He'd never heard of the one which employed her until he'd looked up the address. He crossed the plaza from the tube station and skirted the edge of a modern, partially grassed amphitheatre, in which a few office workers were catching the watery rays of the December sunshine. He made his way to the reception desk and asked for Dawn. He gave his own name as Craig Roberts, the probation officer alias she knew him by. He was asked to take a seat while she was called. He waited ten minutes, and she didn't show. He looked towards the desk, where the receptionist he had spoken to earlier beckoned to him to come to the phone.

Gillard made his way over, picked up the proffered receiver and turned away from the reception desk as far as the cord would allow. He heard Dawn's voice. 'Why have you come to see me at work? I'm really busy.'

'You weren't returning my calls.'

'Why should I? My dad's dead, and if you're his former probation officer, isn't that the end of your interest in him? I don't get who you are and what your interest in him is after all this time.'

He realised he had underestimated her. He had a feeling that she might have guessed who he really was.

'I've got something to tell you. Would you let me buy you a coffee? This will be the last time I'll bother you, I promise.'

She sighed, and then reluctantly agreed. He waited a further ten minutes until she emerged from a lift, very smartly dressed in black trouser suit and white blouse. Even the marker pen eyebrows seemed to be more shaped and subtle. But through her thickly applied make-up, he could see that her face was troubled. Her hands shook slightly.

'This looks a good number you're on to here,' Gillard said, looking around the large corporate lobby.

'This is all the credit card company,' she said dismissively. 'We're on the ninth floor and we don't mix with them lot much.'

'What does your firm do then?' he said as he guided her out into the plaza.

'I couldn't tell you exactly, I just work in the back office on settlements. It's pretty boring to be honest.'

'And from what you said, you do a lot of overtime.'

'Yeah, it's been manic. Two out of the last three week-ends.'

That fitted with Dawn's statement to the police, that she had been at work during the weekend her father had died, and it fitted with what her boss at the company had told DC Michelle Tsu when she'd rung earlier. Done with what he hoped she would interpret as small talk, Gillard asked: 'When is the funeral? I'd like to go.'

'Well that's the thing. I spoke to his GP and his death's not even been registered yet, and there's tests and that. They won't release the body to the funeral directors,' she said, her eyes filling with tears. 'I've got to speak to the coroner or something. All I've got is a leaflet, but no one is telling me anything.'

Gillard knew that they had to string her along for a few more days, not letting her know that the death of her father was now being classified as suspicious. It was a delicate balancing act, and not entirely fair to her. If she did approach the coroner's office, they would no doubt let the cat out of the bag that the police were now involved. If whoever had killed Sutton got to hear that, it could jeopardise Culshaw's grand career-enhancing stakeout. It made Gillard feel uncomfortable for a bereaved family member to be kept in the dark like this.

'When did you last speak to your dad?' Gillard asked.

She looked at him, and her eyes narrowed in suspicion. 'Like I told the police, on the Friday night.'

'And you didn't go back to Thamesway Tower on Saturday.'

She continued to scrutinise him, her face hardening. 'You're a cop too, aintcha? I should have realised before.'

'No, I'm not.'

'My boss said the police had rung him about my movements.'

Gillard was annoyed. Michelle had asked the man not to disclose the fact she'd called.

'Look, Dawn...'

She swore at him, told him where to shove his coffee, turned around and began to walk away back to the office. He could see from the movement of her shoulders that she was crying. *Shit.* He'd overplayed the questions or underrated her intelligence. His attempts to sound purely casual had not fooled her. Maybe being a cop was so stitched into his DNA now that it was never possible to mimic the conversational style of someone less single-minded in the pursuit of information. He now realised he should have left this interview for a few days, when he would have been less compromised, but he hated to leave a murder investigation to get cold. Now what Dawn did with her new information could determine everything.

Chapter Nineteen

It was still dark when the Saudia Boeing 747 cargo aircraft touched down with a roar of reverse thrust and the screech of brakes at London Heathrow, exactly on time. It was 6.05 a.m. The aircraft trundled off the runway, and within ten minutes was in the secure goods area, well away from the terminal building. DC Stacey Daines, flanked by two members of the diplomatic protection service, watched as a specialist lifting truck carefully lowered the wooden crate containing the *Salvator Mundi* from the hold. A forklift then stowed it in the back of a white VW van. Two Saudi security men, in sharp suits and with secret service earpieces, stood and watched. They got into the van, one in the front and one in the back with the painting. Two more identical VW vans arrived, along with a Hallam & Day branded Luton van. The two British protection officers and a Saudi interpreter spread themselves between the white VWs, each of which already contained two security men. Formalities were minimal, and the dummy convoy of the Hallam & Day van plus police patrol car exited the secure goods area within ten minutes, where a team of four motorcycle outriders joined them, two in front and two behind.

By 6.30 they were on the M4 heading into London. The three white VW vans followed a minute later.

At 6.37 a white Audi belonging to Damian Norris was seen by surveillance officers exiting the gates of his home in Epsom. He was alone at the wheel, and ANPR hits were detected on the approach to central London.

At 6.45 Mal Scattergood stepped out of the front door of the Railway Tavern, yawned extravagantly, and climbed into the cab of his white Renault van. He started the engine, put the vehicle in gear, and drove off towards the main road. At the junction, he turned right, heading for London. The tracker attached to the underneath of the van pinged its location to the duty officer in the operations room at New Scotland Yard, and to the iPad of a plainclothes officer in the passenger seat of an unmarked car parked near the pub. The car then set off, following the van.

At 6.49 Scattergood's van pulled into a bus stop, and a large figure detached himself from the queue under the shelter, and climbed into the passenger seat. Officers in the tailing vehicle reported that the passenger matched the description of Horace Mower. The van turned left onto Tower Bridge Road, and joined the roundabout with the A2, heading off towards the Elephant and Castle. By now there were vehicles interspersed between the tailing police officers and their quarry, but the tracker continued to show its position and direction. Traffic lights further distanced the pursued from the pursuers, but the officer with the iPad reported that the van had come to a halt on Elliott's Row just off the A302. That street was a few hundred yards away. Despite that, in the heavy pre-Christmas traffic it took five minutes to get there. When they did, they found the van nose-in at a three-slot private parking bay just off the street, which was otherwise double yellow lined. The officers parked nearby and watched.

They couldn't see whether anyone was in the van and looked around for any signs there could be a half billion pound robbery target in the vicinity. The street was of Victorian mansion blocks, many in a poor state of repair.

'I hope they've not switched vehicles,' one of the cops said to groans of agreement from the others.

At 7.32, Colin Lamb left his flat in Rock Grove Way, Bermondsey. The portly figure was shrouded in his habitual grubby grey anorak and a cloth cap and carrying a white plastic carrier bag. He headed off towards the bus stop that would take him to his place of work. The plainclothes officer sitting in a car across the street radioed in the details to Culshaw's unit.

By 7.40, the security chiefs of all the banks that had been notified by Flying Squad had completed basic security checks. None of them had detected anything suspicious.

At 7.42 security chief Norman Thornton made his way into the British Museum reading room to check that the substitution of the fake jewellery and headdresses had been completed satisfactorily before opening time at ten. The former Special Branch officer had with him two burly security officers. He'd already personally checked the CCTV and found nothing suspicious in the recordings made in last three days. All the cameras were working, as were the alarms which had been tested first thing. The armoured glass cube, its security controlled remotely from the monitoring room, was behaving perfectly. He peered at the replicas, which had been placed on the plinths within. He was no expert, but they looked absolutely identical to the original treasures. But then they should do, for the price they had paid.

At 8.06 DCI Gillard emerged from a packed Bakerloo Line train at Oxford Circus and shuffled with the crowd up two sets of escalators into the ticket hall. He couldn't remember ever seeing quite so many people in one small space, but this was clearly one of the peak times of day on one of the busiest shopping days of the year. There must have been several hundred people waiting their turn at the ticket barriers, shuffling forwards, muttering impatiently. He was due to meet Florence Latimer outside exit five, in Argyll Street, and was already a few minutes late. It was almost quarter past when he finally made his way through the barriers up the stairs to the street and found her by a cafe. She was well dressed for her part, with a smart pale blue woollen coat, sensible brown shoes, a magenta beret, and clutching copies of *The Watchtower*. The evangelical magazines were a masterstroke, marking her out as a member of the Jehovah's Witnesses.

'Sorry I'm late,' he said. 'I've never known the tube so crowded.'

'Trust London Underground to pick this day of all days for barrier maintenance,' she said. 'I even heard the staff complaining about it. I tried five times before it would let me out.'

'Plenty of local councils dig up the roads just before the Christmas rush,' he replied.

'They lost track of the van, you know,' she said. 'We've no idea where Scattergood and Mower are. Probably switched vehicles.'

'So we don't even know what type of van to look out for,' Gillard said. Looking around this, Britain's busiest single junction, on probably its busiest day of the year, he concluded that he wouldn't have much chance of even finding Sam had she been here.

It was 8.15 when big Jackie Norris was seen in the breakfast room of the Swallowtail Hotel. He was dressed casually in a T-shirt, shorts and flip-flops. From the fact his hair was still wet the undercover officer having breakfast there concluded he had been for a swim. Norris took a Danish pastry and helped himself to a mug of coffee before exiting, eating as he went.

At 8.30, Detective Chief Inspector Matt Culshaw checked in by radio with each of the Flying Squad teams. One, four officers in an unmarked van, sat near the National Gallery. Another van was tailing the subterfuge Hallam & Day convoy, a third was opposite the British Museum. In addition, three police riot vans full of uniformed officers were parked in Shaftesbury Avenue, roughly midway between the museum and the gallery. A police helicopter was on standby, currently sitting on the helipad of the Royal London Hospital in Whitechapel.

Finally, he rang the mobile phone of DI Florence Latimer, who was standing with Gillard.

'There's nothing to report, but absolutely massive crowds of shoppers,' she told him. 'So where is the job?'

'We don't know. Nothing to report for any of the suspected target locations. The convoy taking the *Salvator Mundi* is five minutes away from the National Gallery. We'll soon know what the job is, or whether we've been hoaxed.'

At 8.33 the bogus convoy, with its police motorcycle outriders, passed along Piccadilly, turned right into St James's Street, then left into Pall Mall. One minute later the three white VW vans, with the painting in the middle one, took the same route, heading for Trafalgar Square.

At 8.37, unnoticed by any of the police officers, a small white Fiat van, stolen for the occasion the previous day and now fitted with cloned plates, pulled out of the bottom of Great Portland Street, just off Oxford Street. It had been illegally parked for the last three hours while the occupants had been busy elsewhere. It cruised away slowly, turning left into Oxford Street, and then took an illegal right turn into Charing Cross Road, heading for Trafalgar Square.

At 8.39 the dummy convoy passed Nelson's Column, turned left at St Martin's Place, and into the vehicle entryway between the National and Portrait Galleries.

At 8.40 the stolen Fiat van headed south down Charing Cross Road and passed the three white VW vans going the other way in St Martin's Place.

By 8.43 a.m. the real convoy had arrived at the loading bay, and a crate containing the Leonardo painting was moved inside the gallery where the director was waiting to see it unpacked.

It was ten o'clock by the time Gillard was called by Culshaw. 'Sorry, Craig. It looks like we might have been hoaxed. There's nothing happening.'

'No JCBs? No sign of Scattergood's van?' Gillard smiled at DI Latimer, who was standing opposite him, rubbing her hands to keep warm.

'No, that's parked up miles away,' Culshaw said. 'We've got Damian Norris' Audi in the long-stay car park at Gatwick. The financial order on his bank account shows the purchase yesterday of a flight ticket, we can't see where to, and ten grand worth of euros.'

'He's almost behaving like the job's been done,' Gillard said.

'That's right. But we still don't know what the job is.'

'So you can't stop him leaving.'

'I'd love to do a pre-emptive arrest, but the Crown Prosecution Service would be all over me. We'd have to let him go if no crime has been committed.'

'The latest I heard from my team is that Norris senior is still relaxing at his own hotel,' Gillard said. 'Terry Moses has been seen pressure-washing his pub car park. Anything on the movements of Horace Mower?'

'Nothing since he was seen getting into Scattergood's van.'

'They've made monkeys out of us, haven't they?' Gillard said.

'I've not given up – this matters to me. Incidentally, having heard about the assistant commissioner wrangling with big Jackie at some gala dinner in London, I think she's even more determined to nab him than I am.'

'It's good to have her on your side. All right, if you don't need me anymore, I'm standing down. Florence and I will have a coffee, then I'll be heading back to Guildford. I don't see any point me staying here all day.'

–

Gillard was half an hour late arriving at Mount Browne, and as he made his way up to the CID first floor, he ran into DI Claire Mulholland coming downstairs.

'Sorry I missed the incident room meeting,' Gillard said. 'There were two trains cancelled at Waterloo and problems on the tube. The usual Christmas story for the hard-pressed commuter.'

'It's all right, you didn't miss much. There are no fresh clues on the killing of Idris. How was it in London?' she asked.

'Complete waste of time,' Gillard said. 'There's no sign of a job, let alone a half billion pound one. Culshaw's phoned round all the target banks and so on. No sign of anything so far. We did have one piece of intelligence which said it was Sunday, not Friday. But Mal Scattergood was up very early today, and Horace Mower joined him in the van.'

'So no attempt at stealing the *Salvator Mundi*? And all those rubies still in place at the British Museum?'

'So far as I know. I'm just going to get a coffee. Do you want one?' he asked.

–

At the same time, just outside a greasy spoon in Bermondsey, the stolen van pulled up and two men, one very large and one quite small, emerged, wearing standard TfL orange and grey hi-vis jackets. They took off the lanyards which had been dangling around their necks and pocketed them. They walked into the cafe, greeted the proprietor, ordered two coffees and sat down.

'Well 'Orace, that went all right, didn't it?'

'That Ian knew his stuff,' Mower said. 'All I had to do was 'old the screwdrivers and do the testing. It was a piece of cake. Speaking of which.' He turned around in his chair. 'Oi, Mario. Give us two slices of that, wouldja?' He pointed at the glass display cabinet, in which a large and possibly elderly fruitcake sweated under a light.

By the time the cake arrived, Scattergood's phone had rung. He answered it cheerfully. 'Hello Damian. Got your suntan lotion packed, eh?' He chuckled as he listened to the other man. 'Can't believe how well it went. We got in the first one, as soon as it opened, like Colin arranged. Yeah, they fitted perfectly. No one would ever guess. It was a bit busy like, but that's it 'innit, the run-up to Christmas. Everyone fighting to get their pressies sorted.' He laughed. 'They're gonna 'ave a bit of a shock, yeah definitely. So when is it all gonna be in crypto?' He paused. 'All right, the first lot of payments clear on Monday, and they'll be in crypto by Tuesday afternoon.'

He looked up at Mower and smiled as he continued. 'Yeah, by then I'll be lying on the beach in Bali, with a bird in each arm.' He laughed uproariously. 'All those years in the making since you and Ian shared a cell. Yeah. Who would have thought it? See yer, then.'

He passed the phone across to Mower. 'He wants to talk to you.'

'Hello Damian,' Mower said. 'Yeah, I'll do it this afternoon. Should be happy with that. Yeah, it was a tidy job, no mistake. From what I heard, couldn't have done no better myself. Natural causes, yeah. Well, he was old.' He laughed. 'That's what happens if you grass to the filth. See you then, bye.'

Mower handed the phone back then got out his own burner phone. He rang a number, and said: 'Ello, you all right to talk? Yeah, yeah. It's fine. No trouble then? No, Ian did a fantastic job on it, once you'd supplied the data. I've got thirty big ones in cash. Yeah, this afternoon, you'll get the rest next week, in time for Christmas. I 'ope you set up a new account. Yeah. Well, can't teach you nothing can I?' He hung up.

'I want to see if the papers have it yet,' Scattergood said. He picked up his smartphone, typed in London news, and began scrolling. 'Nope, nothing. Not yet. That's all to the good, innit?'

'It'll just be listed as a fuck-up, won't it?' Mower said, taking a slurp of his coffee. 'Not a robbery, at least not for a while. And they'll be scared to admit it won't they?'

'Ian reckons it'll be a week before they're sure. Seeing as the name's the same, innit. Or nearly.'

'So where is Colin heading off to?' Mower asked.

'Mexico, he reckons. First thing tomorrow. Not my cup of tea, but he told me it was nice and sunny, and the criminals they're looking for over there are all from the States, not from over here.'

'Spain is just as easy,' Mower said, biting off half of his cake in one mouthful. 'Not so foreign,' he said, spraying crumbs across the table.

Scattergood laughed, and drained his coffee. 'Right, I'm off to finish packing. You know, 'Orace, who would ever have guessed you could grab half a billion quid in a day or two, like that? It's fucking genius, that's what it is. Can I give you a lift?'

The two men stood up, waved at Mario, and made their way back out to the van.

–

Gillard reversed his car up the drive. It was just gone six, and he was looking forward to a long weekend with Sam. Despite the relatively early finish, it had been a long day, with an early start to get into London, squashing onto the tube, getting cold standing outside Oxford Circus, and once he got back to Mount Browne a series of meetings in the afternoon to review progress, or rather the lack of it, in the Idris case. He wasn't due back in until midday on Monday, for a final half day's work, and then a week's leave over Christmas.

He let himself into his house.

'How was your day?' Sam asked, pausing to give him a kiss.

He held her in his arms. 'Frustrating, I think, is the best description. I don't know how people can commute every day, judging by my experience at Oxford Circus. Anyway, it looks like the robbery was a hoax. No reports of any thefts at the British Museum or the National Gallery. Nothing from any of the big central London banks either.'

'I think there is a bit of daylight robbery going on though,' Sam said. 'You know Moira, sits next to me at work, her daughter just got charged £100 for using the tube.'

'What, was she trying to avoid payment?'

'No, Craig, straight off her contactless card. It was only a three-zone journey.'

'Where to?'

'Bond Street. She works in a gallery there. She tried to phone TfL and there was such a queue for customer service she gave up.'

'Strange.'

'I'd check your card if I was you.'

'Maybe I should. Florence was complaining about the barriers not working properly at Oxford Circus.'

'Who's Florence?'

'Just one of the Flying Squad detectives.' He pulled out his mobile, fired up the personal banking app and checked his balance. His exit charge at Waterloo on the way home looked normal. Then he scrolled further down, past the coffee he had bought Florence, and did a double-take.

'Looks like they got me too.'

Three payments of £100 each to TfL. Then he remembered, he too had needed a second tap to exit the barriers at Oxford Circus and one on the way back in hours later. He been charged for each one, even though the journey cost that had flashed up on the green screen on the barriers looked normal. It certainly hadn't notified him of a charge as big as this.

'Show me,' Sam asked. He did, and she gasped in amazement. 'You'll have to get on to them to get a refund.'

He looked at her, and suddenly his jaw hung open. 'Oh my God, I've just realised what they've done.' He opened Twitter and saw there was a huge outpouring of anger from passengers about being overcharged. A news search revealed one brief article mentioning problems with a new software system affecting passengers travelling to and from Oxford Circus, Tottenham Court Road and Bond Street. Other stations were not affected, and a spokesperson from TfL was quoted as saying that they were still looking into the issue, which seemed to concern 'a relatively small number' of transactions.

'I've got a couple of calls to make,' he said. He disappeared upstairs to use the Internet for a few minutes, and once he'd found what he was looking for, he picked up his phone and punched out a number. He soon got hold of Matt Culshaw, who had just left a meeting, and told him about the card issue.

'I can't see that's anything to do with it,' he said.

'No, listen. How many passengers use Oxford Circus every day?'

'Thousands, I don't know how many thousands.'

'The answer is 100 million a year. That's two million a week, and probably half a million passengers alone on a busy shopping day like today. If everybody got charged £100, on the way in and on the way out, that's £100 million. Add in Tottenham Court Road and Bond Street, leave it running up until Christmas Eve, and I can see that you could get to half a billion.'

'Hang on though, who does the bank app say you paid?'

Gillard looked at his phone. 'TfL (Holdings) Ltd.'

'Maybe they found a way of hacking into Transport for London's accounts,' Culshaw said.

'No, I don't think so. If you can get into its bank you don't need to start charging people who use the tube, you just siphon off money as it comes in.'

'That's logical. Look, Craig, I'm going to call in some financial experts from the City of London Economic Crime Unit. If this was the big job, then we've got to move quickly.'

'I think we've missed the boat on Damian Norris, he'll be on that flight by now. But I can take a look to see if big Jackie is still around.'

'Okay. Let's talk again in an hour.' Culshaw had been keeping it together quite well, but hadn't quite hung up when Gillard heard his string of expletives, each beginning with F and getting louder, before the line dropped.

He concurred with the sentiment. As he stood there, still holding the phone, he realised why the robbery crew which hadn't made any kind of sense now did. It made perfect sense. Even Colin Lamb, in fact especially Colin Lamb, with his job at TfL. It was so simple. Nothing needed melting down, nothing needed fencing, you just needed a couple of herberts in hi-vis to fit whatever type of skimming device had been used, and some banking and data brains behind the scenes. Probably the mysterious Ian.

'So is it true?' Sam asked, peeking around the door into his office.

'Yes, unbelievably. I mean, we were right *there*. On top of them! At Oxford Circus, just like the intelligence said.

Good grief, heads are going to roll for this,' Gillard said, steepling his hands over his face, and blowing a sigh.

'Yours?'

'Well, not initially, but Culshaw, definitely. In the meantime, he's going full Krakatoa. We thought *they* were the old-fashioned gangsters, the jemmy and gelly boys, has-beens, the yesterday's men, and I now realise it was *us* all along. We're the ones who turned out to be obsessed with the big old-fashioned blag. The Met may never recover from this. And the Flying Squad! An old-fashioned name for an old-fashioned game.'

'I think you're being a bit hard on yourself.'

Gillard spread his hands. 'Sam, it's nothing compared to what AC Thompson is going to say! They've made idiots out of us. There we were, staring up into the sky looking for a spectacular half billion pound glamour bank job, and all the time it was there, under our very feet in the grime and filth of the London Underground. And we didn't even notice.'

'Is it too late to do anything about it?'

'We'll see,' Gillard said, punching out some numbers. 'We'll see.'

Chapter Twenty

Detective Constable Brendan Musgrove was sitting with two other plainclothes officers parked in the shadow under a railway bridge outside the Railway Tavern in an unmarked Ford Focus. It was 6.30 p.m. They had been there for two hours, waiting in the December drizzle, which now puddled and ran across the pavements, reflecting the streetlamps. They knew Mal Scattergood was in there because they had heard him belching and singing to himself in the gents' toilet via the bug connected to Musgrove's iPad.

'Is that him making that racket?' asked DC Jason Hart. The skinny young detective was in the driving seat.

'It certainly is. And the song is 'Bali Hai', from the musical *South Pacific*,' Musgrove said. It was confirmation, if such was needed, that Scattergood really was going to Indonesia, as he had been boasting.

'Never heard of it,' said Hart.

'My mum used to sing it,' said the other detective, Tracey Smith. 'And better than that an' all.'

'Yeah, he won't win any karaoke prizes. So what time is his flight?' Hart asked.

'Ten o'clock, Singapore Airlines,' Musgrove said. 'Hang on, what's this?'

A people carrier minicab was nosing its way under one of the railway bridges towards the pub. The side door of the pub opened, and Mal Scattergood emerged, pulling two large white wheeled suitcases. He was wearing a short-sleeved Hawaiian-style shirt, a straw hat, tight white trousers and sandals.

'He really wants everyone to know he is going on holiday,' Tracey said.

'There's nothing subtle about our Mal, nothing subtle at all,' Musgrove murmured. Scattergood greeted the driver and started to stow the luggage inside. He hadn't finished before his mother, Vera, emerged from the side door with some additional luggage for him: a small rucksack and a white plastic bottle that she waved at him, pointing a finger.

'Forgotten the sunscreen,' Tracey said. 'What a master criminal.'

'Well, one of them must be, to have given us the runaround like this,' Hart said.

'You're not wrong,' Musgrove said. Eventually, Scattergood had stowed all his luggage, waved his mum goodbye, and clambered into the passenger compartment, sliding the door shut.

'Right, let's follow him, see if we can get two birds with one stone.' Musgrove wasn't looking forward to the prospect of arresting Horace Mower, and wouldn't countenance it just with these two – an overweight female officer and a callow youth. But if the taxi did stop for Mower, whose London location had so far eluded them, he'd call in to Culshaw to get a van full of uniforms. No, make that two vans. And some bazookas.

The minicab set off on the same route that Scattergood had taken earlier that day. Hart followed. It was a Friday night in the rain and traffic was terrible. It took fifteen minutes to reach Elephant and Castle, and another half an hour to get through Kennington and Vauxhall.

'He's cutting it a bit fine to get the flight,' Tracey said. 'You've got to allow at least two hours to check-in.'

'But he won't be checking in, will he?' Musgrove said. 'We'll be arresting him.'

'He don't know that, does he?' Tracey said.

'Let's hope not,' Musgrove replied. Once they had crossed the river on Vauxhall Bridge, Musgrove was beginning to doubt that Mower would be coming with Scattergood. Mower was a south London boy and wouldn't be at home north of the river. Besides, Mower was probably savvy enough to realise that the further he stayed away from Scattergood, the safer he would be. He had been smart enough to set up a false passport, which already put him in a different league from Scattergood.

–

DCIs Matt Culshaw and Craig Gillard were standing in the main London Underground control room with DI Hunar Desai from the City of London Economic Crime Unit. With them was Andy Padgett, LU's chief technical officer, and they were staring at a screen full of records, which had been captured earlier.

'What's happening here,' Padgett said, tapping the screen, which showed a series of fast ascending lines of letters and numbers, 'is the generation of error codes on the exit gates at Oxford Circus, Bond Street, and Tottenham Court Road.'

'So didn't anybody notice these error codes coming up?' Desai asked.

'They would have done had they not been systematically deleted. We found these in the system dump file. So the error codes were not getting up to the gate management system, which would have alerted the duty technical team.'

'So what exactly caused the errors?'

Padgett tapped the screen again. 'These codes indicate the override signal. Staff at stations all have an admin override card, for when a gate refuses to open. It's a safety thing, and the software has been in place since the days when everybody used paper tickets. Some still do, and just occasionally they jam, and the gates won't open without an override. The same thing happens if you use contactless and the transaction is refused because you've exceeded your credit limit, for example. Someone has to let them through.'

'I see. So somebody has managed to generate all these override codes,' Culshaw said.

'Yes, and I'm not sure how. But this is the beastie which has done it.' Padgett led them over to a desk on which a familiar yellow TfL touchpad for Oyster and bank cards was on display, retrieved from Oxford Circus. He picked it up and peeled off a thin and flexible yellow plastic cap about a millimetre thick. He then turned it over and showed Culshaw. Embedded in the back was a credit card-sized circuit board, including two fingernail-sized microchips, which looked exactly like mobile phone sim cards, and a tiny watch battery linked by a fine wire to the chips.

He pointed to the smaller of the two: 'This one is an EMV chip, exactly like those inside your credit and bank cards, which generates and picks up very short-range radio signals, using a technology called RFID. This is what allows contactless transactions to take place. Now your card has your account number, expiry date, security code and so on, everything required for the receiving system to authenticate a payment.'

'I'm with you so far,' Culshaw said.

'Likewise, the TfL system generates a code through the reader which shows that it is a bona fide payment system, to satisfy the EMV chip in the card. What our fraudsters seem to have done is to interpose, presumably undetectably, a kind of electronic middleman in this system. I wouldn't be surprised if the plastic layer here has a lining which blocks the card and the genuine reader from finding each other. If it didn't, that would confuse the system just as if you were holding two cards over a payment machine at the same time.'

Gillard said: 'So what you're saying is that the passengers were paying a different card reader from the one they thought they were, a bogus one that had been installed on top of the TfL device?'

'Yes, and just like a mobile card reader in, say, a restaurant, it communicates by secure wireless connection as if it were a mobile phone, using this larger microchip. The only interaction between the bogus chip and the genuine gate control mechanism was that this little beastie was able to send an override code to the gates. And to do it time after time after time.'

'How many fraudulent transactions have taken place today at those three stations?' Gillard asked.

'Well, we can't say exactly because the only connection to our system was the generation of an override, and those override instructions were being batch deleted.'

Desai interrupted. 'That alone makes it clear that this is an inside job. If those override codes would normally be accumulated in the TfL management software, but for some reason haven't got there, there wouldn't be anything at the gate end which could cause that, would there?'

'No, that's quite right,' Padgett replied. 'There must either be some malicious code in our system which was just triggered today, or someone has been deleting the files manually. We've got our top people working on it, but it could take some time to find out which it is.'

Culshaw smiled tightly. 'I think we can approach this from the other direction. I understand TfL has an employee called Colin Lamb.'

'I've no idea. I can't get hold of the personnel database from here.'

'Well, let's get to somewhere where we can, and quickly,' Desai said.

'While you're at it,' Culshaw said, 'I want a list of everyone in the organisation called Ian.'

'What? Everyone in TfL? We've got twenty-eight thousand staff,' Padgett squeaked.

'Let's just start with those in technical or computer departments,' Gillard said. 'That should help a bit. And let's hope to Christ we can get some CCTV that helps us narrow it down.'

–

Colin Lamb had just got off the bus at 6.35 p.m., and was hurrying through the rain the last 200 yards to his flat, when two well-dressed young women, one blonde, one brunette, approached him. From their friendly smiles, he at first he thought they were trying to raise money for charity. He wasn't used to being approached by attractive women.

'Are you Colin Lamb?' asked the blonde.

He hesitated, and glanced from one to the other, with a look of panic on his face.

'Colin Aloysius Lamb, we are arresting you—' said the brunette as she held up a lanyard with a police ID card. He pushed her hard, causing her to stagger back, and barged into the other, as he headed to his front door. Lamb's idea of sprinting was not that impressive, and they caught him within five seconds. He didn't see which of them kicked his leg away, but the pavement came up and hit him hard in the face. His arms were forced behind him and someone knelt on his back while handcuffs were snapped on while the rest of the caution was read out to him.

'I'm innocent,' he bleated. With his face to one side on the wet pavement, he was able to watch the stream of blood from his throbbing nose mingling with the rain and spreading into a puddle.

'I didn't do nothing,' he said, as they gradually hauled him to his feet, dabbed his nose with a tissue for him, and pushed him into the back of a grey Peugeot saloon, illegally parked right next to the flat. As the car pulled away, driven by the brunette, Lamb looked at the familiar damp Bermondsey streets and wondered when he would see them again.

Chapter Twenty-one

By eight o'clock, the three detectives and TfL's Andy Padgett were in the British Transport Police office at TfL headquarters, together with a group of BTP officers, all looking at CCTV footage from each of the three Underground stations where the problems had arisen.

The first was Bond Street, where the camera showed staff opening the sliding external gates just after five in the morning. There was only a trickle of passengers for the first half hour, and then three men appeared, wearing blue overalls and orange and grey hi-vis tabards, which had on the back the familiar Underground logo of a circle with a line through it. They were carrying toolboxes and wearing baseball caps which made it harder to see the faces. When they passed beneath the camera, the operator froze the image.

'That's Horace Mower, and Scattergood is the little one,' Gillard said, pointing at the screen.

'But who is the other guy?' Culshaw asked. The man in question was average height, with designer stubble and spectacles.

'Maybe that's Ian,' Gillard said. 'The technical expert who was mentioned. He doesn't resemble any of the Ians we've been looking at.'

'The names on the security cards issued to them were Harold Mole, Michael Goode and Ian Booker,' Padgett said. 'They were booked in formally for maintenance work, supposedly.'

'Mower as Mole, Scattergood as Goode,' Culshaw said. 'I don't suppose Booker is his real name either.'

'Let's see some more,' Desai asked.

The three moved under the camera and reappeared on another one. The one they'd labelled Ian was speaking to a member of staff and showing him what looked like an official letter. Each of the three waved their lanyards and ID cards. Two other members of staff came over, and after a conversation and perusing the sheet of paper, began to hazard-tape off a section of five exit barriers. The three men soon got to work fitting new round push-on yellow caps over the top of the circular card contact plates. Each one took only ten seconds to fit, and all five were done within two minutes. Ian stood back, took a card from his pocket and tested each one in turn. The gates opened, though not always on the first touch. The three criminals then moved on to the next. Even within this camera shot there were at least twenty barriers to do.

'That's incredibly quick,' Culshaw said. 'They must have had a dummy gate to practise on.'

'It must help that the contact plate stands proud from the panel, so you can fit something on it,' Padgett said.

'Never mind that,' Gillard said, pointing at the screen. 'We've got our evidence in black and white, Matt. Let's get them all arrested before they leave the country.'

Culshaw pulled out his phone and called the operations room. 'Get on to Musgrove,' he barked as it was answered. 'Get Scattergood before he gets on the plane.' He listened to what was said back to him and then turned to Gillard.

'Norris junior has already flown out, but Scattergood is stuck in traffic on the M4. Musgrove is half a dozen cars behind, but they'll get him. We've already nailed Colin Lamb.'

Gillard had been on the phone himself. 'Big Jackie hasn't shifted from the hotel. We've got a female officer staying there incognito. I don't think we've got anything on him.'

'Always the way with Mr Big,' Culshaw said. 'Always the way. Still, if he's not going anywhere we've got a little more time.'

Gillard peered closely at a frozen CCTV image of the unknown conspirator. 'It's this Ian Booker character who fascinates me. Who the hell is he, and where do we find him?'

'I've shown Musgrove this footage and he swears blind that he's never been seen in the Railway Tavern. He's got a pretty good memory, so we can trust him on this,' Culshaw said.

'Okay, so where did Damian Norris find him?'

'I don't know. I've forwarded stills to Peckham's Safer Neighbourhoods Team. If the SNT don't recognise him, I don't know where to go next.'

The meeting quickly broke up. Culshaw had to get back to Scotland Yard to brief senior officers, while Desai said he needed to get on to the credit card companies to see how the fraudulent payments had managed to get past them. Gillard walked out with him, realising that he had two still unsolved murders on his plate: that of Jordan Idris, which Claire Mulholland was looking after, and that of Keith Sutton. With a lack of DNA evidence in the killing of Idris, the best they had was that Mal Scattergood's van had been in the area at the time of the killing. For Sutton, they had even less.

He rang Claire to get the latest on her case, which wasn't much. As he hung up, he wondered if the Sutton case could be returned to the Met police, now that there was no longer any need for secrecy. Someone had killed a grass, and it didn't appear to be Mower. Gillard decided it would be better to talk it over with Culshaw before contacting Peckham Police Station to formally hand it over.

It was half past eight when he first gave a thought to Sam, whose planned long weekend had just been ruined by this case. He really wanted to get back and apologise, although he'd had no choice. Maybe he should be like some of the other officers he knew, whose diligence tailed off rapidly after normal working hours. Many of them were cynical, coasting on towards an early retirement, and then some rather easier job as a security consultant.

TfL's Andy Padgett was checking his phone, and said: 'That's good, we can finally reopen Oxford Circus. It's been closed for four hours while we rechecked the gates. So it's all systems go!'

'Hold on,' Gillard said. 'Has a forensic team checked over those barriers? We want fingerprints, DNA, all that stuff.'

'No idea,' Padgett said. 'My job was to get back online as soon as possible.'

Gillard pulled out his phone and rang Culshaw. It went to voicemail. He must already be in that meeting. He then rang DI Florence Latimer, who picked up immediately.

'Hi Craig, I'm just off to interview Colin Lamb at Peckham nick. Do you want to join me?' she said.

'I would, yes, but can you tell me whether any CSI team has been dispatched to get some dabs and DNA off the tube gates?'

'I don't think so.'

'Come on Florence, it's a crime scene!'

'Look, there will be a million people's traces all over those gates. It wouldn't prove anything.'

'Not true. Get them to test the undersides of these yellow plastic caps. Joe public wouldn't be able to touch them. Mower and Scattergood were wearing gloves, but on the CCTV I saw, it looks like our mysterious Ian wasn't gloved-up the whole time.'

She was silent for a moment. 'Good point.'

'Tell them they have to find some with the bogus caps still in place, not those handled by all and sundry.'

'I'll make the call.'

'Thank you. I'll see you in the dungeon at Peckham.' He hung up.

–

Colin Lamb looked distinctly uncomfortable in the interview room. Gillard was looking through the one-way glass and saw a man clearly out of his depth. Lamb's doughy face was mottled red, there was a plaster across his nose, and a little dried blood across his upper lip. His head slumped forward onto the table and he rested it on his podgy arms.

DI Latimer arrived with the paperwork, and followed Gillard's gaze. 'They've already taken photos, DNA and fingerprints,' she said. 'But I'm not sure there'll be anything we can do with them.'

'We'll find out what he has to say.' They had twenty-four hours to hold him without charge, plus another twelve once a senior officer had signed off on it. 'He doesn't look that tough to me. In fact, has someone been roughing him up? Looks like he's got a broken nose.'

She opened the paperwork and looked at the arrest report. 'He tried to run away apparently. Tripped and fell on the pavement.'

'That's what they always say.' Gillard shook his head. 'Doesn't look good in court.'

'He'll look a lot better by the time we have to go to a magistrate. So let's see what he's got to say.' She led the way down through the corridor, greeted the duty solicitor as John, and made her way into the interview room. She introduced herself and Gillard, and prepped the tape.

'What am I in here for?' Lamb said.

'You have been arrested in connection with a major fraud, in which thousands of people have been rooked of at least a hundred pounds.'

'I don't know what you mean.'

'Yes, you do,' she said. 'You and your mates, down at the Railway Tavern, cooked up this scheme which needed you on the inside at TfL for it to work.'

The duty solicitor spoke. 'Can I ask what evidence there is?'

This was of course the crucial question. It was the same one that the custody sergeant had asked when Lamb was first brought in. There was not as yet any CCTV evidence of exactly where Lamb had been today. It was being sought through the TfL bureaucracy. Gillard had been told by Padgett that Lamb's computer login had been used that day, but that his ID number was not against any of the deleted files. That didn't necessarily exonerate him, but it left them with only what Musgrove had overheard.

That had been good enough for the desk sergeant, but the Crown Prosecution Service would certainly want more.

'We are not at liberty to disclose that evidence as yet,' Florence said. 'Now, Colin. You have a golden opportunity to co-operate. Name names, let us know how it worked, and you will do much less time.'

'You've got nothing on me.'

He was right. Gillard just hoped that something could be found quickly. Florence began by reconstructing his day's journey, writing down the times of his departure from home, what he would normally do, and which buildings he worked in. His replies made it sound like he was a basic erk with no responsibility for anything. 'It's simply admin,' Lamb said.

'Does the name Horace Mower mean anything to you?' Gillard asked. Lamb flinched at the name and blinked several times.

'I've heard of him, obviously.' More blinking.

'How have you heard about him?' Gillard asked.

'He's got a reputation, but I think he lives in Spain now.' Lamb folded his arms.

'So you've not seen him?'

'I wouldn't know. I don't know what he looks like.'

'Let me help you,' Gillard said. He passed across a mugshot of a much younger Mower, glowering into the camera, his face as impregnable as an Easter Island statue. 'Ever seen him?'

'No.'

They tried the same with pictures of Mal Scattergood. Lamb did admit knowing him from the pub. When it came to both Norrises, he only shook his head.

'What about Ian?' Gillard asked.

'Ian who? I know a few Ians.'

'Ian Booker, but we think that's an alias.'

Lamb shook his head. 'Not an Ian I know.'

'List the ones you do, then.'

Lamb screwed up his face, and looked at the ceiling in a mockery of concentration as he trotted out half a dozen of his mates, some from the pub, some from work. Gillard wrote them down, pretty sure that he was wasting their time. After half an hour of further questions, they hadn't made any progress. So he decided to turn up the heat.

'You know they've all buggered off abroad, don't you?' he asked. 'They raked off hundreds of millions of pounds, with your help, and left you to take the rap.'

Lamb didn't look happy to hear this. His face tightened, and he looked down at the table.

'How much did they pay you, Colin? Fifteen grand? Twenty grand? Thirty?'

Lamb's eyes flicked up at thirty. Gillard chipped away at the weakness they had exposed. 'Thirty grand isn't much for what's going to happen to you. You haven't been inside for years, have you? Three months in Pentonville for receiving stolen property back in 2006. Bad enough, wasn't it? Now think about a fifteen stretch. Let me help you with the maths; that's sixty times as long. If we can't get them, the justice system will come down on you like a ton of bricks.'

Lamb's eyes focused on the table in front of him. His mouth was downturned. Gillard decided he'd given him enough to think about. He and Florence stepped outside to confer.

'He's thinking about it,' she said. 'But he's clearly terrified of Horace Mower.'

'Understandable.'

'I've arranged to give him half an hour break and a bite to eat, then I'll unleash DCs Hogg and Glover on him, the two Peckham ladies who brought him down and smashed his nose. We'll keep working on him, through the night if necessary.'

Gillard glanced through the one-way window, seeing Lamb slumped over the table. 'My guess is you'll get a result.' He thanked her, checked his watch, and rang Sam. Time to apologise for the ruined weekend. He was supposed to be off, apart from Monday afternoon, right through Christmas week. He doubted whether that would happen now.

Chapter Twenty-two

Peckham Police Station wasn't the best place to spend the Friday night before Christmas. It has some of the busiest custody suites in the capital, and the sound of booze- or drug-addled young men being booked in downstairs punctuated Gillard's concentration as he caught up with paperwork in a borrowed office.

An email had arrived from Claire. The detective inspector had one fresh piece of news to report, courtesy of Carl Hoskins. Terry Moses' car hadn't shifted from the car park at his pub all day. The karaoke was in full swing, with Moses giving his best to the aged Engelbert Humperdinck number 'Please Release Me'. It made Gillard chuckle to hear that the superannuated jailbird should choose such a song. However, the fact he hadn't shifted seemed to pour cold water on any idea of Moses' involvement. The text exchanges on the burner phone supposedly stolen from his pub had turned out to be wrong in every respect. No JCB. And not deferred to Sunday. The reference to BM was wrong too, if that was meant to be the British Museum. Above all, the name at the end: Tel, if it was indeed short for Terry Moses. Wrong again.

The bug in the gents at the Railway Tavern had picked up Mower's remark about 'Your old man giving the filth the runaround'. As the man he was speaking to sounded like Norris junior it could well be big Jackie's idea to implicate Moses instead of him. He had a motive to do so, and it had indeed given them the runaround.

If so, it was an elaborate sting, and it worked like magic.

But that led into another thought. Why say anything at all? Underworld activity required zipped lips, keeping your mouth shut sometimes even for years after the job. The hatred of grasses. This was different. It could only be because big Jackie Norris had heard that there was *already* a rumour about the job. Maybe he even had eyes and ears in the Met. It wouldn't surprise Gillard. One motivation for the rather elaborate attempt to implicate Terry Moses could have been to dilute the intelligence that was already out there with a load of false data. The equivalent of fighter jets scattering shreds of silver foil known as chaff to fox the radar of pursuers.

–

Mal Scattergood had apparently been plucked out of an airport queue kicking and screaming, and he wasn't in any better a mood by the time he been brought to Peckham. Gillard and Florence Latimer interviewed him.

'What the fuck is this about?' he said as they first came in. He was wearing exactly the same holiday gear as when he left the Railway Tavern.

'You know full well what this is about, Mal,' Gillard said. 'We have CCTV of you, Horace Mower and a third man working on London Underground barriers at three stations this morning. We know what you are doing, so why not make it easy on yourself and just co-operate?'

'Fuck off,' he said. 'I've got nothing to say.'

'We've spoiled your holiday in Bali, haven't we?' Florence asked. Scattergood merely scowled at her and folded his arms.

'Let's face it, this job was a bit too sophisticated for your mob wasn't it?' Gillard said. 'Inside job, with Colin Lamb to dish out some security cards, lanyards and some convincing paperwork. Something like that?'

'I don't know what you mean,' Scattergood said. He maintained that demeanour of wounded innocence throughout and was eventually taken back to the cells to think about it.

After he was gone, Gillard kept thinking: who is this Ian, the hands-on guy at the tube station barriers? Where did they know him from? He must be the crucial key to unlock the whole mystery.

–

At 9.30 p.m. Gillard was sitting in the incident room at New Scotland Yard, with Culshaw, DI Latimer, and detective constables Stacey Daines, Jason Hart and Brendan Musgrove. The whiteboard displayed the mugshots of each of the conspirators, bar two: 'Ian' was represented by a close-up of the Oxford Street CCTV, which didn't really show his face very well, and there was a question mark over the label 'finance guy'. It was this last unknown that occupied them as they listened to Detective Inspector Hunar Desai.

'I've just been with the credit card companies. Those who were charged at entry or exit gates were paying a company with the plausible name of TfL (Holdings) Ltd. It appears on the payment advice, though the actual company is based in Guernsey. Needless to say it is not among the registered subsidiaries of Transport for London.'

'So who owns it?' Culshaw asked.

'That may take a little bit longer to establish. However, the Guernsey company has a British trading subsidiary, which is a VAT-registered retailer called JRK Phone Repairs. Its registered address is in Station Road, Woking. Now while it is tempting to go racing around there, my guess is that it is simply a staging post on the payment cycle. That company is only needed to provide credentials of being a bona fide retailer with a credit card history, so payments can be approved.'

'So is that all they needed to have?'

'No. There are many parts to the approval process, and they're all looking to flag up something unusual, and individually these transactions weren't. They were to a known and approved retailer, and were below the contactless threshold. It's just that there were hundreds of thousands of them every hour.'

'And do they already have the money?' Culshaw asked.

'Not all, no. Debit card payments at the contactless limit or below have already been transferred. Credit card approval has been made for the majority of the rest, where there is no exceeding of balance limits, but payments would not normally be made for several days.'

'What kind of numbers are we talking about here?' Gillard asked.

'Well, Visa and MasterCard between them registered over two million payments up until three o'clock this afternoon. That is two hundred million quid. TfL data show that sixty per cent of journeys are made on debit cards, twenty-three per cent on credit card and most of the rest on Oyster card.'

'I still think we should get someone to that address,' Gillard said, picking up his phone. 'We have missing conspirators. Only two are in custody so far. I'll get a patrol car to take a look over the place.'

While Gillard made a hurried phone call, Desai continued. 'We've got the banking details of the Guernsey company, and I've got my people applying for a court order to freeze it. However, I'm pretty sure that if the conspirators know what they're doing, the cash has already been moved.'

'Where to?' Culshaw asked.

'That depends,' Desai responded. 'It could be going the money-laundering route. On the other hand, if they just wanted to do a quick and dirty transfer, it may have been converted into crypto. Either way, it could be hard to trace.'

'This is very disappointing,' Culshaw said. 'We've been caught with our pants down despite all that warning we had.'

'Why don't we get big Jackie Norris in?' Gillard said, having just ended the call.

'On what grounds?'

'We've got as much undercover intelligence on him as on anyone else,' Gillard said. 'You never know, he might make a mistake.' He picked up the nearest phone. 'I've already got the warrant. Now I think perhaps we'll use it.'

Chapter Twenty-three

The Swallowtail Hotel still had its lights on at 2.15 a.m. on Saturday morning when the two police patrol cars and a vanload of uniforms swept into the car park. Jackie Norris' own Bentley was parked there, along with a few other high-end vehicles. Detective Inspector Claire Mulholland, warrant printout in an envelope, was in the lead car, which pulled in under the ornate faux Greek portico, and screeched to a halt. A dinner-jacketed doorman with a smart beard and an earpiece pulled open the car door to let her out.

'This is an unexpected pleasure,' he said smoothly, giving the impression that a raid had been expected after all. Perhaps it had. She was the one who was in the dark. Two hours ago she had been sitting at home watching TV with her husband, thinking about going to bed. Following Gillard's call, and the lack of availability of the duty DI, John Perry, who was tied up with a stabbing in Redhill, she had found herself pitched into the adrenaline-filled world of a raid on Britain's best-known retired gangster.

Flanked by two uniforms, Claire made her way along the carpeted corridor towards the reception desk. Awaiting her there, in a white dinner jacket and with what appeared to be a martini in hand, was big Jackie Norris. His wife Sally Winchester, wearing a black cocktail dress, was talking to a couple of other glamorously dressed women in the entranceway to the ballroom.

'Ah, Claire,' Norris called when he saw her. 'I'm afraid we didn't order a kissogram.'

She didn't recall ever having met him, but it didn't surprise her that he would know who she was. There were only half a dozen detectives of her rank in Surrey Police, and his sources inside the police would undoubtedly have helped him in his research.

'Mr Norris, I have a warrant here to search these premises, in connection with an offence of conspiracy to defraud committed in central London this morning.'

'Make yourself at home,' Norris said. 'Have a drink on the house. Would you like to start with the massage area? The swimming pool? Or the bedrooms? I have to warn you that we have two dozen guests staying tonight.'

'We are also arresting you in connection with the same offence. You are not obliged to say anything, but it may harm your defence if you do not mention when questioned something—'

'You can't do this,' said Sally Winchester, making her way over. 'This is harassment. If you'd intended to interview my husband, it could have been done voluntarily. But you barge in here, making a scene in front of guests.' Another woman seemed to be filming the confrontation on her phone.

Behind Winchester was a striking dark-haired Asian woman in a green dress. 'I'm Amina Kulkarni, Mr Norris' legal representative, and I shall be challenging this arrest, and the warrant. You had better make sure you are on firm legal grounds.'

At Claire's direction, four of the officers headed off further into the building, two to search Norris' private apartment at the back of the building, and two to search the office behind reception. Their immediate target was the hotel CCTV, and its records for the previous few days.

Claire, meanwhile, spent the next ten minutes arguing the toss with Ms Kulkarni, whose proffered business card showed she was a principal at a high-end London firm. Norris himself seemed quite relaxed by comparison, and when they took him in fifteen minutes later, he simply drained his drink, picked up an overnight bag that a member of his staff offered him, and walked smilingly with two escorting officers back to the patrol car. Ms Kulkarni, as his legal representative, came with him. Somehow, Claire felt they were better prepared for all this than she was.

—

It was gone four in the morning when Gillard arrived at Staines Police Station to speak to the man himself. Norris, seen through the one-way window, looked quite relaxed in his white evening jacket and bow tie, laughing and joking with his glamorous brief, as if they were sitting at a table in some expensive bistro rather than a basement interview room in a suburban cop shop.

Accompanied by Claire Mulholland, Gillard stepped into the room feeling quite definitely underdressed. He sat down, prepped the tape, and then began. 'Mr Norris, we have evidence that you, your son Damian, and at least three other conspirators were yesterday involved in the defrauding of hundreds of thousands of customers of the London Underground.'

Still looking amused, Norris turned to Ms Kulkarni before answering. 'I'd like to see that evidence. Can you produce it?'

'Don't worry, it will be produced when the time is right.'

'DCI Gillard,' Ms Kulkarni interjected. 'This is a completely heavy-handed arrest. My client was more than happy to speak to you from his home, about something with which he obviously has no connection. The only time he left the Swallowtail Hotel today was when you and your officers dragged him out.'

'We have a number of questions to put to you,' Gillard said, ignoring the lawyer. 'First of all, do you know Horace Mower?'

'I've heard of him, yes,' Norris answered.

'More than that, I think,' Mulholland interjected. 'You used him as an enforcer during your time as a gangland boss, did you not?'

'I was a businessman. You can't expect me to know everybody who was on the payroll,' Norris said, smirking.

Gillard brought out a polythene evidence bag and placed it in front of Norris. Inside was a yellowed and somewhat dog-eared business card. The big man glanced at it. 'Ah yes, "Horace Mower, I cut grasses." Just a little joke isn't it?' Norris said.

'We can place Mower at the scene of the crime. Likewise Malcolm Scattergood, whom I think you know.'

Norris smiled indulgently. 'I know his mother, Vera. My mum and her were just like that.' He held up a crossed index and middle finger. 'Solid bloke, Mal. Not seen him for a few years, mind.'

Gillard was beginning to see the outline of Norris' strategy. The police couldn't prove that he had anything to do with the conspirators. The plan had all been laid out sometime in advance, probably via meetings in person, in obscure locations. Virtually nothing on the phone, nothing on computers. Gillard was almost certain that the officers who had bagged up computers in Norris' home and hotel office would find nothing incriminating. It would however certainly inconvenience the business on the last weekend before Christmas.

He placed down before Norris a series of enlarged photographs, from the Oxford Street tube CCTV. Mower, despite the baseball cap, was obvious, as was the diminutive Scattergood. It was the final picture, the close-up of Ian Booker, that Gillard tapped his finger on. 'So who is this then, Jackie?'

'I have no idea,' Norris replied, then looked across to Amina Kulkarni. 'This ain't a very good pub quiz, is it? I don't know any of the answers.' He straightened his bow tie, and then steepled his fingers over the table.

'We think you do,' Mulholland said.

'It must be very clear to you by now that my client has been brought here on a fishing expedition for which there is simply no excuse. I am going to be getting him released at the first possible opportunity,' she said.

'We can hold you for twenty-four hours,' Gillard said. 'And when you do get police bail, we'll be keeping your passport, as you are clearly a flight risk.'

'You haven't charged him with anything yet,' Kulkarni said, slapping her hand on the table. 'In this country you are innocent until you are proven guilty.'

'You will be charged in due course,' Gillard said, although he felt far from confident. All along the line, Norris had kept one step ahead of the police. If they couldn't find anything to clearly link him to the crime, this would go down as a career-damaging PR disaster.

Chapter Twenty-four

'This is extraordinary, and for us unprecedented,' said IT security manager Edison Frear. It was a Saturday morning, and Gillard was sitting with DI Matt Culshaw in the executive offices of one of the world's largest credit card companies. With Frear was the company's chief technical officer, Bill Consett, and the head of PR, Karen Blair.

'I can now see what's happening here,' Frear said, pointing at the screen. 'I got a disk image and a memory dump which tells me what's running across the network.' He typed in a couple of codes, and the screen image changed. He tapped it with a pen. 'Our managed service provider uses a VPN, a virtual private network, to reach what is called a jump server. This is an intermediary and gives access to all servers in our network.'

'So this managed service provider is another company?'

'Yes, it's a specialist subcontractor.' He squinted at the screen and tapped his pen at a particular line of code. 'This unidentified program, here, is the one which is communicating to an alien command and control server, outside the system. That's very bad. Of all the servers to be infected, the jump server is the worst, because of its unique access. I presume what it is doing is deleting all of the management systems' oversight controls. For example, error logs, unusual activity reports, failed payment flags. Essentially the malware is putting its hands over the eyes and ears of the systems' own software security guards.'

'See no evil, hear no evil—'

'But not speak no evil. It hijacks the system to do its dirty work. The first place to look is in the temp folder. If your hackers have been lazy, that's where you will often find the malware. And here we found a password-scraper called mimikatz.exe, which basically finds passwords in any Windows system, where they are stored in plain text.'

'What, just readable English?' Culshaw asked.

'Yes, dim isn't it? That's how Windows is. Anyway, we looked at the output file of the malware, and it shows all the passwords taken. The next step is to take a look at all the files that have been modified from the time that mimikatz was initialised.

'Finally we found a malicious DLL file. This is a very well-known technique for infiltrating a system, because certain programs on Windows reach out to look for familiar DLL files, just like you or I would reach for wallet or car keys when we leave the house. By substituting a lookalike for those items, the program pockets them by mistake, and already you have the system working on your behalf, putting malicious keys into the car, false credit cards into the machine, so to speak.'

'So who could have done this?' Gillard asked.

'Clearly, it originates at the MSP, the managed service provider.'

'I spent an hour on the phone with their technical team,' Consett said. 'They insist their system is watertight, none of their other clients have reported any problems.'

'All it takes,' Frear said, 'is someone with system clearance to open the wrong email with a malware attachment. It doesn't have to be insider fraud.'

'But surely to work within a credit card company's system, the virus or malware must've been developed by someone with knowledge of it?' Consett said.

'Yes and no. I've worked at Visa, MasterCard and American Express in my career. All credit card company systems work in the same approximate way, so doesn't have to be a disgruntled employee of our own. There are most of the pieces of software you need out there on the dark web, for sale to the highest bidder.'

'So how are we going to get to the bottom of this?' Karen Blair asked. 'We can't take the system offline while we look, we can't go public on this,' she said. 'Everything needs to carry on as normal, the chairman has made that quite clear to me. The reputational damage would be enormous.'

'A crime has been committed,' Gillard said, fixing her with a stare. 'Computer Misuse Act 1990, malicious and unauthorised access to stored data. You are not the primary victim, hundreds of thousands of members of the public have had money stolen from their accounts. I don't think you're going to be able to keep a lid on this.'

Frear shook his head. 'This is in many ways a clever fraud because the size and shape of each transaction is absolutely normal. So some of the safeguards would not be alerted, as they would for example to a single transaction of unusual size.'

Gillard couldn't pretend that he'd understood everything that had been said. But there was one thing sticking in his mind. 'So who is this service provider?'

'QIJ International.'

'Don't they share a building with you in Paddington?'

'Yes,' Blair said.

Gillard turned to Culshaw. 'Keith Sutton's daughter Dawn works there.'

'That seems a bit of a coincidence,' Culshaw said.

'Too much of one,' Gillard said, getting up. 'Do excuse me.'

–

Dawn Sutton lived on the seventh floor of a block of flats. The building was shrouded in scaffolding, which Gillard recalled was due to the replacement of cladding required after the 2017 Grenfell Tower fire. He ascended in the lift accompanied by two uniformed officers from Peckham Police Station. It was quite a tidy place, with carpeted corridors. Unlike the social housing block where Dawn's father had lived and died, there was no smell of urine. Arriving in her corridor, they could see through the external windows, between the sheets of plastic, distant views over Waterloo East and the London Eye. Gillard pressed the doorbell to her flat.

There was no reply.

It was quite possible she was already out of the country. DC Stacey Daines had added her to the list of conspirators, and referred them all to the Border Force for passport usage enquiries, but there had been no joy so far. Dawn's employer, QIJ International, had told him when he rang earlier that she had left on Friday at the normal time, and with time off in lieu and holiday booked over Christmas, was not expected back until the second week of January.

He rang the bell again, pressing harder. He had a warrant, should he need to effect an entry. Mentally he added her to the list of people who'd made a fool of him. He was beginning to suspect that Dawn was the finance specialist that had been referred to in overheard remarks by the male conspirators. Okay, she didn't have an MBA, but she was a lot smarter than she made out. All she would have needed to do was to insert a data stick with the malware to neutralise the defences of the credit card company. He hadn't understood everything that Frear had explained, but the analogy of blinding the defenders of the system was clear enough.

Right now, he knew that the digital forensics anoraks of the economic crime unit would be working with the tech specialists of the credit card companies to find out exactly how this half billion pound job had been constructed. The more he thought about it, the more marginal the roles of Mower, Scattergood and Damian Norris had been. The real genius was in the conception. That could only be Ian.

'I don't think she's there, sir,' said one of the PCs. 'The locksmith will be here in a minute.'

'Righto, let's get in there soon as we can. If we don't find any sunscreen or swimwear, then we'll know she's off to the Caribbean.'

He turned away and stared out between the flapping stained plastic and steel poles, to the rainswept London horizon. So much for my long weekend with Sam, he thought. I better ring again and see how she is. He stepped away to make a call, but his mobile rang before he had a chance.

'You're not going to believe this, sir,' said Carl Hoskins. 'We found the woman that tried to kill your wife.'

Lydia Marasova! 'Is she alive?'

'Very much so. She's been staying at the Swallowtail Hotel. Got her on the CCTV.'

Chapter Twenty-five

The CCTV stills that Hoskins emailed Gillard were from yesterday, the day of the robbery. They showed Marasova in a bathrobe, in what looked like one of the hotel corridors, and three hours later leaving the hotel by the main entrance, wearing a light-coloured raincoat and pulling a wheeled suitcase. Gillard clicked on a short video, from which the second still had been taken. It showed Marasova coming into view by reception, greeting somebody who was out of shot, and then leaving. The shopping centre images of Marasova Gillard had previously seen showed a washed-out unkempt individual. Here she was well dressed, her hair had been highlighted and styled, and she seemed composed. There were no obvious signs of the tattoos on her neck.

What on earth was the connection between Marasova and Jackie Norris? Maybe there was none. She had simply come into money, presumably someone else's, and had decided to spend her time at the spa. However, the fact that her partner in crime, Jordan Idris, was dead, presumably killed by Horace Mower, made it seem just too much of a coincidence.

Gillard called the detective constable back. 'This is great work, Carl. Was she down as a guest?'

'No. There was no one of her name on the booking system.'

'That either means she's using someone else's credit card, or she must be staying with big Jackie's approval.' Gillard tried to recall Marasova's educational background. He didn't remember a degree or anything beyond GCSEs. Could she really have had a role to play in the fraud? It was hard to believe. Perhaps she was more intimately connected with the killing of Idris, and she was being given somewhere to hide until things cooled down. The fact she was leaving with luggage on the Friday might well indicate that she was being treated as part of the conspiracy.

Hoskins told him that the female undercover officer who had been staying at the hotel had not noticed Marasova, probably because she wasn't looking for her and hadn't been part of the Greenway shopping centre case team. Instead she had kept her eyes open for Norris himself, as well as his son.

Gillard remembered that there was no car registered for Marasova, and she didn't even have an address to go to. Her own rental flat had been abandoned, and that belonging to Jordan Idris was still sealed with a police padlock. He rang DI John Perry, who had conducted the initial search for her. Perry, who was off duty, had already heard from Hoskins that the young woman had reappeared. 'Maybe she's gone back to her father's place,' Perry said. 'I can't think of anywhere else.'

'She must know we're still looking for her. I think it's a long shot that she would go to a place we've already visited. Still, can you arrange for some uniforms to go round there? I've got a different female fugitive to locate.'

–

DCI Matt Culshaw drove himself and Gillard back to Peckham Police Station, where they convened a quick incident room meeting with Florence Latimer, Stacey Daines and Jason Hart. They all looked exhausted except for Florence, who looked like she could go forever without getting bags under her eyes.

'We've got strong evidence from CCTV against Scattergood and Mower, and our mystery Ian,' Culshaw said, standing before the whiteboard. 'And we have just heard from QIJ International, which handles a lot of the computing services for the big credit card companies, that not only do they employ Dawn Sutton, but that her sign-in details correspond with the first system log of what turned out to be the malware program.' He put a tick underneath her name on the whiteboard. 'We need a lot more information to nail this down, but it's a good start. Now we just have to find the woman.'

'We had uniforms at her late dad's flat, and she's definitely not there,' Stacey Daines said. 'She's not at home and her passport has not been registered against any airline or travel company booking that we are aware of. Border Force are watching out for her.'

'She has a son, called Adam, aged fifteen,' Gillard said. 'We should be able to trace her through him. The next step is to find out who her friends are.'

'I've got uniforms asking,' Daines said, making a note of the son's details.

'Right,' said Culshaw, rubbing his hands together. 'I've already got an extra twelve hours from the superintendent, so that's until roughly midday tomorrow. Let's go and work over the three we've got in custody. I've just had Norris senior transferred here.'

'I'd concentrate on Lamb,' Gillard said.

'*You* are the weakest link,' DC Jason Hart said, imitating the catchphrase of the TV show. 'Goodbye.'

'We'll let DCs Hogg and Glover interview him a couple more times,' Culshaw said. 'It's clear he can't handle a couple of tough women.'

–

It was mid-afternoon on Saturday, just the kind of time when Colin Lamb might normally be watching the footie down at the Railway Tavern. But here he was, getting a mauling from Hogg and Glover. Gillard watched through the one-way glass as the two detective constables softened Lamb up. They'd been doing it for an hour before he arrived. They asked the same questions again and again, even though the duty solicitor kept reminding them that his client had already responded. Lamb went from quiet and surly through to frustrated and angry, shouting and insulting the two women. Finally, he flopped forward onto the table, resting his head on the backs of his hands.

'Are you tired, Mr Lamb?' Hogg asked.

'Tired of you, that's for sure,' he muttered.

'Would you like us to stop, Colin?' Glover asked softly.

'Yes.'

'We will, as soon as you tell us who you were working with,' she said. The murmured response was inaudible.

'Speak up for the tape!' Hogg yelled, slapping the table.

'I don't know anything.'

'On the evening in question, in the Railway Tavern, you were seen to hand Malcolm Scattergood an envelope. What was in it?' Hogg demanded.

'It was the TfL ID cards you had prepared, wasn't it?' Glover asked.

'No.'

'What was in it then?' Hogg yelled. 'Was it drugs?'

Lamb actually lifted his head at this point. 'What you mean, drugs? It wasn't drugs. I ain't got anything to do with drugs.'

Glover turned to Hogg. 'It wasn't drugs, it was just a few cards.' Then she turned back to Lamb. 'Isn't that right, Colin?'

Lamb nodded, his head still resting on the table.

'For the tape, the interviewee nodded a "yes",' Hogg announced.

'Would you like a cup of coffee?' Glover said.

Lamb lifted his head. 'Yeah.'

'I was asking her,' Glover said, indicating her colleague. 'You can have one when you've told us some more.'

'I'd like one of those nice iced buns they have in the canteen,' Hogg said to her colleague as she stood.

Lamb eyed them, like a labrador scenting dinner. 'Are we done?' he asked.

'We are,' Hogg said. 'Interview terminated at 14.33.'

As the two detectives exited, Lamb stood up. But as soon Hogg and Glover left, Gillard and Florence Latimer came in.

'Sit down, Colin,' Florence said. They prepped the tape, while Lamb groaned.

'Full name and address?' Gillard asked as soon he had sat down.

'You know all that,' Lamb whined.

'Just confirming, Colin,' Gillard said. Lamb mumbled out his address.

'Right, let's start at the beginning,' Florence said, pen in hand. 'Tell me everything that you did yesterday from the moment you got up…'

Colin Lamb started to whimper.

–

Three hours later, and well past teatime, Culshaw, Gillard and the others reconvened at their temporary incident room upstairs at Peckham Police Station. A large Indian takeaway had been ordered in at Flying Squad's expense, and the team sat around gorging themselves on lamb bhuna, chicken dhansak, saag bhaji and fluffy pilau rice. There was a side order of chips for DC Jason Hart, and a whole tandoori chicken shared by DCs Glover and Hogg. Gillard thought about how much Carl Hoskins would have enjoyed it all, at least before his diabetes diagnosis. The meal was to mark a significant piece of progress on a stubborn case.

'You've done well,' Culshaw said through a mouthful of curry. He was principally addressing the two female detectives, but extended his gratitude to the others. They had made no progress with Jackie Norris or Mal Scattergood, but Colin Lamb had finally cracked. He'd admitted supplying security cards and lanyards for the conspirators, and booking them in without authority on the TfL contractor works schedule. He confessed to receiving £10,000 upfront, with the promise of twice that once the job was done. Most importantly of all, he named Damian Norris, Mal Scattergood and finally – after a good deal of snivelling – Horace Mower. 'He'll fucking kill me,' Lamb had said.

'You won't be sharing a cell, don't worry,' DI Latimer had cheerfully reassured him. Gillard fully expected Lamb to recant the testimony entirely, once the full enormity of grassing up Horace Mower sank in. Lamb said he had no idea whether big Jackie was involved or not, and neither did he know anything about Ian, just enough to create the false ID badge in the name Ian Booker.

Daines, currently halfway through a peshwari naan, had scoured the entire UK crime database and could find no Ian Booker, at least not one with even the faintest resemblance to the man who led the work at the tube stations. Hart shouted for everyone's attention; he was staring at his email inbox.

'We got the DNA results from the tube barrier swabs.' He said nothing while his eyes scanned the results. 'Blimey! There's hundreds and hundreds of 'em.'

'Of what?' Culshaw asked.

'Traces with links to individuals on the DNA database,' Hart said.

'Not surprising, given that half a million people pass through a day. What about traces from under the rims of the false caps?' Gillard asked. 'Those tests should be labelled separately.'

Hart shook his head. 'They ain't. It's all mixed in together.'

Gillard swore. 'I told them. For God's sake!' He let his head fall into his hands.

'How many Ians are there?' Florence asked him.

'Good point,' Culshaw said.

'Three, counting middle names.'

'Let's see the mugshots,' Culshaw said, coming over to sit next to Hart. They trawled the police national computer and found the three. One drug dealer, who was Black, a white teenager convicted of affray and a struck-off dentist with a paunch. None of them looked anything like the suspect.

Then, finally, Gillard had a brainwave. 'We're approaching this from the wrong direction. Let's use lateral thinking. I've got an idea. This Ian has clearly got a particular talent, right?'

'Obviously,' Florence said with a grin.

'There are two avenues he might have come into this by. One, that he is intimately connected with the development of this kind of technology, maybe a supplier to TfL, right?'

'I've already been on to the two companies that TfL use,' DC Daines said. 'They don't recognise the guy from the CCTV stills we sent them.'

'Okay. And we know that he wasn't a TfL employee, at least in recent years,' Gillard said.

'We're still with you,' Culshaw said. 'Carry on.'

'The other avenue isn't skill specific, but crime specific. In other words, this guy must have done something like this before. And I don't mean just card skimming, I mean something that really gets into the guts of how these systems work. On the CCTV, he was clearly showing Mower and Scattergood how to do it.'

'Sounds reasonable,' Culshaw said. 'What are you suggesting?'

'That we look through unsolved cases of sophisticated credit card fraud.'

'We've already done that,' Daines said. 'There's nothing with an MO quite like this.'

'Yes, I understand that. The nearest thing to this, I reckon, is the cash machine card skimming that used to be done by some of those foreign gangs. Remember the Moldovans? There were quite a few others. There was a group caught in 2019, who just came over here on holiday visas, installed a lot of skimming devices into card readers at ATMs, scooped up tens of thousands of card details, and used them to create cloned cards. Where they were able to use cameras to pick up the PINs too, they would get straight into the victim's accounts. Tens of millions of pounds were siphoned off.'

DC Stacey Daines nodded. 'I'll get on to it now.'

–

By 8.30 p.m. they had a list. One was a very successful Romanian gang, most of whom went down in 2009. Then there were the Moldovans, the majority of whom were still inside, and a couple of Liverpudlian engineering graduates who had served their sentences and got out in 2016.

'No Ian Bookers, nor indeed any Ians at all,' Daines said.

'Are you sure?' Gillard asked.

'It's not hard, I typed in the three letters and there were no matches,' Daines said.

'Let's pull up some mugshots,' Culshaw said. 'Maybe we will recognise him.'

The first one they alighted on was a Moldovan called Pavel Ivanchuk. 'He's got a beard,' Daines said. 'And he's done time over here.'

'Not sure,' Gillard said, looking over her shoulder at the screen. The images were in most cases around a decade old. Add or subtract weight, hair loss, spectacles on or off, facial hair on or off, even a few dentition changes. It wasn't always easy.

'What about this guy?' Gillard said of a shorter than average Romanian, dark eyed, shaven headed. There was still something familiar about him.

'The name's Marasova,' she said. 'Ionatan Marasova.'

'Marasova!' Gillard exclaimed. 'The same surname as Jordan Idris' girlfriend.' There was a little bewilderment amongst the Flying Squad team. 'A shopping centre pickpocket was murdered a couple of weeks ago. Do you remember? That's where the Terry Moses tip-off was found, on a phone in Idris' flat.'

Gillard was aware that the London-centric nature of the robbery inquiry tended to dominate, but he was a little annoyed that the Surrey end of the investigation had left so many glazed expressions.

'Yes, of course,' Culshaw said. 'We rather left that end of things to you.'

'This is your Ian, mate,' Gillard said, tapping at the screen. 'No wonder the gang called him Ian, with a difficult name like that.'

'He's from Bucharest originally,' Daines said. 'Maybe that's the Booker part of the name.'

'Ian Booker. That makes sense,' Culshaw said. 'Let's find out everything we can about him.'

'Ionatan means Jonathan,' Daines said, having googled it.

'Hold on,' Gillard said. 'Somebody went round to see Lydia Marasova's father in the early days when we were looking for her. I think we'll have an address.' He started to tap out a number on his phone. He spoke to the desk sergeant at Mount Browne, and asked him to look up on the local system any statement from anyone called Marasova. It took a couple of minutes, but the officer located the statement, attached it to an email and pinged it off to Gillard.

He lived in Slough. Ian Booker was Lydia Marasova's father. For God's sake, Gillard thought, had nobody done a criminal record check after they visited him?

Chapter Twenty-six

While patrol cars were sent screaming round to Ionatan Marasova's home, Gillard took a good look through his 'previous'. Marasova and his wife had come to Britain in 1996, where they got residency status through her British-born father. The first crime reported was in 2002, when he was cautioned for a shoplifting offence, and then in 2006 he was caught on CCTV cameras outside a Lloyds Bank ATM in Reading installing a card skimmer. He and three other Romanian nationals were caught and in the following year sentenced to four years. Curiously enough, there was no DNA record for him on the PNC. Perhaps an oversight, and possibly the reason that the samples taken at the tube station barriers had not found a match for him.

'I definitely think this is our man,' Gillard said. 'It now makes sense that his daughter, who we feared was murdered, turned up on the CCTV at Norris' hotel.'

Gillard spent the next half an hour pulling together the various loose threads of the investigation. He pulled up the paperwork for last night's police raid on JRK Phone Repairs. The VAT number and business address of the business, based in Station Road, Woking, had been used on the payments. Surrey's economic crime unit had established that the money was being pumped out of JRK's bank account as fast as the payments came in from Visa and MasterCard. More than £10 million per hour had been transferred via the Guernsey-registered TfL (Holdings) Ltd to an offshore account. They had only been stopped at eleven a.m. this morning after £282 million had already disappeared abroad. Looking through the details, Gillard could see that one of the directors of the Guernsey company was a man called Ian Booker.

While Gillard and Culshaw had been trying to track down the mysterious Ian, City of London forensic financial specialists had been working with Surrey's economic crime unit to try to stop any further cash being collected.

Gillard was notified of one other loose end. There had been no luck tracing Dawn Sutton from her mobile phone. It seemed to be switched off, and perhaps she was using another one. There was more luck with her son, Adam. Uniformed officers from Peckham had, with the assistance of his school, tracked down a few classmates and school friends and visited them at home. They soon discovered his mobile number, and when the officers said that they were trying to trace him, one of the girls in his class had contradicted them. 'He's not missing,' she said. 'He's going on holiday to Spain over Christmas.' She showed some of the recent message exchanges, which confirmed what she said.

'Can I ask you a favour?' one of the officers asked. 'Send him a text, from you, not from us, and ask him exactly where in Spain he is going. Don't say the police have been asking because he might have been abducted.'

'Oh my God,' the girl said. She readily agreed to what they asked.

'Horace Mower has just been spotted,' Stacey Daines said, looking at her phone. 'Trying to board a ferry at Portsmouth this afternoon.'

'Have they got him?' Gillard asked.

'No. But it seems they have ANPR on the vehicle he was driving. There was a woman with him.'

'How long ago was that?'

'Two hours, in the queue for the nine p.m. sailing.'

'Why has it taken so long to tell us?' Gillard asked.

Daines grabbed her phone. 'I'll ring the Border Force now.'

'Make sure we get the CCTV and ANPR details.'

She nodded.

Gillard was furious. The conspirators had made fools out of them at every turn. First, sending them this way and that in the search for the location of what was expected to be a conventional robbery. And now most of them were managing to slip abroad before they could be arrested. Mal Scattergood and Colin Lamb were pretty poor crumbs of comfort, unless they could catch the main conspirators and find some way to nail Jackie Norris to the job.

Border Force was quick to make amends. The CCTV it sent of the passport booth showed exactly what had happened. Culshaw, Latimer, Hart and Daines gathered round Gillard's screen as the video attachment opened. The camera was mounted in the immigration officer's booth and gave a high-up view of a blue BMW saloon, with a sunglassed and baseball-capped driver of Mower's build passing up some passports which disappeared out of view. There was no sound, but Mower could be seen tapping the side of the car door with impatience as a minute elapsed, then he shouted something. The officer's hand appeared in view minus the passports. Mower then reversed at speed out of the queue, smashing into the vehicle behind, before doing a rapid U-turn and racing out of view.

'He bottled it, didn't he?' Latimer said with some glee.

Gillard was reading the main body of the email. 'It wasn't his passport that was the problem. He was travelling under the name of Maurice Cutler, which we know must be a false passport, but it was good enough to get him into Britain a few weeks ago. However, the woman's passport had been stolen, and that's what the officer picked up.'

'Do we know anything about Mower's girlfriend?'

'Nope,' replied Florence Latimer. 'Nothing recent on the file. Presumably because he's been in Spain.'

'Let's see the ANPR hits,' Gillard said. He clicked on the attachments which showed them. 'Right, three hits leaving the port, M27, M3 heading north. This is still an hour ago.'

'He could be anywhere by now,' Culshaw said.

'I'll check in with Thames Valley Police, and the Hampshire force as well as our lot,' Gillard said. 'And perhaps I should get over there, if you're happy to pick up the rest of this?' He turned to Culshaw.

'That's fine.'

–

Half an hour later Gillard was racing west along the M4 in a borrowed Flying Squad car, with the twos and blues going. In the passenger seat beside him was DC Stacey Daines. The Lexus IS-F may have had a dented side panel, but it had been tuned to perfection, and roared along the motorway at 110 mph without trouble. Daines was on her iPad checking on the ANPR hits of the BMW Mower was driving.

'He's on the A34, crossed under the M4 fifteen minutes ago.'

He glanced at the satnav. They were at junction eleven, just past Reading. Mower was half an hour ahead, tripping just as many speed cameras as they were. Gillard was also listening to police radio activity for the Thames Valley force, where a report had just come in of a vehicle hijacked on the edge of the Oxfordshire town of Wantage.

'That'll be Mower, changing cars,' Gillard said, listening for the next radio snippet.

'...the driver of the hijacked vehicle was assaulted and is reportedly unconscious, and being attended to by paramedics...'

'That's definitely Mower,' they said in unison.

Daines rang the Thames Valley control room. 'Can you confirm the registration number of the hijacked vehicle? You can't. Ah. Are there any witnesses? Good. And was a BMW left there? Yes.' She spent a few minutes longer, and when she finished turned to Gillard.

'The new car is white, description of the male occupant matches Horace Mower. The witness is an elderly woman, and the driver is still unconscious. The incident was in a suburban street where there is no known CCTV—'

'Great,' Gillard said sarcastically.

'But the fugitives left behind a blue BMW saloon.'

'Make sure they tape it off and don't touch it until CSI get there.'

It took ten minutes to confirm the registration number of the hijacked car. It turned out to be a Subaru saloon. There were no ANPR hits reported before Gillard's car arrived in the residential cul-de-sac where the crime took place. CSI had just arrived, and a square of blue tape on traffic bollards marked out the abandoned BMW, whose front two doors were open, keys still in the ignition. He walked around the vehicle, and held his hand just above the bonnet to feel the heat still coming off the engine. Donning blue nylon gloves, he carefully popped the boot open. There were two large suitcases inside. He didn't touch them, but made his way around peering into the back seats, where a woman's jacket could be seen. Squatting down between the open passenger door and the seat, he pressed the button to release the glove compartment lid. He could see a torch, a bottle of what appeared to be sunscreen and a pair of women's sunglasses. Going to the corresponding driver side, he found a French motoring atlas in the door pocket, along with a hammer. Useful for hitting people with.

He wondered who the woman with him was. Nothing was known about Mower's girlfriends, but it would be odd if she was sufficiently well known to need a false or stolen passport. And then it struck him. Of course. If the woman was Dawn Sutton, then she *would* need a stolen passport.

-

Gillard left CSI to their work and returned to the Lexus. Stacey Daines was busy on the iPad. 'The car driver is now conscious. An officer is with him at the hospital, and I've asked them to find out whether the car has satnav. It may take an hour or two, but we can get on to the manufacturer to trace the GPS position.'

'That's great thinking. Mower is probably going cross country now, though I've no idea where.'

'Maybe Northern Ireland on the ferry?' she said.

'You still need a passport,' Gillard said. 'And the Border Force has got Mower's forged one.'

'Maybe he's got a mate who will drive him across in the boot.'

'True. But I think our Horace is probably a bit of a hot potato right now. And having Dawn Sutton with him makes him easier to catch.'

Daines chuckled. 'That would be handy. We're not doing brilliantly so far, are we?'

Chapter Twenty-seven

'You've left all my luggage behind,' Dawn Sutton complained as Mower floored the accelerator of the hijacked Subaru.

'You brought too much stuff anyway, woman. It's bad enough that we had to bring 'im,' he said looking in the mirror at Adam, petulantly staring out of the window.

They headed off down a darkened country lane, with Mower stabbing away with a finger at the satnav. 'We go this way, switch cars once more, and then we'll be away.' He cackled to himself, a habit that Dawn didn't like.

'Why do we have to switch cars again?' she asked.

'It's pretty simple. The filth got our BMW plate at the ferry, right? So they could follow us on those road cameras. When I liberated this, there was a bit of a to-do about it—'

'You hit that bloke really hard,' Dawn said. 'You could have killed him.'

'He shouldn't of fucking argued, should he? No one argues with 'Orace without needing new teeth.'

'Yeah, it was amazing,' Adam said. 'One punch, and he just flew through the air.' He mimed the action, with some sound effects.

'Yeah, anyway. There was a witness, right? This time when we switch there won't be no witness. Park the car nice and quiet, in a car park in a little town, where there's no CCTV, and we'll choose a new car. So that we get a few days head start, not a few hours.'

'So Uncle Horace, can you break into any car?' Adam asked.

'Not some of them new ones, no. Give me a ten-year-old Ford, or an old Cavalier. Can do them in me sleep.' They turned off the lane, heading towards Witney in Oxfordshire. The dark woods either side of the road almost closed over the top of the road. The passed a pair of semi-detached roadside cottages, and saw that a vehicle was just pulling out from the drive of one of them.

'Hang on a minute,' Mower said, pulling in to the left and stopping. They watched the car pull away, and head back in the direction that they had come from. The house left behind was darkened.

'You're not gonna break in there, are you 'Orace?' Dawn asked.

'Nah, not that one. The next-door house.' The next-door home was brightly lit, and the glare of a TV could be seen through the curtains. 'See that little silver Toyota there. Old ladies' car, perfect. Not suspicious. And the neighbours are out, as we've just seen 'em leave. Stay there.' Mower exited the car and crossed the road towards the cottage.

'Does he know someone here?' Adam asked.

'No, I don't think so,' Dawn said.

'Why aren't we going to Spain like you said?'

'There was a problem with me passport.'

'I don't want to go to Wales. It's boring.'

'None of us want to go to Wales, Adam. But it's the only place that's safe.'

'But it's so boring.'

'How do you know, you've never been.'

263

'I ain't been to Spain neither, but I know it ain't boring.'

Mower rang the doorbell, and Dawn could see movement behind the curtains, and then a hall light come on. The door opened, and there was a glimpse of an elderly woman. There was a brief conversation, then Mower jumped right in, and slammed the door behind him.

'He's not gonna kill her is he?'

'No, I don't think so.' She felt much less sure of it. 'You keep your mouth shut when he comes back, all right? Don't ask any difficult questions.'

'All right, Mum.'

Dawn watched the house, and saw a light go on upstairs. Then a minute later the light went off. The downstairs lights also went off. Mower emerged, walked over to the little silver Toyota with keys in his hand, and then opened it, got in and drove the vehicle out into the road in front of their own.

'Is that our new car, Mum?' Adam asked.

'For a while, I suppose.'

Mower emerged from the car, and beckoned Dawn to follow him. She moved over to the driving seat, started the Subaru and followed. They went only a mile before turning left in a tiny farm lane. There was a copse of young hazels off to the right, accessed by a gate. Mower stopped and walked back to the Subaru. 'Right, get in the other car, and stow your stuff. I got to dump this one in there.' He indicated the copse.

While Dawn and her son grabbed the remaining bags and moved across to the smaller car, Mower used a screwdriver to lever off the front and rear number plates from the Subaru, and stowed them in the Toyota's boot. He then drove the Subaru into the copse as far as he could, about twenty yards. He opened the boot, took out a bottle of lighter fluid, and sloshed some of it around the inside of the car. With a lighter from his pocket, he then set it ablaze.

Once they were all back inside the Toyota, Mower reversed back to the lane.

'What did you do to that woman?' Dawn asked.

'Did you murder her?' Adam asked.

Mower stopped the car once they were at the junction. 'Course I facking didn't. I tied her to a radiator with a few pairs of her tights, gagged her an' all. Borrowed her car. And got us a new phone.' He held up a smartphone.

'She must've been terrified,' Dawn said.

'Nah, she was all right. 'Cept when I killed her stupid little dog. Fucking thing kept barking and I couldn't have that, so I wrung its neck. Never could abide Yorkshire terriers. Not even a proper dog.'

'Oh, 'Orace,' Dawn said.

'What you going on about? She'll be all right. I told her I'd ring the cops in a few hours, so they can come and rescue her.'

'Will you?' Dawn asked.

'Will I fuck,' Mower said, with a laugh. 'After a week, maybe, once we're safely away.'

'That's terrible. The poor woman,' Dawn said.

'You've got a nerve,' Mower said. 'The woman who suffocated her own fucking father.'

Dawn's jaw fell open. *You promised not to say.*

'Mum, you didn't kill Grandad…?'

''Orace, I told you not to say anything,' Dawn hissed. 'Not in front of him.'

Mower turned round and stared at Adam. 'Yeah, son. She put a plastic bag over his head, gripped it tight round his throat, and forced him down on the bed, until the old sod choked.'

Adam was in tears now. 'You couldn't, Mum, you couldn't.'

Dawn was unable to speak, the overwhelming guilt stuck in her gullet.

'Let me tell you, son,' Mower said, pointing a huge finger at the boy. 'Stop your squalling, right. Your grandad was a traitor to his family. Squealing to the filth, grassing us up. All I ever wanted was to provide for me and my own, in my own way. And along comes your grandad, sitting in the Railway with his ears open, listening to bigmouth Mal Scattergood boasting about a half billion pound job to his mum. Now your mum here, an important part of the operation, comes into your grandad's flat one day, and him being a bit deaf like, he doesn't know. So she hears him on the phone to the cops. She realises that this bloke what has been befriending your grandad is actually a copper. Gillard, that's his name. I tell you, I'd like to ring his neck like that dog.'

'You're both bastards. You killed my grandad,' Adam said, sobbing.

'We had to, Adam. We're in debt up to here.' Dawn indicated her chin. 'I told you about those huge bills, the cladding and that. What were we gonna do for money, eh? PlayStations don't grow on trees. Holidays, a proper car. For the first time ever, we are going to have some money. And your grandad jeopardised it, even though he didn't realise I was involved until I confronted him.'

'Money's not everything!' Adam shouted.

'It is when you haven't got none,' she snapped.

'You killed him!'

'He was dying anyway, love. It was euthanasia, really.'

'But you murdered him!' Adam yelled and began to cry.

'I've just about had enough of you,' Mower said, pointing the warning finger at Adam. 'If I smack you one, you will know all about it. What a crybaby!' He turned to Dawn. 'You know, I can't believe he's mine.'

Adam's jaw fell open. Dawn threw her head into her hands. *You idiot, I've never told him that either.*

'My dad died,' Adam said, through angry tears. 'From cancer, when I was a baby.'

Mower laughed, leaning with his elbow over the seat back. 'Is that what you think?'

Adam's face contorted with rage. 'You're both bastards!' He flung his door open, and started to get out. 'I'm not going to Wales.'

'Get in and shut the fucking door!' Mower yelled.

Adam did move back in, but only to hurl a fist into the middle of Mower's jeering mouth. He roared like a bull, and reached for the boy, who ducked away, and jumped out of the car.

'Adam, don't!' Dawn shouted.

'I hate you!' Adam yelled at his mother, adding a mouthful of the worst swear words.

Mower, bellowing fury, burst out of the car, leaving it rocking. Adam sprinted away down the lane like a deer and disappeared into the darkness. The big man ran after him, but after twenty yards stopped, and jogged back to the car.

'Right, we'll chase the little bastard down.' Mower put the car into gear and headed off in pursuit.

'Leave him, 'Orace.'

The headlights, on full beam, picked up the running boy 200 yards ahead, confined within high bare hedges on the narrow lane.

'I can't fucking well leave him, can I? The filth will pick him up.' He accelerated.

'No, 'Orace, please no.'

'I'm gonna kill him.'

'Please, no.' She reached out for the steering wheel, but the slap he gave her threw her sideways.

Her eyes flicked up to the road, and her sprinting son, running for his life down the middle.

'You brought this on yourself,' Mower said, as he hit the accelerator. They were quickly catching up. In the glare of the lights, Dawn saw Adam just a few yards ahead.

'No, no!' she yelled, reaching out to pull on Mower's arm.

She opened her eyes to see Adam jink sharp left, leap across a ditch and scramble through a gap in the hedge. Mower swore, and hit the brakes. The Toyota screeched to a halt, a dozen yards further on. He burst out of the car, scrambled over the ditch and fought his way through the hedge. Dawn followed. The ditch was three feet deep and wet, the far side was slippery, and she had to grasp at spiky branches to haul herself up. She wished she'd worn trainers now instead of canvas holiday shoes. Through the hedge she saw Mower, a dark silhouette against an overcast pewter sky, standing with his hands on his hips, gasping like a steam engine, wreathed in breath and curses. There was no sign of Adam, just in the far distance the orange glow of the burning car, smoke billowing.

Mower made his way back to her.

'I should have ditched the pair of you, and right now I'd be on my way back to the Costas. Nothing wrong with *my* passport.'

'Mal said he got mine done proper.'

'That was bollocks, weren't it? Liability, that geezer.'

'So where is Adam?'

'I've no idea. Little bastard. Oi, what's this?' Looking behind Dawn, in the direction they had come, Mower made his way back to the hedge. He crouched down and picked something up, which emitted a faint blue light.

'Look. He dropped his phone. At least he can't call the cops then.'

'I told him not to bring it,' Dawn said. 'They can trace us with that.'

Chapter Twenty-eight

DC Jason Hart dropped the handset into the receiver rest after a half hour wait trying to get phone triangulation results from an overstretched service provider. He had a huge list of mobiles of interest, and was gradually working round the various networks. There had been no luck with devices registered to Damian Norris or Dawn Sutton, and they couldn't even find a listed phone for Horace Mower or Ionatan Marasova. As for his daughter, Lydia, Surrey Police had struggled for weeks with that. Most of the phones they had succeeded in tracing were for people already in custody: Jackie Norris, Mal Scattergood and Colin Lamb. Finally, he had been told that one of the lower priority items, an up-to-date trace for young Adam Sutton, had been found.

'Better than nothing,' Hart said, as he waited for the email. After five minutes, it arrived, giving a map of the various pings. When he saw it, he suddenly realised its significance.

'Adam Sutton was in rural Oxfordshire fifteen minutes ago, according to his phone,' he yelled across the office to Culshaw, who was staring at a different screen.

Culshaw turned to him. 'That's where Mower is. Let's have a look.' He made his way across to Hart's desk. 'Mower could have borrowed the phone to avoid being traced on his own. But I think it's more likely that he has

Dawn and Adam Sutton with him in the car. It would make sense for the ferry. Give Gillard a ring, he might not be far away.'

–

Gillard was just outside Burford, west of Oxford, when he got the call. 'That's great news,' he told Hart. 'Trouble is with triangulation it's always at least fifteen minutes behind.' He knew patrol cars were all over the patchwork of small rural roads, just in case Mower had gone to ground. But it was like looking for a needle in a haystack. Daines was soon scrutinising the detailed map on her iPad. 'The trace hasn't moved in ten minutes,' she said. 'We could be there in five.'

She tapped in the co-ordinates to the satnav, and they set off at speed, but without the siren or blue lights. They were heading through darkened country lanes, many of them wooded, with high hedges, and pockets of new housing development. There were a few other vehicles, none of them a Subaru. Gillard kept his eyes peeled, looking down every side road, however small. Then, in one, he saw the shadowy figure of a slim man walking towards him. He turned the car to get the figure in his lights. Full beam showed a youth of exactly the build that he recalled for Adam Sutton. He was underdressed for the chill December evening, in jeans and a polo shirt. No coat. The lad had his hand up to mask the lights, so Gillard dipped them as he coasted the Lexus up towards him. The boy looked around nervously, as if getting ready to run, and retreated across the roadside verge behind a telegraph pole. Gillard brought the car to a stop, with the window down.

The boy looked terrified.

'Are you Adam?' Gillard asked.

'Yeah.' He looked nervously up and down the lane. 'Who are you?'

'We've been looking for you…'

'Where am I?'

'Oxfordshire. We're looking for your mum. Do you know where she is?'

'Are you the filth?'

'We are police officers, but don't worry, you're not in trouble.' Gillard recognised the reflex suspicion bred into almost everyone from Adam's south London neighbourhood. 'Get in, out of the cold, we can get something to eat.'

'I've lost my phone. I think Mower got it when he chased me.' Adam opened the car door and slid into the seat behind Gillard.

'So Horace Mower is with your mum?'

Gradually the story came out: the planned escape to Spain, the change of plan to go to Wales, he didn't know where exactly, some relative of Mower's. Stacey Daines found a packet of Hobnobs of uncertain vintage in the glove compartment, and offered them to the boy, who gobbled them down without hesitation. There followed two of Gillard's cereal bars, and some boiled sweets from Daines' own collection. Gillard scrutinised the young man in the driving mirror: pale, shivering with cold, and out of his depth. No wonder he looked upset.

'I think we should get you back to the nearest police station and get you some soup,' Daines said.

His face began to dissolve, and he angrily wiped away tears.

'Are you all right?' Daines asked kindly.

'She killed my grandad. Murdered him with a plastic bag over his head. Horace made her do it.'

Gillard had suspected something like this. 'The sooner we find her the better, eh?'

'He's a fucking madman.'

From the mouth of babes, Gillard thought.

'I'll see what we can get on the mobile now,' Daines said.

Adam leaned forward. 'Horace stole a car from a house near here, somewhere.'

'Do you have the registration number?' Gillard asked. 'Or even the make?'

'It was a silver Toyota, a Yaris I think, not one of the new ones. He tied up an old lady to get the keys and killed her dog. He set fire to the old car, over there somewhere.' He pointed out of the back window.

'Can you guide us?' Gillard said.

Five minutes later they could see the glow of the fire, and arrived by the small area of woodland to find a farmer's four-wheel-drive already there. He was on the phone, to the police as it turned out. Gillard showed him his badge, and after a short discussion the farmer agreed not to approach the still smouldering car until the uniforms arrived with some CSI investigators. Gillard got back in the car and followed Adam's directions to the cottage. He told Adam to stay in the vehicle and went with Daines to the house. There was no reply to the bell, and the door appeared to be locked. The boy had already explained to them that the neighbours were absent, and Daines confirmed that by ringing their doorbell.

Gillard donned a pair of blue neoprene gloves, then peered through the letterbox and called out. He could hear some kind of metallic noise, and decided that was enough excuse to go in. He tried to feed his arm through the letterbox to reach the interior of the Yale lock, but it had been years since his arm was slim enough for that. Instead, he was able to use a plastic card, judiciously bent, to fit into the flange of the door, to jiggle the lock until it opened. Once the door was open, he slipped on a pair of plastic booties, and went inside. There was the body of a dead Yorkshire terrier at the foot of the stairs. He called out again, then headed upstairs, following the sound of the metal ringing. He found an elderly lady bound to her bedroom radiator by four sets of knotted tights, with a fifth used as a gag. He cut her free with a pocketknife and called for Daines to ring for a family liaison officer.

'Are you okay?' he asked once the gag was off.

'He killed Bertie,' she said.

Gillard nodded. 'He died trying to save you.'

The woman cried briefly, as Gillard was freeing her. He went downstairs, slid the dog into a plastic bag, then placed him by the front door. He helped the woman down until, once sitting at her kitchen table, she described what had happened. She hadn't been otherwise assaulted, but Gillard had to break the news to her that her car had been taken. 'Does it have a satnav?' he asked. It didn't, but she was able to give him the registration number, which was quickly passed on to Thames Valley Police by Stacey Daines. She also asked for an ambulance to be sent to give the lady a quick check over.

–

Gillard didn't want to leave her alone and used twenty precious minutes waiting for the uniforms and paramedics to come. Daines spent the time questioning the boy about his knowledge of Welsh relatives, friends or any other connection which would give them a clue where Mower was heading. He had little information to give. Gillard checked in with Culshaw, who was co-ordinating the fast-expanding multi-force police operation, while he made a cup of tea for the shaken victim.

A first responder car arrived, and a patrol car moments afterwards. After briefing them Gillard and Daines headed off. Culshaw had given him two pieces of information. The bad news was that the boy's phone appeared to be turned off, because there was no longer a signal. The good news was that having passed on the registration number of the Toyota Yaris, it had just pinged an ANPR camera near Chipping Norton, a few miles north of them. That was ten minutes ago. Oxfordshire had allocated half the county's available patrol cars to the pursuit, Culshaw had said.

'We're definitely going to get the bastard,' Gillard said to Daines.

'Good thing too,' said Adam, from the back seat. Gillard had forgotten the boy was still there, and should really have handed him over to the liaison officer. Too late now.

'Put your seatbelt on,' Gillard said. A call came through on the hands-free, which Daines answered. The Toyota had been spotted at a garage, refuelling just three minutes ago.

'How close is the nearest patrol car?' Daines asked, as she tapped in the postcode she been given onto the iPad. Five minutes was the answer.

'We're closer than that,' she said to Gillard. 'Take this next left, and step on it.'

Gillard did so, and opened up the Lexus. He was aware of the boy leaning forward so that he could see between the two front seats. He seemed excited. It was a winding road, cutting through dense woodland. It was nearly midnight and there was no other traffic. They could see the lights of a car in the distance, and slowed down as it approached.

'Is it them?' Adam asked.

'Could be,' Gillard said. It was certainly a small saloon, and the shape of the headlamps seemed to accord with what he hazily recollected from the car identification course he had done years ago. The car flashed by, and Gillard only got the first two letters of the registration. But they matched. He screeched to a halt, pulled a tyre-smoking U-turn in a farm gate entrance, and headed off in pursuit, with the twos and blues going. It certainly was a Toyota Yaris, and no match for the Lexus. The fugitives turned left onto an even narrower road. And they followed.

'This is a dead end,' Daines said, looking at her iPad. 'Leads to a farm in half a mile.'

Gillard could see the brake lights of the Yaris and slowed down to forty. 'Is he carrying a gun?' Gillard asked Adam. Should have checked that before.

'I don't think so,' the boy said. Gillard could now see the intimidating figure of Horace Mower silhouetted in his headlamps. He had something in his hands. Dawn still appeared to be in the car.

'Yeah, that's right, he *has* got this massive spanner,' the boy said.

Great! Gillard stopped the car twenty yards away and kept the lights on full beam. He looked in his mirror, no sign of the cavalry as yet. 'Right, here we go,' Gillard said, as he got out of the car. Daines emerged from her side and tossed Gillard a stab vest.

'Fucking copper, you stay away, right!' Mower bellowed, gesturing with the adjustable spanner.

'Drop that weapon, and lie down on the road. It's all over, Horace. Time to give up.'

Dawn had emerged from the car. 'I recognise him. 'E's the one that my dad grassed to. I recognise the voice. That's Gillard.'

Mower gave a huge bellow of fury. With a sinking feeling in his stomach, Gillard watched the man rumbling towards him like a tank. He took a deep breath, made sure his handcuffs were to hand, and waited, balanced on the balls of his feet. Where was a Taser, just when you really needed one?

Chapter Twenty-nine

Ionatan Marasova was sitting in his white Mercedes saloon, with his daughter Lydia in the passenger seat. She was sleeping, and he was listening to music with his hands behind his head as they rumbled on in darkness under the English Channel. They had managed to get on Le Shuttle using their Romanian passports and were on their way home to a new life. He had set up the transfers into crypto currency, and using a new burner phone bought in duty-free, had managed to establish that £50 million, half of his share, had already cleared into BullionBase. All he had to do when he got back to Bucharest, where he was going to stay at his brother's place, was insert the sixty-eight digit code for the online vault, and sell the first £1 million for Romanian leus. There was no shortage of Romanian criminal buyers of crypto. He'd had years to work it out. He had no idea whether the other conspirators had made it out or not. He wasn't really interested, and apart from having set up the crypto account, needed to have no further involvement with them.

The big breakthrough was fifteen years ago, when he was on remand, and for two days shared a cell with a small-time drug dealer called Damian Norris. They had discussed their dreams for a big blag, as Norris had called it. But even then it was clear to Marasova that Norris was living in the past. Cops and robbers, security vans, gold bullion. That was all nonsense in the twenty-first century. Traffic cameras, phone tracing, CCTV everywhere. You can't get away with it anymore. The future was financial sleight of hand, electronically diverting money from point A to point B while no one was watching. He'd seen how easily it could be done with card skimming at bank ATMs. The trouble with that, especially in the early days, was that you could only clone a limited number of cards in one go, and there was a danger of being caught on CCTV installing or retrieving the device. But the first time he travelled on the London Underground after they started using Oyster cards got him to thinking about a bigger application. That was in 2003. He had friends in banking technology back home who assured him that contactless cards were on the way for all transactions. He vowed that he would be ready when that happened. But it wasn't quite as simple as card skimming. You needed a couple of inside contacts. One on the card processing side, obviously, and one on the London Underground side, who could provide them with credentials to modify the gates that wouldn't raise suspicion. Once he was out, Marasova made contact with Damian. Norris was no rocket scientist, but he did have contacts, and could vouch for him to them. Putting all the various pieces together had taken five years, and for at least three of those he was dubious it was ever going to happen. They did eventually get the contacts they needed on the inside, but having to work with gorillas like Mower and idiots like Scattergood had made him very nervous.

He was hugely relieved that he would never have to see them again.

He looked across at his sleeping daughter. Marasova's original idea was to just to rescue Lydia from that drug den, and hide her away from the police search. Big Jackie had agreed she was a dangerous distraction, and if she was caught could lead the police first to him as her father and then on to the conspirators themselves. 'I can take care of it,' big Jackie had said. 'I don't want you distracted, and we can look after her here, in a little flat at the back of the gym in the basement. If she keeps her head down for a couple of weeks before the job, then you can take her with you when you go.'

It hadn't all gone well. Jackie Norris said she'd been a handful at first, unwilling to be locked up, even in a luxury room. But that was the drugs talking. She was healthier now, much safer away from that awful boyfriend. That at least was one favour that Damian had been able to get through his father. Ionatan had only ever had one face-to-face meeting with big Jackie, to ask for that courtesy of accommodating his daughter, and he had been favourably disposed.

As it turned out, Jordan Idris had been murdered. Horace Mower's doing, apparently. It was stupid because it increased the risk of distraction, not diminished it. Marasova was horrified when he read the newspapers. He thought the police would be back to him, poking about again. They had wanted to see his workshop in the garage, and it had been less suspicious to agree to it. There, laid out, were all the essential electronic pieces of an old London Underground barrier, removed as defective, made available to him by Colin Lamb. He had repaired it and used it to test his emulator. He had spent two years pulling apart contactless payment terminals to try to find the smallest, lowest power-consuming device he could, one that could fit under a false cap on the barrier and communicate with the TfL host system through an intermediate chip, in order to trigger the emergency opening signal. In the end he got one which would run off a watch battery. It had all been there for the cops to see, under the model railway, if they had any idea what they were looking at. He had passed it all off as part of the electronics for the railway, and if they knew any better, they didn't say.

After half an hour in the tunnel there was a change in the rumbling noise, a higher frequency, almost a note of excitement that mirrored the feeling he was having. The lights of France were sporadically visible. He felt a sense of growing relief now, to have got out of Britain. To have committed the once-in-a-lifetime job. The crime of the century.

Lydia stretched in the seat and opened her eyes lazily towards him. She smiled. The detox that big Jackie's wife recommended looked to have done her a world of good. She was no longer pale, but had a healthy glow in her skin. Norris had recommended laser removal of her neck tattoos, which had been very successful, leaving only a faint red mark which had faded after a few days. With a new hairdo and blonde highlights, she looked to be once again the loving daughter that he had lost.

'I've been dreaming,' she said. 'About that woman in the shopping centre.'

'The one you tried to kill?'

'Yes. In the dream, I'm coming up the escalator towards her, and Jordan is at the top as before. But this time, I start to fly, going high above her, looking down across three different floors of the mall, with all the shoppers scurrying around beneath me. I soar upwards to the glass roof, and out into the bright sky. Then I turn down to her, and say how sorry I am.'

'You know she is the wife of one of the detectives who is chasing us? She and her husband visited the Swallowtail Hotel when you were there.'

'I know. Sally told me. That's why they made me stay in the room the whole time. It was a kind of luxury confinement.'

There were clanking noises, lights within the shuttle came on, and the brake lights of the vehicles ahead turned to red as engines started. He drove the Mercedes carefully down the ramp and off the side of the carriage, joining a long tail of vehicles that made their way past unused customs and immigration booths, the French checks having been made at Folkstone. They slowed to a walking pace, directed by officials in high vis who were walked up and down the queues. A white Mercedes a few vehicles ahead was directed off to the right. And then so were they. With a rising sense of fear, he coasted into an open-ended metal shed just as the previous Mercedes was leaving. Five officials, two in recognisable gendarme uniforms, were staring at the car. One approached, with another man, and Marasova buzzed the window down. 'What seems to be the problem?'

Passports were requested and the non-gendarme looked carefully at both the documents before addressing them individually by name. He seemed to be English. 'Mr Ionatan Marasova and Miss Lydia Marasova, you are under arrest.'

Chapter Thirty

Gillard jumped to the left as Mower approached, and kicked out hard with the heel of his right foot against the big man's kneecap. Any normal man would have stumbled, but Mower was no normal man. His knee seemed like rock. Mower's upper body pivoted, and the spanner-wielding right hand shot out towards Gillard's jaw. He stepped back, and with his own right hand seized the shaft of the weapon. Mower's left jab hit him agonisingly hard in the ribs. The detective knew you couldn't outbox this man, but he might outfox him.

Suddenly he was aware of another figure by his side. Adam Sutton.

'You murdering bastard,' Adam said, trying to throw his own punch.

The momentary distraction, as Mower batted away the boy, was enough for Gillard to twist the wrench out of his grip. Gillard knew better than to use an illicit weapon during an arrest, except perhaps to save the life of another officer. As Mower attempted to grab it back, a second kick by Gillard to the same kneecap produced a satisfying crunch, and a twist of pain flashed across Mower's countenance. Adam was doing a tremendous job of distraction, waving his fists and shouting. Stacey Daines, meanwhile, was behind Mower.

Mower glanced back towards her, and elbowed her in the face as she approached. As Daines yelped and fell, Gillard took the opportunity to punch him on the jaw. His fist felt like he had rammed it into a brick wall. Adam grabbed Mower's right arm, stopping a fist that was heading towards Gillard's head. Daines, still on the ground, grabbed one of the big man's ankles. Caught off balance, he only had time to grasp Gillard's head in his left hand before tumbling backwards. Falling onto him, Gillard wrestled as best he could. Daines now had a good grip on one leg, and Adam on the other. Even on his back Mower showed enormous strength, lifting Gillard's whole body up with his knees. It took all the detective's strength in both hands to stop Mower's right closing around his throat. Adam repeatedly lost a hold of one leg, as Mower tried to pull him off with his left hand, while Stacey fought hard to retain a grip on the other leg. The breakthrough was the ultimate low blow, with Gillard forcing Mower's knees apart and then dropping with his own knee right onto the big man's groin. The howl of pain coincided with the sound of sirens and two patrol cars arrived. Finally, with two more officers piling in, Mower was subdued.

–

Meanwhile, back in Peckham Police Station, Culshaw and Latimer were having their turn at interrogating Jackie Norris.

'We've got most of what we need, Jackie,' Culshaw said. 'We know that Colin Lamb provided the credentials, we know that Mal Scattergood, Horace Mower and Ionatan Marasova worked together on the electronic gates. We know that Dawn Sutton was involved in interfering with the credit card computers, probably by inserting a

USB stick given her by Marasova. And we reckon that you pulled it all together.'

Norris smiled. 'That's a very nice bedtime story, and it's making me sleepy, so if you don't mind…'

'You're not getting any sleep until we know how you pulled it together,' Florence said.

The crime boss had a few hours earlier been taken from Staines by Serco van, so that all the conspirators were held in the same place. With the signature of a superintendent, they had extended the detention to thirty-six hours, and that gave them until breakfast time on Sunday morning. Despite being shuttled from cell to cell, Norris looked less tired than the two police officers. Even his bow tie was still straight. Kulkarni's firm had dispatched a new brief, a middle-aged man with sandy hair, to sit in with Norris, so that she could get some sleep. He was already earning his keep: 'My client is entitled to reasonable rest, as you well know.'

The detectives ignored him. 'We have evidence that you organised the whole thing, your name was mentioned—'

'Hearsay is not evidence,' the brief said.

'—not only by Colin Lamb, but by Malcolm Scatter-good and others.'

'This is all circumstantial,' the lawyer said.

Norris turned to him and smiled, before returning his gaze to Culshaw. 'No fingerprints, no DNA, no forensics, nothing. You've got nothing on me.'

'You tried to frame Terry Moses for this didn't you?' Latimer said.

'No no no. I mean, I understand that you've got Terry's phone, discussing details of this robbery. That's what I've heard. But you ain't got anything on *my* phone, have you? Maybe he's trying to frame *me*.'

–

While Norris was giving the two detectives the runaround, Surrey's DC Rob Townsend was at the Mount Browne CID office looking through the electronic data gleaned from the raid on the Swallowtail Hotel. He put Norris' mobile to one side. He was pretty sure that the crime boss was too smart to have left any evidence on his own phone. There was nothing incriminating on the CCTV either, Hoskins had looked through all of it. What was left was a laptop from Norris' flat at the hotel, and that of his wife. He pulled up the search history of both, including that which had been done on private browsing. There had been a few searches on Norris' machine on Terry Moses, just a few weeks ago. That on its own was not incriminating. Word searches on the names of the conspirators turned up nothing, either. No search terms were recorded that related to credit card fraud or the London Underground. There wasn't even a cryptocurrency account that he could see.

The laptop had, however, an app which allowed Norris to connect to the hotel CCTV system. Seeing as Hoskins had already been through that footage, Townsend didn't initially open it. However, the laptop's file history showed that Norris had made plenty of use of it. He had browsed several file clips, one of them repeatedly. Townsend clicked on that file, which opened a video window. He immediately thought he had stumbled on Norris' porn collection. The camera gave a view from above of a massage table, with an attractive semi-naked woman, seemingly pregnant, murmuring with pleasure as she was being massaged by a young man in a bathrobe. Townsend double-checked the file label, which gave a camera number which was not on the main hotel system. He closed the clip and opened another one on file history. This was a different camera number and showed what appeared to be a different room, this time with a man being massaged by a woman. The towels were largely in place across the man's back, but there was something familiar about him. The detective watched, until the masseuse asked the man a question. He didn't quite catch what she was saying, so it was only when the client lifted up his head that he realised the man being massaged was his boss, DCI Craig Gillard. Townsend replayed the footage, donned his headset and turned up the sound until he could determine what was being said. The woman was clearly offering 'extras' and Gillard politely declined.

Townsend chuckled. That was a wise decision given the secret camera. Clearly, Norris was not only a voyeur in general, but he had also been after some highly compromising material on a senior police officer. He did recall that Gillard had said he and his wife had undertaken a reconnaissance, but he hadn't realised that it was quite such deep cover. It hadn't fooled Norris, anyway. It was then that he realised who the woman on the first clip was. He clicked back to it to confirm: Yes, Sam Gillard. Clearly enjoying herself. The final towel had been removed and she was naked.

He leaned back in his chair, with his hands steepled over his nose. This was all quite delicate. The common sense course of action was simply to stop now, let Gillard know, to leave it to him to review the evidence. On the other hand, there was temptation. To just watch a little bit more. It was 9.30 p.m. and there was no one in his section of the CID office.

When he next looked up, five minutes had passed. His main feeling was one of guilt, for everything he had seen and learned about his boss's wife. It was information he could never share. He heard movement in the adjacent office, the arrival of DI John Perry. To make himself look busy, he clicked back to the list of files recorded from the two illicit cameras and opened another file at random.

At first it just showed the same massage room, empty. At first.

What it revealed next made his jaw drop.

Chapter Thirty-one

It was Sunday morning, 9.15, and Culshaw and Latimer were in the Peckham interview room having another go at trying to crack Jackie Norris, when a text arrived from Gillard saying he was five minutes away. That was good news, Culshaw reckoned. The prisoner didn't look quite so comfortable now, but still wasn't saying anything. They had been covering the same ground for over an hour, and got nowhere. Norris' face looked pale, he was no longer wearing his bow tie, and he had his collar open. A seemingly junior lawyer, who looked almost teenaged, but was from the same legal firm, sat in and said nothing.

Culshaw had hoped that after a night in the cells Norris would be a little less smug. The prisoner's breakfast had been a cereal bar, and a plastic cup of stale coffee with powdered milk. Poor fare, but as the desk sergeant had explained, staff shortages meant the normal service had to be suspended.

The two detectives decided to keep Norris on the go until Gillard arrived. 'Are you tired?' Culshaw asked, after seeing him yawn. 'If you haven't the stamina for this, we can carry on later.'

'I'm fine,' Norris said.

Culshaw had guessed that this would be his response. A big man, full of pride. Definitely time to take him down a peg or two. Gillard's first text had mentioned the emergence of some apparently decisive evidence, which he wanted to present himself. Culshaw himself was in desperate need of sleep, though Latimer looked like she could go on for a week.

Finally, the desk sergeant messaged them the news of Gillard's arrival, with DI Claire Mulholland in tow. Culshaw and Latimer excused themselves and left Norris in the room. They went out to greet Gillard and Mulholland. Gillard, as always, looked capable of running a marathon even though he'd been up all night. He showed them a video on his phone which had just been sent to him by Rob Townsend.

'Fantastic,' Culshaw said. 'I'd like to see him get out of that one.'

—

'I'm charging you with conspiracy to murder,' Gillard told Norris, almost as soon as he had prepared a tape and sat down in the interview room.

'What's this then, "bad cop, worse cop"?' Norris sat with his arms folded and a look of contempt on his face.

'I'd like to show you a video,' Gillard said, turning round his iPad so that the prisoner could see it. The screen showed a massage room in the Swallowtail Hotel, complete with a dishevelled massage table heaped with used towels. For a few moments nothing happened, and then there was the sound of a door opening. Two men could be heard talking, but could not be seen. By their voices, one of them was Jackie Norris and the other was Horace Mower.

> 'It's nice and private in here,' Norris said.
> 'Good flight?'

'All right,' Mower replied. 'Brilliant pass-port you got me, looked totally legit.'

'No problem. Look, Horace, I've got a little problem. I'm assembling the team, including this genius Romanian engineer. Trouble is, his daughter's a junkie, and is hanging around with this low-life pick-pocket. It's already brought unwelcome attention from the filth, who went round to see him. I need him focused. So here is the plan. I need you to deal with the pickpocket. Nice and tidy like, no mess. We need you to bring the girl here, so we can look after her until after the big job. Mal Scattergood will drive while you do the business. But there's a little twist.'

'Right, what's that?'

'Did you ever hear of Operation Mince-meat?'

'Nah.'

'It's a film, but based on a true story from World War II. This dead body is found by the Germans, bearing all sorts of secret Allied papers about the plan for an invasion. But it's cobblers, disinformation, designed to mislead. Our Jordan Idris is going to be found in possession of the phone of Terry Moses.'

Mower laughed. 'Are you gonna stuff him up?'

'Definitely.'

At this point the two men moved further into the room, and became visible on camera, Norris showing a device to Mower.

'This is the phone, Horace. Your standard cheap burner, on which I've already recorded some bogus text messages to another unknown phone.'

'What's the point of all this?'

'The word is out, Horace my friend. I've got a little mole in the Met police, who says they heard whispers about the big job. Not what it is, thank God, or where. But simply the fact there is one and it's big. I need to steer the filth in the type of direction that they would probably go anyway. Different day, bogus story, that kind of thing, and with the added bonus of dropping Terry Moses in it.'

'So what do I have to do?'

'Simple. I need to prove to the plods that this is Terry's phone. What you need to do is break into Terry Moses' pub, it's not far away. The place has been thoroughly cased, so it shouldn't be that hard. The difficult thing is, I need you to get Terry's DNA onto that phone, and then put the phone in a plastic bag.'

'How do I manage that?'

'He's got a big Barbour jacket he hangs on the back door near the bogs, ain't been washed in a century. Rub the phone round the collar. Bound to pick up some.'

'Right. I'll need a day to make some arrangements.'

'We need to move sharpish, Horace, time is ticking on.'

At this point, Norris took a phone call, and the two men exited the room. The last sound was the click of the door closing. Gillard paused the video and looked up at the prisoner. Norris had turned grey, though his jaw was still set firm.

'You forgot about your own secret cameras, didn't you?' Gillard asked. 'Your voyeurism is your downfall. We've got everything we need here: conspiracy to murder, the planning of a fraud. You're going to go down for a long time.'

–

After terminating the interview, Gillard and Mulholland joined Culshaw and Latimer, looking through the one-way glass at Norris. He was as tough as they came, but had slumped slightly since being confronted with the evidence of his own guilt. They were going to give him fifteen minutes to think about it, before re-interviewing him. Eventually, he'd be taken back to a cell, at the far end of the corridor from Scattergood. With Mower and Dawn Sutton now in custody in Oxfordshire, and Ionatan Marasova and his daughter arrested at the French border, there was only Norris' son Damian to round up.

'Did you find out where Damian had flown off to?' Gillard asked Culshaw.

'Croatia.'

'We'll soon get him back,' Claire Mulholland said.

'Not so fast,' Culshaw said. 'He's a wily one. Turns out he's had a small holiday home there for ten years and has managed to get Croatian citizenship. Since Brexit, Croatia is among a dozen EU countries that will no longer extradite its citizens to the UK for crimes committed here.'

'What? That's crazy,' Claire said.

Culshaw shrugged. 'We've had problems all over with this. France, Germany, Poland, Slovakia, and Portugal. We're no longer part of the European arrest warrant, so a French burglar could come over here on a day trip, do a load of houses in Canterbury, and so long as he is back before we catch him, we can't touch him.'

Gillard sighed. 'Thank God Spain isn't one of them, given the number of British criminals living on the Costas.'

'Too true,' Culshaw said. 'You know it's a funny thing, big Jackie could have got Croatian citizenship too, at one time, seeing as his first wife, Damian's mother, was of Croatian descent. But he was so confident that we couldn't pin anything on him, he decided to brazen it out.'

Culshaw's mobile went, and he turned away to answer it. It was several minutes before he turned back to Gillard, with a look of shock on his face. 'That was Thames Valley Police. They took a DNA sample from Mower, and it matched the unknown DNA found at Idris' flat.'

'That's great news,' Gillard said, and then frowned. 'The unknown sample? But Mower's DNA is on file.'

'Ah, but Thames Valley said it didn't match the sample on file for him.'

'What?' Gillard exclaimed.

'Yep, it seems that the sample against his name was from someone else, a small-time thief called Harold Mawer.'

'So what's that? An admin screw-up, or something more sinister?' Gillard said.

'A typing mistake possibly. An H. Mower for an H. Mawer, so Thames Valley reckons.'

'That kind of thing isn't supposed to happen,' Claire said.

'Well, it certainly explains why we could never get Mower on forensics for previous crimes,' Gillard said.

'But wouldn't any samples found at Idris' flat have fingered this Harold Mawer instead?' Claire asked.

'Wrong way round,' Gillard said. 'It's Mower's name against a sample that hasn't been found anywhere, except on Harold Mawer's crimes. Mower's own original sample sounds like it's been lost.'

'That's exactly right. All I can say is that Thames Valley Police are looking into it,' Culshaw said, with a shrug.

'Sloppy practice, certainly,' Gillard said. 'If Mower had been retested every time he'd been arrested, the discrepancy would have shown up before.'

'Well, the big picture is you've got him now,' Claire said.

A familiar voice in the corridor outside made them stiffen, and the door behind them opened to reveal the desk sergeant. Behind him was Assistant Commissioner Kay Thompson. 'Relax, this is just a flying visit. I just wanted to have a quick look at Mr Norris.'

She peered through the one-way glass, down into the interview room. 'How are the mighty fallen,' she said, laughing softly.

'Ma'am, I think he was surprised we managed to get him on camera, his own secret spy camera, talking about the details of the crime,' Gillard said.

'Yes indeed. Did he really think he was going to get away with this?'

'I'm certain that's what he thought,' Culshaw said.

'In fact, he nearly managed it,' Gillard added. 'The killing of Idris was highly forensically aware, especially considering it was done in something of a hurry. None of us had thought that this crew of old-timers could be caught up with a twenty-first century fraud. The conception of stealing hundreds of millions on a single day from unwitting Christmas shoppers was an act of genius.'

'And that's down to Mr Marasova, isn't it?' she asked.

'Yes, a very clever individual,' Gillard said.

'DCI Culshaw, have you made any progress on finding out how it was that our Mr Norris got to hear about our suspicions?'

'No, ma'am. I've checked all the phone records from the department, but obviously...'

'I suspected that, so I've got no alternative but to call in the Anti-Corruption Command.'

'Yes, ma'am,' Culshaw said dejectedly.

She turned to Gillard. 'From what you said, no one at Surrey Police bar you knew of all the details of the Flying Squad investigation, is that right?'

'Yes, ma'am. I'm pretty sure the mole isn't at Mount Browne.'

She nodded and began to leave. Just as she reached the door she turned and said: 'There will be commendations for this, by the way. This is just the kind of big-league crime that we need to be seen to be dealing with. It's quite a PR coup.'

'Thank you, ma'am,' they replied in unison.

She closed the door behind her.

Chapter Thirty-two

It was two days before Christmas, and Gillard was back at the scene of the crime. He and Sam emerged from the crush at Oxford Street tube into a grey and drizzly afternoon, but the Christmas lights and the bright shop windows lifted their spirits. Sam was delighted to finally get some time with her husband. She had a little Christmas shopping left to do, but the main destination was one of their favourite restaurants, a little Greek place just north of Oxford Street. Gillard had, as many times before, made his apologies for the intrusion of work into almost all of their leisure time. But he was now on leave until the new year, definitely, and she intended to take full advantage of it. They made their way to Selfridge's to look at the window display. She took a selfie, and they kissed. Then he gave her a small wrapped gift. 'It's an early Christmas present, and a bit of an apology,' he said. She opened the box and saw a small but expensive-looking emerald bracelet. She was thrilled. He put his arm around her, and mingling with the crowds, they retraced their steps along Oxford Street. Just as they reached the corner of Duke Street, Sam heard someone call out to her husband.

A lad in a car coat and a woolly hat crossed the street towards them. He had a narrow face, and a big youthful smile.

'Well, Jason, fancy meeting you here,' Craig said, then turned towards Sam. 'DC Jason Hart, from Flying Squad.' Sam noticed a middle-aged couple who seemed to be with him.

'This is my mum and dad,' Jason said.

'Nice to meet you both,' his mother said, shaking both their hands. 'We've heard so much about you!'

'Michael Hart,' the father said shaking Gillard warmly by the hand. He was a big man with a craggy face. 'I remember you, Craig. You were a young recruit in Croydon when I was in the force.'

'That was a long time ago,' Gillard said, scrutinising him carefully. He recalled the name, but hadn't before put it together with Jason's. 'I should have guessed that Jason had a dad in the force.'

Hart senior waved a dismissive hand. 'I retired a good decade ago.'

'He's still a mine of information,' Jason said. 'Aren't you, Dad?'

'I do what I can,' he replied.

Gillard nodded. They chatted for a few minutes, then waved their goodbyes before heading off.

'That's a bit of a coincidence, running into them here,' Sam said. 'Jason looks like a schoolboy. Is he a trainee?'

'You know what they say when you start noticing how young policeman are?' Gillard said.

'I'm not old,' Sam said, elbowing him gently in the ribs. 'What is it?' she said suddenly. He was now scrolling through his phone.

'Just checking something.'

'Craig, you're off duty!' she said emphatically, leading him off up Duke Street towards the restaurant.

He put his phone away until they were sitting down in the little taverna, and she had gone to the ladies. When she returned, he was poring over his phone, sorting through emails. Was the workaholic ever going to take a day off?

'Sam, I just want to show you something. It'll take one minute.'

'Go on then.'

He opened a video attachment, looked at it himself for a moment, and then hit pause. He showed it to Sam.

'Do you recognise that man?'

It was a CCTV image of a solidly built middle-aged man in a smart jacket and jeans with dark glasses, turning away from what looked like a hotel reception desk. 'No, should I?'

'You've just met him. It's Jason's dad. He's got a distinctive mole just above his right ear.'

'Can't see it on that!' Sam said squinting at the display.

'True, but when I first saw this it was on a bigger screen. This footage was taken from a security camera at the Swallowtail Hotel. I didn't know who he was until now. I'm just wondering what Michael Hart would be doing there?'

'Isn't he allowed to be a normal guest?'

'He is, but it's a bit of a coincidence. Especially with the dark glasses, wouldn't you say?'

The waiter had approached and asked them if they wanted to order. Gillard put down the phone and chose a lamb kleftiko, while Sam opted for the souvlaki. When he had gone, she said: 'Can't you pass this on to somebody else?'

He smiled and said: 'Of course. I'll message this to Claire, she's on duty today.'

It was first thing next morning when three officers from Anti-Corruption Command arrested DC Jason Hart at home. The bewildered young detective was ashen faced as he was taken in for questioning. He protested that he had done nothing wrong. When interviewed, he readily confessed that he had mentioned to his father that they were investigating a potentially huge robbery. He also admitted that on a second occasion he had made the mistake of discussing with him in detail the Flying Squad's reaction to the various contradictory pieces of intelligence that were emerging.

When he heard about it, Gillard felt quite sorry for the young officer. His career close to being ruined, almost before it had begun, and all because he had trusted his own father. He just hoped that the inevitable publicity from young Jason Hart's disciplinary would not overshadow the PR coup at having foiled the biggest card fraud ever perpetrated against the British public.

Epilogue

The conspirators pleaded guilty to most charges, given the incontrovertible CCTV evidence. Colin Lamb and Mal Scattergood each got eight years. Horace Mower went down for life with a minimum of fifteen years for the murder of Jordan Idris, and eight years for the fraud, to run concurrently. Damian Norris was sentenced to fifteen years in absentia, while his father big Jackie went down for life, with a minimum of fourteen years. Dawn Sutton got four years for her involvement, which she insisted was merely inserting a USB stick into a computer at her workplace a couple of times. The CPS declined to prosecute her for the murder of her own father, because the only clear evidence was Mower's comment overheard by Adam in the getaway car. As the chief CPS lawyer said, this was simply hearsay. There were no clear forensics to show that she or anybody else had suffocated him.

Michael Hart was sentenced to three years for assisting an offender. His son Jason received a final written warning from the Met Police for breach of confidentiality.

AC Kay Thompson was as good as her word. DCI Matt Culshaw was commended for his role in the case, and soon promoted to detective superintendent, while DI Florence Latimer was promoted to a DCI. Some moved sideways, at their own request. DC Brendan Musgrove slipped quietly away from his undercover role in London and returned to Northumbria Police as a desk officer.

As for the money, Britain's banks and credit card providers grudgingly coughed up over £300 million for the many passengers on the London Underground who had been defrauded. Transport for London was forced to thoroughly review its operating and security procedures, as was the credit card industry, and its suppliers. The Metropolitan Police has so far managed to recover just over a third of the money which had been transferred into cryptocurrencies.

Completing that work is expected to take years.

However, the first trial to take place was that of Lydia Marasova, for the attempted murder of Sam Gillard. Lydia, smartly dressed in a charcoal grey dress and matching jacket, had entered a plea of diminished responsibility and when she took the stand to give her defence, she was asked by her own barrister why she had made that plea.

Lydia turned to Sam, who was sitting with Gillard in the public gallery, and said: 'I was very upset that day, and wasn't thinking straight. I'd taken some painkillers, and some vodka.'

'So it would be fair to say that you were under the influence of drugs, at that point?'

'Yes.'

'You've seen the prosecution CCTV footage, which shows you following the victim, and going up the escalator after her. Why was that?'

'She'd taken my picture, after Jordan handed me the purse. It made me angry.'

'So you wanted to deprive her of the phone, is that correct?'

'Yes.'

'Witnesses claim you had a knife.'

'I did, yes.'

'But wasn't it true, Lydia, that by the time you had got to Mrs Gillard, you had already seen Jordan Idris take her phone?'

'Yes.'

'So what on earth was it that possessed you to attack her, when you could simply have run away, as indeed Mr Idris did?'

Lydia chewed her lip, and glanced at Sam. 'She was pregnant.'

There was a gasp throughout the court.

'You attacked her because she was pregnant?'

Lydia put a handkerchief to her nose, and began to sob. Asked the same question again, she nodded in assent.

'Why on earth would you attack a pregnant woman?'

'Because I'd just lost my own baby, two days before. I was jealous.'

'So, in your grieving state, your mind was unbalanced?'

She nodded. It was a plea the jury eventually accepted. Lydia Marasova was sentenced to six years.

February

Sam was just heading out to a late shift, her last week before taking maternity leave. She had just drained the last of her coffee. She heard the letterbox as she went out to grab her post. Just one letter, postmarked HMP Bronzefield. She opened it.

> *Dear Mrs Gillard,*
> *This is a very difficult letter for me to write. I know that I did you a great wrong, something that*

303

will live with me for the rest of my life. I feel guilty every day, that I tried to end not only your life, but that of your unborn baby. And it was all for selfish reasons. As I said in court, I had recently had a miscarriage, so felt angry and resentful to see someone like you. I was on drugs and alcohol, and going through a difficult time with my boyfriend. I know none of this excuses what I tried to do. I'm just so hugely relieved that I did not succeed. I will serve my time, knowing I deserve it, and hopefully come out a better person.

I wish you, and your baby, all the luck in the world.

Yours
Lydia Marasova

Sam read and reread the letter, then placed a hand on her swollen belly. Only a couple of weeks to go now. She felt the child move within her. Not even born yet, but what stories she would have to tell her!

Afterword

Please don't read this until after you have read the book – there are spoilers! Many frauds tend to be a single large illicit transaction, but I realised that contactless technology offers a completely different MO for a criminal, at the epicentre of a blizzard of diverted payments. And where has more transactions in a single day than London's Oxford Circus tube station in the run-up to Christmas? I hope readers weren't too bewitched by the technical details of the 'how' of the fraud; I merely wanted to show that such a theft, while unlikely and hard to organise, is not impossible. After some initial and understandable hesitancy, Transport for London agreed to look over the technical details and gave me some useful pointers. I would like to thank Tom Canning and Danielle Eddington at TfL, Natalie Bruce at UK Finance, Kim Booth, and Home Office forensic pathologist Stuart Hamilton. I'm grateful to Dave Browett for checking the computer and technical descriptions. I would also like to thank my readers' circle Tim Cary and Valerie Richardson. Any mistakes remaining are my own. I am grateful to Michael Bhaskar and the rest of the team at Canelo, and to copyeditor Miranda Ward. Last but not least, my wife Louise, for her boundless patience and support during the gestation of each and every book.

CANELOCRIME

Do you love crime fiction and are always on the lookout for brilliant authors?

Canelo Crime is home to some of the most exciting novels around. Thousands of readers are already enjoying our compulsive stories. Are you ready to find your new favourite writer?

Find out more and sign up to our newsletter at canelocrime.com